SAVING LIBERTY

HELENA NEWBURY

First Edition

ONE

Emily

SOMETIMES I think: five minutes earlier or five minutes later. That's all it would have taken. If Kian hadn't strolled towards me right when he did, we'd never have met... and I'd be dead.

It was a gloriously warm September day. No one expected any trouble, so I only had the normal level of protection: five guys from the Secret Service plus a perimeter guarded by the Washington DC police. The park had been swept at dawn for bombs, there was a helicopter circling overhead, and two streets had been temporarily closed.

You know: *normal.* When you're the President's daughter.

Anacostia Park was a sprawling oasis of green in the heart of DC's gray. The science fair's organizers had made towering sculptures of DNA strands from red and yellow balloons, bright and glossy against the blue sky. The press photographers were going nuts, snapping picture after picture of me talking to the kids. I nodded enthusiastically as they told me about their solar-powered radios and battling robots. I wasn't faking it, either. The exhibits blew me away: they made my own vinegar-and-soda volcano back in high school seem pretty lame. Choosing just one winner was going to be heartbreaking.

I checked out the final entry, told the kids I had to consult with the other judges and stepped away to get some water. And that's when I saw him for the very first time.

I actually saw the guy he was with first: just another corporate sponsor in a suit, hurrying towards me to get a picture shaking my hand. He fitted the scene. Then I saw the guy following just behind him and my brain went *wait, what?* Because that guy didn't fit the scene at all.

Everything about him raged against the neat, safe, family-friendly atmosphere. He wasn't wearing handmade Italian shoes like all the senators who'd stopped by; he was wearing lace-up leather boots that could have come straight from the Army. And not as some kind of fashion statement: these looked worn and battered, like they'd actually been to a warzone. His blue jeans had that perfect, lazy fit that you only get from a favorite pair that's been worn *a lot,* when the fabric goes super-soft and barely seems to be there, the next best thing to being naked when it's a warm day. The blue denim was stretched tight over muscled calves and hard thighs that could have graced a linebacker.

I blinked and stared at those strong legs as he strolled towards me. His walk didn't fit, either. All the guys in DC walk like they're trying to prove something, whether they're a senator or a lowly aide. It's all the testosterone in the air and the constant eyes of the press. But this guy strolled through the scene as if oblivious to the cameras. As if he was experiencing life instead of acting it out. He looked... *real*.

I blinked as the sun glinted off his belt buckle. That didn't fit either: big and brash and definitely not picked out by some overpaid personal stylist. And then the breeze lifted the bottom of his t-shirt a few inches and my eyes were drawn inexorably *up*....

His abs looked hard as rock: smooth, warm, rock, tanned from the sun and so very strokable—God, I could see the deep crease of his Adonis belt leading diagonally down towards—

The t-shirt dropped back into place but my eyes kept following the line—

No, I'm not going to look at his—

But my eyes were already on the heavy bulge between those strong thighs. Heavy and... *hard*. I could feel my face heating up.

Everyone else in Washington is oddly sexless. Oh, sure, power is an aphrodisiac and senators will bend their naive young assistants over the desks just to prove how goddamn awesome they are, but it's all done in a polite, carefully-choreographed ballet. This is a city where husbands and wives only argue over their affairs when one of them is indiscreet and threatens the other's chances for re-election.

This guy was the polar opposite of that. Raw and wild, untamed. He didn't hide his sexuality behind double-talk and mind games. He wasn't hiding the fact he was getting hard, under that tight denim. Whichever woman he was checking out would know, when she looked down and saw that bulge, that he was thinking about—

Wait, who *was* he checking out? He seemed to be looking my way. I twisted around, frowning, but I couldn't see anyone behind me.....

My eyes widened. He was looking at *me*... and he was still approaching.

I snapped back to front and hauled my eyes desperately *up*. The breeze was plastering the soft cotton of his t-shirt against his torso, now, a vertical cliff as solid and unyielding as granite. I could see the shallow depression where the fabric blew into his navel: an *inny,* same as me. We'd match. *Wait, why am I even thinking that?*

I found my eyes being drawn up, hypnotized by the swing of his pecs under that tight black cotton. Wide shoulders and broad, huge pecs that didn't make me think of DC gym bunnies who get up at 5am to pump iron. It put me in mind of a soldier, a *warrior:* muscles that weren't just for show. And, yep, I could see ink on those thick biceps, tattoos that looked like they could be military.

The guy was *big,* bigger than any of the suits around me, bigger than any of my Secret Service detail. And a *lot* bigger than my own small frame. In fact: if I stood up against him, like *right up against him* with my front pressed to his front, and someone looked at him from behind, I'd disappear, completely hidden by that big body. I reeled a little, imagining it. My nose would be near the tops of his pecs, my lips perfectly positioned to kiss across that warm expanse of flesh, my breasts would be brushing that hard torso and, further down, his groin would be—

What the hell is going on? I didn't normally react

to guys like this. Or stare at them like this. I dragged my eyes away from his body and looked at something safer, like his face.

Big. Mistake.

I looked up just as he reached me. Even his jaw didn't fit the scene. Strong and gorgeous and sporting a thick layer of black stubble, gleaming in the sunlight. None of the other guys around me were unshaven. I wondered if it would be scratchy, when he—

Get it together, Emily!

But I couldn't get it together. Because set right into that beautiful jaw were the most perfect set of male lips *ever*. Just the right combination of hard, strong upper and soft, sensuous lower. I unconsciously licked my lips, then realized what I'd done and blushed.

He was wearing sunglasses so I couldn't see his eyes, but he had soft, tousled hair, the blackest I'd ever seen. The wind was playing with the strands in exactly the way I wanted to.

"Miss Matthews," said a voice. It was weird, because he'd said it without moving his lips. And the voice didn't match his face at all. It was a refined, Boston accent, slightly nasal. It would fit better with—

Realization hit me. I twisted around to look at the guy in the suit—mystery man's companion. I'd completely forgotten about him and, immediately, I felt awful. *What's the matter with me?* "Hi! Yes!" I said enthusiastically. The breeze blew a lock of hair across my face and I scrambled to push it back.

The suit told me that he worked for one of the chemical companies sponsoring the science fair and we both agreed that, *yes,* the kids were wonderful and it's *so* important to get them interested in science at an early age and meanwhile a photographer to my left was snapping picture after picture of us shaking hands... and my mind, however hard I tried, kept drifting a few feet to my right, where mystery man was lurking.

I forced myself to focus on the suit, to nod sympathetically about how the new clean air bill was going to affect his company and reassure him that, yes, my dad totally understood the needs of industry and he was working very hard to make sure the right balance was met (after a whole day of saying it, the words rolled off my tongue like song lyrics).

Talking to the suit wouldn't normally have bothered me at all. It's part of being the President's daughter. But right then, all that small talk seemed so... stupid. False and meaningless. It was because *he* was standing there, just out of my eye line, his presence rolling off him in waves and slapping up against every inch of my body. Talking to *him*... that wouldn't be meaningless at all. It was suddenly all I wanted to be doing.

But I'm not someone who can be rude to anyone. So I took my time with the suit, listened to his concerns and promised I'd pass them on. And only when I'd finished did I flick my eyes in the direction of mystery man and raise my eyebrows to ask....

"Oh!" said the suit. "That's my protection."

As if he wasn't even worthy of a name. I *hate* people who do that. I felt a deep, hot rush of anger on mystery man's behalf. I turned to him and stuck out my hand. "Emily Matthews," I said.

He seemed surprised. I couldn't see behind the sunglasses but I imagined him blinking at me. Then he took my hand in his much bigger one and it was *so* much better than the suit's handshake: warm and strong and comforting. "Kian O'Harra," he said. "Ma'am."

That voice fitted. It was strong whiskey poured over slabs of rough-hewn rock, American but edged with something else, something beautiful and silvery I couldn't place. It burrowed deep into my brain and throbbed straight down to my groin. I'd never heard anything so good in my life.

"Emily," I said in a *don't be silly* tone.

"Ma'am," he rumbled stubbornly. And for some reason that sent a hot rush through me. I think it was the combination of old-fashioned politeness and the feeling that he really, really wanted to rip all my clothes off.

I swallowed. "You don't *look* like a bodyguard," I thought. And then realized I'd blurted it out loud.

He grinned as if he was very proud of that fact and took off his sunglasses. I found myself looking up into the clearest, bluest eyes I'd ever seen. A blue that put me in mind of frozen lakes of pure, glacial water... and yet his gaze wasn't cool at all. I could feel it heating up my skin, like I'd just opened an oven door. He didn't gawp, didn't glance down at my body. And yet I swore I felt that heat slide right down me.

"You don't look like *other* bodyguards," I said. He must have some sort of security clearance: there was a huge pistol holstered on his belt and you don't carry a weapon anywhere near the President's family without some very thorough checks. "Are you with a security company?"

He shook his head, not taking his eyes off me for a moment. "Private," he said. "Just me." He gave me a wry grin, showing white teeth. "I don't play well with others."

"Well," said the suit a little hotly, "we should let you talk to someone else." And he walked away, jerking his head to indicate that Kian should follow him. As if Kian wasn't worth wasting words on.

Kian and I both tensed in reaction. He scowled at the guy's retreating back, those glorious pecs lifting and his biceps swelling. I could see the anger building in those pure blue eyes and for a second I thought he was going to thump one big fist down on the suit's head, knocking him into the ground like a tent peg. But then he glanced back at me and we exchanged a look: *asshole!* And the anger seemed to drain from him. He sighed, gave me one last grin and ambled after the suit. I could hear the suit muttering something about *not paying you to flirt.*

That made me flush... but I grinned a little, too, turning away so that the cameras couldn't see. Guys don't flirt with me. Guys barely speak to me: they're too intimidated by my dad. And I spend twenty-four hours a day in a bubble of security, everyone I interact with carefully screened and vetted and every conversation watched. The idea of even meeting someone is far-fetched; *dating* would be absurd. Especially since I finished college and moved into a room at the White House. I mean, sure, it's *The White House,* but it's still living with my parents. I was looking forward to starting my new job in a few months and getting a place of my own.

What kind of name was *Kian* anyway? I was sure it was spelled that way, too: he'd said it *Key-an,* not *Kane.* It sounded hundreds of years old, maybe something from England or Scotland. The sort of name you'd give to some ancient warrior, standing on a windswept clifftop about to lead the charge against his foes. It suited him: there was something old-fashioned about Kian.

I sighed and turned back to the science fair. Time to get back to my duties. And stop thinking about rough, gorgeous, totally unsuitable men. Especially ones I'd never see again.

I took a step towards the other judges. The press moved in and I heard a flurry of shutter clicks.

And that's when the first gunshot rang out.

TWO

Kian

Asshole.

Businessmen annoy me at the best of times—which is a problem, because they're the ones who hire me, these days. But now he'd dragged me away from *her* and that made me royally pissed.

"I'm not paying you to flirt," bleated the guy. "I'm paying you for protection. She's right, you don't even look like the other bodyguards. Couldn't you have worn a suit?"

I ignored him. He didn't need protection. He'd only hired me because he'd wanted to feel big and important. What he really wanted was a guy in a suit with a bulge under his jacket to stand by his side and say *yes sir, no sir, the limo's here, sir.* He didn't notice—or care—about the actual protection stuff I did, like checking the sightlines and watching the crowd, sweeping under his limo for devices or planning escape routes.

I was tempted to tell him where to shove it but I

was painfully aware I needed the job. So I walked silently beside him, soaking up his bitching and moaning, and keeping myself calm by thinking about Emily.

I don't like politicians. And back when I used to protect them, I found that most of their families were pains in the ass, too. Back-slapping, guffawing senators who'd get wasted on brandy and need help sobering up before they could get into a strip club, then more help tottering from the limo to their house. Meanwhile their trophy wives would be sleeping with the gardener or the personal trainer and the poor kids were forgotten about aside from photo opportunities until they grew up to be carbon-copies of their folks. I'd never met the President but it made sense that he'd be even worse. And therefore that his daughter, by her twenties, would have become a power-hungry, backstabbing bitch.

And yet she hadn't been like that. *At all.*

She had an infectious energy about her that made me want to grin. I'd seen it in her as we approached, as she talked to the kids and shook hands with the businesspeople. The sort of person who lights up the whole room when they walk into it. And she was... I couldn't think of a better word than *good. Good,* in a city where every damn person was either trying to win power or cling onto the coattails of someone already there. She'd treated me as if I deserved respect. I hadn't had that for a long, long time.

And all the goodness, all that energy, was wrapped up in a body that made me instantly hard. Long, graceful legs, from what I'd glimpsed under that summer dress, and pert, luscious breasts, not big but perfectly shaped. She had a gorgeous wide mouth... I could have stared at those lips all day and when she'd licked them I'd caught my breath. All that soft, mahogany hair that hung down her back... I wanted that to be the only thing she wore. I wanted her sitting naked on the edge of my bed with that hair trailing down her naked back and pointing to that hot little ass like an arrow. And then I'd grab her waist and pull her to me and try to decide whether she or I would go on top.

That voice: sweet and earnest and so soft it seemed to wrap around you. It had a warm shaft of Texan sunshine running through it, but a very particular kind... I couldn't imagine her whooping or hollering. She sounded more like the innocent young schoolmarm who'd just arrived in town, all laced up tight in a bodice.

She was *good.* And that made part of me want to do very bad things to her.

Worryingly, it made another, deeper part of me come alive in a way I hadn't expected. It almost made me want to pick myself up out of the gutter and climb up to her lofty heights. Which was nuts. I'd made peace with what I was a long time ago.

Damn... so *that* was the President's daughter. I sighed. Some oil tycoon or CEO was going to be a lucky SOB, someday soon.

We reached the limo and I opened the rear door for the suit. He was just climbing in when the first gunshot rang out.

Everyone looked up. That's what happens with civilians: they're so completely unused to gunfire, they think that it can't possibly be happening *here, now,* to *them.* So their first reaction is to look around for the backfiring car.

15

I'd already gone into autopilot. I stuffed the suit into the limo before the shot had finished ringing in my ears. I started to climb in after him. One leg was already in the car when I turned and looked at the scene.

One man—a Secret Service agent, from the look of him, was down on the ground, blood staining his white shirt. And standing maybe six feet from him, looking down at him with huge, horrified eyes, was Emily.

As I watched, a second shot rang out. Another Secret Service agent was hit in the shoulder. He'd been running towards Emily and the impact sent him sprawling on the ground.

Now everyone started moving and screaming, running for the exits of the park or pressing themselves to the ground. Everyone except—

Emily just stood there, frozen. I could see her chest heaving as she took big, panic-stricken breaths. *Move!* I screamed in my mind. *Move, damn you!*

"Come on!" yelled the suit next to me. His voice was hoarse with fear. "Get in!"

I barely heard him. My whole world had narrowed down to Emily, standing motionless in the line of fire. Gut-wrenching fear hit me, a kind I'd never felt before. Twisted in with it, anger that anyone would dare put *her* in danger.

She was going to die. She was going to die unless someone did something *right now.*

I hurled myself out of the car, slammed the door behind me and rapped on the roof for the driver to go. And as the limo screeched away, I started to run.

THREE

Emily

Move!

I knew it was what I was supposed to do but I was staring down at Agent Hale. He'd been the head of my security detail for months now. He liked Krispy Kreme donuts and ice hockey and, the first time he'd ever flown on Air Force One, we'd hit turbulence and he'd thrown up and no one had ever let him forget it.

And now he was dying, right in front of me, clutching at the wound low down on his side. His shirt was slowly staining red. His fingers were dripping red where they covered the wound. Even the green grass beneath him was turning red. "*Run!*" he croaked.

But I couldn't. Everything was happening too fast. It had all been fine, I'd been goddamn *flirting* like some happy idiot and meanwhile someone had been plotting violence, planning to kill people I cared about. Planning to kill *me*.

Move!

Everyone was screaming. I heard a hiss of air, like

when you're playing softball and the ball flies right past your face. When I turned, another agent was falling behind me.

Move!

I finally managed to make my legs work and ran, but I had no idea where to run *to*. A building? There were none: only a few tents and wooden stands.

I can tell you exactly what being under fire from a sniper feels like: it's like being in a horrible, sick game played by the cruelest mind imaginable. The people in the park were now just ants, crawling across a tabletop: we could run, but it made no difference to the fist that slammed down every few seconds, picking one of us to crush. All of us were pleading the same thing in our minds: *please, please not me.*

And then I saw the kids. And I started pleading *please, please, not them.*

Most of them had been scooped up by terrified, sprinting parents but a few were just standing there as I'd been. I swerved and ran straight towards the nearest one.

Another shot. This one went so close that the hiss hurt my ears. Another Secret Service agent tumbled to the ground. I was so scared my muscles were locking up and I could barely run. But I kept stumbling across the grass, focused on the kid in front of me. Another ten paces and I could grab him and take him somewhere safe. Eight. Seven. Six.

I felt it right at the center of my left calf, as if someone had drilled a hole there and poured boiling water right into the core of the muscle. I screamed and tried to take another step but my leg wouldn't support me, anymore. I went down in a clumsy mess of arms and legs. The grass felt like concrete: every little jolt jarring my leg and making the pain ten times worse. Then I was sprawled on my side, panting, the pain seeming to pump its way higher and higher up my leg with each beat of my heart.

I actually thought my leg had cramped up. That's how in shock I was. It was only when I saw the blood on my calf that it sunk in that I'd been shot.

I knew I had to move but just *thinking* about moving tensed my muscles in preparation and white-hot pain seared through my calf. I rolled on my back and howled.

The shots had been coming at regular intervals. It was almost time for another one and, however much I wanted to deny it, I knew this was the one. I was an easy target, now, lying there on the ground. I looked towards where I thought the shots had been coming from and saw a tiny glint of light, off in the distance. I imagined the shooter racking the bolt, loading another round, lining me up in his crosshairs....

I squeezed my eyes shut and waited to die.

FOUR

Emily

A HUGE, WARM ARM hooked under my armpits and heaved me off the ground. My heels kicked once on the ground, sending a jolt of pain up my injured leg, and then I was fully airborne, lifted right off my feet. I felt the press of a body against my back, a hip rubbing against my ass, and it hit me that I was being carried under someone's arm like a piece of luggage. Who the hell was strong enough to do that? I still had my eyes squeezed shut but I could feel us moving: the darkness rose and fell in a fast, pounding rhythm. Who was strong enough to lift me and carry me *while running?*

I started to open my eyes but, just at that second, another bullet hissed by us. Hissed by *me.* I hadn't heard the hit when I was shot but I heard this one, a sound I never want to hear again, like a side of beef being slapped. My rescuer, whoever he was, had just been hit. I squeezed my eyes tight shut again, waiting to fall.

And heard, very clearly, a voice say *Motherfucker*. The syllables were twisted by pain and brutal anger but I recognized that whiskey-silver accent.

Then there was a deafening boom, the sound of a gun being fired only a few feet from my head, and I clung to the arm that held me as tightly as I could, my hands wrapped around a bicep that felt like warm rock. The gun roared again and again, a flurry of shots, as if my rescuer was pouring all his anger into it. And then I was flung down on my back on the grass and a huge, warm body was hunkering down on top of me.

I finally opened my eyes.

"You're going to be okay," said Kian O'Harra.

FIVE

Kian

I'd hurled us down behind a big wooden stand. It was only waist height but it was long enough for us to lie full-length behind and still be hidden. "Stay down," I told her. And then I tried to think of what to do next.

I was panting and not just from the run. I wasn't ready for what I was feeling. Since the second I saw her under fire, I'd been gripped by the need to protect her, primal and all-consuming, stronger than anything I'd ever known. I had my body completely covering hers, as low to her as I could without crushing her, and I never, ever wanted to move again. As long I stayed there, she was safe. I'd soak up bullets all day long, if need be.

I could hear her panting. Her face was close to my chest and I could feel each panicked breath as a warm gust pushing my t-shirt against me. I looked down and I was looking right into big, green, terrified eyes.

God, even like this she was so beautiful it hurt.

And it hit me that I could feel the soft mounds of

her breasts, pushing up against my abdomen. And our legs were scissored together, which meant our groins were almost touching. I could feel the heat of her body through the thin cotton of her summer dress. My head was focused on the danger but the message hadn't reached the rest of me—she was too gorgeous, too soft and fragrant beneath me. Her scent was amazing: warm skin, sun-kissed rocks, and desert winds.

I used my arms to lever myself up off her and then crawled backwards, taking care to stay behind the stand. "Let me see your leg," I said gruffly. She tensed as I reached for her ankle, then hissed in pain as I gently rotated it to see the back. I felt sick when I saw the twin holes, that beautiful, elegant calf I'd admired now shining with blood. The anger surged up inside me. I was going to personally eviscerate the guy who'd done this.

"It'll be okay," I told her. "The bullet went straight through. I know it hurts but you'll be okay."

I hunkered down over her again and searched the park with my eyes. Another shot rang out and I saw a guy in the distance fall to the ground: a cop. Most people had cleared out, by now, or were in hiding.

I looked down at her again. I could tell she was close to going into full-on shock. I put my hand on her cheek and she felt cold—she actually pushed her face into my hand a little and a hot little bomb went off in my chest.

"Just hang on," I said. "Help's coming. Okay?" Her eyes were going wild—she almost seemed to be looking through me. I'd seen this before: her mind was closing down to protect itself. I couldn't bear to see that happen, because I knew the kind of damage that would lead to. "Hey!" Barely a reaction. *"Emily."*

She focused on me. I cupped her cheek in my hand and stroked my thumb across the soft skin. "Listen to me: *they're coming.* You are the *President's daughter.* At the *very first shot,* the entire Secret Service and the DC police went into full-on red alert fucking crisis mode. There are squad cars *screaming* here. Trucks full of SWAT guys. Helicopters with counter-snipers. In about thirty seconds this park is going to be the safest place on earth. You just have to hang on."

She blinked and then slowly nodded. Looked around her. And then, to my horror, she tried to move.

I grabbed her shoulders and pushed her back down to the ground. "No," I said gently. "Stay down."

She shook her head and pointed. "The kid," she croaked.

I followed her finger.

There was a kid stumbling through the trees, maybe thirty feet away. I realized that's who she'd been trying to reach, when she was shot. And even now, lying here injured, she was trying to get to him. I looked down at her, speechless.

"No," I said. I knew exactly why the kid was still standing. The cowardly bastard who was sniping us was using him as bait. He'd be watching for anyone running towards the kid. It was the oldest trick in the book.

Emily answered by gritting her teeth and heaving herself a few inches along the ground on her elbows, wincing in pain.

"Stop!" I hissed. Then, "*I'll* get him."

She nodded in thanks and stopped moving.

I got awkwardly to my feet: there wasn't a lot of room, behind the stand. I crouched there between her legs and took a second to think and assess, like they'd taught me in the Marines. I slotted a fresh magazine into my pistol and measured the distance to the kid. It would be close to a suicide mission even if I could grab him and keep going. Stopping, turning, and running back to Emily would make it much more likely that I'd get hit. But leaving her undefended wasn't an option. I was bleeding: a bullet had winged my left shoulder but I'd been too busy carrying Emily to notice at the time. Picking a kid up off the ground was going to *hurt*.

I looked down at Emily. *"Stay here."*

She nodded.

I took a deep breath... and ran, squeezing off a shot in the direction of the sniper as I went. I had no hope of hitting him at this range: I was pretty much firing blind at the distant glint of metal. But it might make him keep his head down.

A bullet sliced through the air three inches in front of my face. *Or not.*

I thundered towards the kid, firing off two more wild shots. The kid had stopped and was just standing there, the bottom of his t-shirt twisted in his fingers, looking at the bodies around him. I thumped into him and kept moving, hoisting him over my shoulder. At least he was too scared to struggle.

I slid behind a tree like a baseball player stealing third base. Bark exploded from the edge of the tree, the shot missing us by a quarter-second.

I panted and scrambled to my feet. The longer I stayed there, the more time the sniper would have to prepare. I ducked my head and *ran,* charging like a bull. I didn't bother firing back, this time, just went for raw speed. Emily and the safety of the stand were only thirty feet away. Twenty feet.

A bullet punched a hole straight through the hem of my flapping t-shirt.

Ten feet. I resisted the urge to close my eyes.

A bullet skimmed my hair, so close I swear I felt the heat of the round against my scalp.

And then I was pressing the kid to Emily's chest and throwing myself over both of them like a protective blanket. My whole body was soaked with sweat. But at least now we'd be safe. How long had it been, since the shots started? Three minutes? Four? An almighty army would be descending any minute. All we had to do was to stay put.

That's when I heard the footsteps scrunching through the grass. Confident and assured. Not the steps of a man watching out for a sniper. The steps of a man who's protected by one.

There was a second shooter.

I heard a scream and a gunshot and now I *did* close my eyes. I could picture the plan, now, as if it was laid out on a military map. One sniper, to take out the Secret Service and any other heroes. One man on the ground to walk around and take out those who made it into hiding. With the sniper watching his back, he was untouchable. Hell, if they had radios, the sniper could direct him right to each hiding place.

The footsteps were coming closer.

He was heading right for us.

SIX

Emily

I LAY THERE PANTING, the kid pressed to my chest. He'd started to cry and I was making wordless little *shh*-ing noises and wishing I knew something about being a mom.

The panic was like cold, black water that kept threatening to push me down and drown me. It had nearly taken me a couple of times already, but Kian had brought me back. The press of his body against mine was my life raft. As long as I could cling on to him, I'd be okay. It was something that went beyond his physical size or the fact he had a gun, even beyond the fact he was a bodyguard. From the second he'd grabbed me, I'd just felt so... *protected,* in a way I never had before, not even when I was in the White House before all this started.

And then I felt him slowly draw away from me and sit up, pressing his back against the stand. And I realized it wasn't over.

"Someone's coming," he whispered. "Stay where

you are."

I nodded and put my arms around the kid. I could feel his tears wet against my neck and wondered why I hadn't started crying myself. I think I was too scared to.

Then I heard the footsteps myself. Heavy footsteps—a man almost as big as Kian. They were as slow and relaxed as if he was out for a stroll and that only made it scarier.

Kian was staring at something opposite our stand. A display the kids had made about pollution, with clouds made of silver card dangling on strings. There were hazy reflections in some of them: I caught glimpses of the man, walking up behind us. The stand was only waist high. In another few seconds he'd reach it, lean over and....

Kian sprang to his feet and twisted around to face the stand. He and the gunman fired at the same time.

And Kian missed.

I let out a scream as I saw a bullet hit him in the shoulder and knock him back on the ground, his pistol bouncing out of his hand. Then the gunman was right up against the stand, looking down at me and the kid.

My arms tightened around the kid. I rolled us over, wincing at the pain in my leg, so that the kid was hidden beneath me. I stared up at the gunman with fear and desperate, irrational anger. "*Why?*" I begged, my eyes finally filling with tears.

He had close-cropped blond hair and strong, craggy features: he'd almost have been good looking, but the cold deadness in his eyes made him terrifying. "It's just business," he said with a shrug. And leveled his gun at me.

SEVEN

Kian

I WAS DOWN. My right arm was useless: I could barely move it. That left my left, and I was a lousy shot with my left even when it *hasn't* been clipped by a bullet.

But a lousy shot is better than no shot.

I gritted my teeth and rolled towards my gun, crying out as my injured shoulder mashed into the ground. I clawed my pistol from the grass, came up to sitting, aimed one-handed at the gunman and emptied the magazine. Every shot sent pain reverberating through my arm and I gritted my teeth and panted through it.

On my final shot, I managed to wing him. It was enough to make him duck down behind the stand.

And then, behind me, I heard the most welcome sound in the world: sirens. And the thump of helicopter blades. They were coming.

The gunman peeked over the top of the stand. I was hoping he hadn't heard my gun click empty and thought I still had a few rounds left. We glared at each other. He was definitely ex-military: I could see it in the way he carried himself, in the way every decision was coldly tactical.

Including the decision to retreat. He turned and fled, disappearing into the trees just as a small army reached us.

They swept in on both sides of me: Secret Service agents in suits, DC police in uniform and SWAT guys in full tactical gear. Everyone was suddenly pointing guns at me, which was when I remembered I was sitting there in civilian clothes with a gun in my hand, six feet from the President's daughter. I let my gun fall from my fingers and four guys pinned me to the ground.

I saw them separate Emily and the kid and then Emily was lifted into the air and carried off at a run by two Secret Service guys. She stared at me until she disappeared from view. Her eyes were huge and terrified, as if she'd never feel safe again.

EIGHT

Emily

I live in the White House.

Not the part of the White House you see on TV, with its grand white columns and Oval Office. Deeper. The residence, where the President's family lives while he's in office, a place the press aren't generally allowed and where your public tour won't take you. Deeper still inside that are the bedrooms and the last room you come to, right at the end of the corridor: that's mine.

I was protected by a fifteen mile aerial exclusion zone, backed up by anti-aircraft defenses. Inside that, the most fiercely-guarded, closely-monitored ground perimeter in the world. Inside that, bulletproof windows to guard against crazed gunmen, tire shredders to deal with suicide bombers in vans and reinforced doors to protect us from rampaging mobs. Within the walls, hallways patrolled by armed Secret Service agents who could swap their handguns for assault rifles in the event of a breach, security doors that could seal off the residence and evacuation routes down to the secure bunker in the basement in case of absolute, total security failure.

I was the best-protected woman in the world, beyond anything envisaged for a princess in a fairy tale.

And I still didn't feel safe.

Things after the park are a little blurry. I don't remember spacing out, or going catatonic, or whatever you want to call it. But I can only piece together about half an hour of memories of that afternoon and apparently I was at the hospital for over six hours, so clearly I wasn't *there* for some of it.

I know that I was taken to the designated emergency evacuation hospital for the President and his family, and that I was treated in a closed-off corridor guarded by the Secret Service, so I didn't see any of the other people who'd been hurt. I know some were taken to other hospitals and that there were twenty-two injuries in total, enough for the hospitals to call on all of their trauma staff.

I know that I was lying face-down on a bed with a doctor working on my wound when I heard that the number of deaths was confirmed at six. Four Secret Service agents, one cop and one man identified as a private security contractor. I threw up, when I heard that, especially because no one had been able to tell me where Kian was, or how badly he was hurt. When I eventually found out that the guy killed was a park security guard in his sixties, I slumped on my bed in relief... and then immediately hated myself for being relieved, as if the fact it wasn't Kian made it any less awful.

No kids were hit. No one knew if that was by design or by sheer luck, but I offered up a prayer of thanks.

Hale, the head of my Secret Service detail, would live, but the bullet he'd taken in his side took him off active service: he'd be working a desk for the rest of his career.

The Secret Service's first move, almost as soon as the first shot was fired, was to evacuate the President to the bunker: they were worried about coordinated attacks and were fully expecting shooters to start advancing across the White House lawn. The First Lady was in Texas, giving a speech: she was rushed off stage and secured in her hotel room.

All of which was sensible and understandable and they were only doing their jobs. But it meant that I didn't get to see my mom or dad for over two hours, until my dad overruled the head of the Secret Service and said he'd damn well drive *himself* to the hospital if they didn't agree to take him.

Part of me almost didn't want him to come. I knew there was a very real possibility that the entire attack, including me getting shot, had been just a ploy to lure my dad to the hospital without adequate security measures. Like everything in my life, things that happen to me are seen through the lens of how it might affect him. That's why I'm *the President's daughter* to most people and not *Emily*.

Kian had been right about my leg: the bullet had gone straight through the muscle and out the other side without touching the bone. With some physiotherapy, I'd be fine. I remember thanking the doctors again and again and trying to persuade them to go help someone who was hurt worse. I did everything I could to find out where Kian was but there was too much confusion and the injured were spread between too many hospitals: eventually, I heard he'd been treated, questioned for a long time by the FBI and then released.

The FBI were everywhere. It was the worst attack on American soil for years. What drove me mad was how the news media kept relating it to *me*. They kept referring to an attack on the President's daughter until I finally screamed at a reporter that they should be focusing on the twenty-two people who hadn't been as lucky as me.

At first, the media just called it an *attack,* but within about eight hours it became a *terrorist attack.* A group calling themselves the Brothers of Freedom claimed responsibility and the media went *nuts* for a solid week with pundits speculating on where they'd come from and how they'd managed to strike so viciously, so effectively, right in the middle of DC. The group was a homegrown, extremist militia whose idea of freedom seemed to be anarchy: they wanted the end of government and, specifically, the flag and the constitution, the end of taxes, the end of laws and a society based on all-out dog-eat-dog chaos. There was a heartening lack of sympathy for them—the entire nation seemed to be firmly allied against them. But that didn't make them any less dangerous.

Neither shooter was apprehended. Helping the FBI to put together a photofit of the second shooter was easy because his face was burned into my memory forever. I went through hundreds of mug shots, too, but couldn't identify him. Somehow, both men had sneaked out of the city and vanished. The media, always desperate to find someone to blame, raged against both the FBI and the Secret Service, demanding to know how this could happen. The director of the FBI made some defensive comments about needing more funding and better surveillance. The Vice President surprised everyone by turning it into his personal cause. For years, he'd been pushing for more surveillance and tougher laws, but now he brought it all together into a bill. Given the climate, there were no end of co-signers eager to jump on the bandwagon.

And me? That night I went home to the White House, patched up, medicated and as safe as a person could be. I hugged my mom and dad, went to the most secure bedroom on the planet and waited to heal.

But I didn't heal.

I got worse.

Helena Newbury

NINE

Emily

IT STARTED the night I got home from the hospital. Maybe I should have expected it. The doctors had expected it: they'd given me details of people I could talk to if I needed to (I nodded and promised I would) and offered me something to help me sleep (I turned it down). But I was focused on my leg and how lucky I was that the bullet hadn't shattered a bone or shredded a nerve and left me in a wheelchair for life, or just hit me in the chest or head and ended me right there. I thought I was okay.

And then, at about two a.m., when the residence was quiet and still, a man broke into my room and stabbed me in the chest.

It wasn't a nightmare. I'd had nightmares. This was something else. I felt the weight of him on top of me, felt the knife slip between my ribs, When I woke up I could see the dark blood on the sheets and on my hands and it took long seconds before it faded.

I climbed out of bed: I couldn't stay in it because I

was *sure* the sheets were blood-soaked, no matter how many times I checked to make sure they weren't. Three times, I told myself angrily not to be so freaking silly and forced myself to limp back into bed and get under the covers, only to stagger out again a few moments later, physically shaking with fear. I wound up sitting in the doorway between my bedroom and bathroom, hugging my knees and trembling. I stayed like that until the dawn broke through the drapes and then I breathed a little easier because I assumed the fear would disappear with the night.

I was wrong.

When I hobbled over to the window, I saw the sun rise on a world filled with threats. Every slow-moving car could contain a gunman, the window whining down to reveal a dark barrel pointed right at my head. Every man—every *woman*—walking down the street was hiding explosives under their coat, ready to swerve towards me and cover the distance between us in less time than it took to scream.

I'd always known I was in danger. But it was the first time I really felt it, in all its bone-deep, horrifying certainty. When you know something like that, you can't think of anything else.

I couldn't go outside. The dreams were bad enough, but at least I could tell myself that they couldn't hurt me. Outside, the threat was real.

At first, it wasn't too bad. My injured leg meant that no one expected me to attend events anyway. I hunkered down in the residence. If someone asked how I was doing, I said *fine,* because I'd convinced myself that this was just a temporary glitch and normal service would soon be restored. For the same reason, I didn't call the therapists the doctors had recommended. Six people had died and it was *my fault* because, ultimately, it had been *me* the gunmen had been targeting. I'd been lucky enough to survive: what right did *I* have to be messed up? *It'll get better. Give it time.*

There was another factor, too. I'm not just *Emily*, I'm the President's daughter. A lot of the time it's like being a freakin' fairy tale princess: I know how lucky I am. But there are strings attached. Ever since my dad took office, I'd done my best to support him. I'd been to every press event, watched every word I said to the press... I even agreed to take a job with my mom's charitable foundation, even though it wasn't what I wanted. And I'm okay with the sacrifices: my family is a team.

If I let myself crack up over this, if I had to go to therapy, I felt like I'd be letting the team down.

But the nightmares didn't go away. I slept because I was exhausted but I woke several times a night. Sometimes I was out of bed and across the room, cowering in a corner, before I fully woke up. I dreamed that I was shot and stabbed and poisoned. I dreamed that men tied me and tortured me and raped me, that they killed the people I loved. And every time, it was worse because it was somehow my fault.

I could barely function, much less go out. But the longer I stayed inside, the more frightening the outside world became. The day before, I'd been itching to move out of The White House and get a place of my own. Now, it was my one safe haven.

The first warning sign was the memorial service for those killed, in the Rose Garden, I stood between my mom and dad and shook hands with the relatives, I told them how brave their loved ones had been and how we'd never forget their service and I meant every word. But I felt like the facade was shattering in slow motion, big jagged cracks with nothing but a dark void between them. Not bolting for the safety of the White House was like trying to stand my ground as an 18-wheeler truck roared straight toward me. Every time the cameras clicked, my stomach knotted as I waited for the first bullet to slam into me.

That day was a turning point. Something snapped inside me and, from then on, I *couldn't* leave. I couldn't take the chance that something awful would happen. So I made excuses: I said my leg hurt, I told them I had to prep for the new job I was due to start soon with a charitable foundation... anything but the truth.

***

It had been a full month—it wasn't as if the date could pass without me noticing because the TV news channels were full of the "one month anniversary." A full month of me being weak and stupid and people growing silently frustrated with me.

Tonight's the night. This has to stop.

Tonight, I had to go out. A concert by the New York Philharmonic at the John F. Kennedy Center. A limo ride, a thirty-second walk across the red carpet and a few hours in a big, safe room listening to great music. *Easy.* Except that thirty seconds would feel like thirty years. Except every camera click would make me want to throw up.

I dug my nails into the palms of my hands and marched off to see my dad. The more people knew I was going, the harder it would be for me to back out.

I caught him coming out of the Oval Office. "Emily!" He gave me big, warm, Texas smile. "Feeling okay?"

My dad is in his sixties and what people call *intimidatingly tall.* Six-foot-four with hair that's still got some black in between the silver. He has a way of looking at you that makes you feel like no one else in the world exists.

"Great," I lied. "Didn't mean to disturb you. I just wanted to say I'm definitely coming tonight."

I saw the relief break across his face and it cemented my decision. I'd been cooped up long enough: I had to fight this thing.

And then, just as I was feeling good, a hand landed on my shoulder. "That's great news, Emily," said the Vice President. "Good to see you getting back to your old self."

I gave my best fake smile and counted the seconds until I'd be free of his hand. I could feel my guts twisting, the *wrongness* throbbing down from each finger that touched me, like being plugged into evil.

Let me tell you about the Vice President.

Edward Kerrigan is handsome in a safe, bland sort of a way. He has curly blond hair that probably made him a really cute kid and big gray eyes that look good in photos, but are utterly soulless when you see them in real life. If you stranded a choirboy on a desert island at age eight and left him to grow up by himself with no parents, no moral compass, killing animals with his bare hands to survive, when you came back in thirty-five years he'd look exactly like Kerrigan.

Other women go nuts for him: women in their thirties, even women in their twenties. I sometimes wonder if there's something wrong with me because I can't stand him. The guy's got it all: he's rich (and it's not daddy's money, like a lot of politicians: he built up his company from nothing and was CEO for years), he dresses well and he's never been hit with a scandal. His wife is beautiful. His kids are adorable.

And yet....

Imagine the most enticing cake you've ever, ever seen. Smoothly frosted with thick chocolate frosting, intricately decorated with sugar flowers. It looks *perfect*. Everyone's inviting you to take a big ol' bite.

But you know—you just have this instinct—that it's a trick. That just beneath the frosting, instead of light, perfect, sponge, it's a solid block of squirming, crawling maggots and roaches. It doesn't matter how good it smells: the thought of biting into it makes you want to hurl. But *only you know*. Everyone else wonders what the hell's the matter with you. *Don't you like cake?*

That's how Edward Kerrigan made me feel. Every. Single. Time.

The hand on my shoulder rubbed. Not in a sexual way. More like he was stroking a puppy. "I'm going to see to it," he told me, "that those bastards can never do this again."

Both my dad and I stiffened because we knew exactly what he was talking about: *The Guardian Act.*

It was the Vice President's bill, the one he'd announced in response to the attack in the park. Lately he'd been all over the media talking about it, using phrases like *a new era of security* and *leaving the bad guys no place to hide.* The bill promised to end terrorism by putting a huge new security force on the streets, together with more surveillance. To a public in shock, it sounded like a good idea. And while there was plenty of opposition from grassroots protestors and people like the ACLU, the media were divided... and starting to lean his way. Stoking the public's fear of more terror attacks was a good way to sell papers.

My dad, like me, could see the true horror of what he was proposing: martial law... but much, much worse than anything our country had ever known after a disaster. Because the Vice President wasn't proposing that we use the army to protect us: he wanted to use private military contractors. Tens of thousands of them, enough that there would be no way they could all be adequately trained. Every street corner would have a goon with an assault rifle on it, with the power to stop and search anyone they wanted. Suspects would be interrogated where necessary, and the bill contained passages that overturned the ban on *enhanced interrogation techniques*—in other words, torture. Without the training and oversight of the real military, abuse of power would be rife.

There was another side to it, too. The Vice President was promising a massive increase in surveillance, with facial-recognition cameras on every street. We would all become permanent suspects: watched, judged and, where necessary, spirited away to secret detention centers. There were very few checks and balances—anyone suggesting adding more was accused of being on the side of the terrorists. So the people watching the cameras would quickly become as corrupt as the goons on the streets. You'd find yourself dragged into a van, screaming and helpless, a bag over your head, because some guy at a monitoring station disagreed with something you'd said... or, terrifyingly, because you met him in a bar the night before and turned him down.

It was terrifying. But the scariest part was why Kerrigan was doing this.

Before he took office, the Vice President was CEO of Rexortech: the world's largest private military contractor and surveillance company. They'd get the contract if this whole thing happened: every security officer, every camera. Rexortech would make billions of dollars and Kerrigan would return to them and become a billionaire. That was one reason. It was sickening, but it wasn't the worst one.

The worst reason was something you only got a hint of if you were around Kerrigan long enough, as I had been. Just occasionally, when he looked away from the cameras and dropped his smile for a second, you'd catch a glimpse of something... *vicious*. A child's cruel anger. Something must have happened to him when he was young: maybe he was bullied, maybe the prom queen laughed at him when he asked her for a date, I don't know. But someone had made him feel small and he'd never moved past it. I figured the Guardian Act was his revenge: if it went through, he and Rexortech would have total control over everyone in the country.

Fortunately, he was facing off against my dad. And the look on my dad's face said it all: no way was he going to let Kerrigan turn America into—as he put it— *a goddamn police state*. His hand landed on my other shoulder, warm and possessive. Kerrigan's hand slid away, leaving my skin clammy under my blouse.

We both watched him walk away. With every step he took, I felt a little better. I had to resist the urge to shudder. "You can't let him push his bill through," I muttered.

My dad pulled me into a hug and then kissed the top of my head. "I won't," he told me.

Except it wasn't as easy as that. In theory, the VP should support the President. In practice, my dad needed him: his youth and tech-savvy was the whole reason my dad put him on the ticket when he ran for election. And Kerrigan's rose-tinted vision of an ultra-secure America sounded *good* to a lot of terrified voters. They couldn't understand why my dad wasn't jumping on board.

My dad drew back and looked at me. When he saw the worry in my eyes, he pulled me into the Oval Office and pushed the door closed behind us. "I have to humor him a little," he said. "That's the climate, right now. But I'm not going to let him turn this country into a prison, especially not one guarded by his private goon squad." He squeezed my shoulders. "Not on my watch."

I smiled and relaxed a little. Of course he'd never let it happen. And I was aware that part of the reason I was so focused on Kerrigan was because it took my mind off the freezing, dark fear that rose up every time I thought about going out in public.

"You sure about tonight?" my dad asked.

I nodded quickly. "Absolutely." I kissed his cheek and ran off to get ready before I could change my mind.

***

A few hours later, I was sitting in the back of a limo

with my dad, gliding through the DC streets. Sitting across from me was my new Secret Service bodyguard, Daniel "call me Dan" Hudson. Technically, he'd been assigned to me for a month, ever since Hale had been shot, but this was the first time I'd been out. He seemed nice: serious and yet friendly, but...

... but he didn't make me feel protected the way Kian had. I could feel the panic churning inside me, ready to explode, and looking at Hudson did nothing to calm it.

Beside Hudson was Harlan Tate, my dad's chief bodyguard since the day he took office and the chief bodyguard of two presidents before that. Harlan reminded me of a big, solemn, utterly faithful Labrador. Of all the Secret Service, I liked him the most. He almost felt like an uncle.

But even his presence didn't make me feel safe. The closer we got to the John F. Kennedy Center, the more I tensed up. I could feel the freezing black water rising by the second, threatening to drown me, and I couldn't stop it no matter how hard I tried. I had my heels pressed against the floor of the limo to stop them from shaking and the tendons in my legs felt like they were straining so hard they were about to snap. I knew the limo was bulletproof but, the second I'd stepped outside the White House, I'd felt like I was an ant again, crawling across a tabletop, waiting for the fist to strike. *We'd have no warning....*

The limo came to a stop. I knew the exit order because we'd been through it a thousand times. Harlan first, then my dad. Then me, then Hudson behind me. Easy.

I watched my dad step from the limo. I swung my

legs out so that I was facing the red carpet and heard the constant clicking of the cameras for the first time.

It'll be fine.

I pushed myself upright and the scene turned white as the cameras turned towards me and a hundred flashes went off at once.

It's all fine.

I took a step forward, cautious in my heels. I was still a little shaky without crutches but I could do it if I concentrated and I was determined to prove I was back to normal. *One foot in front of the other.*

The cameras went *clickclickclickclickclick*.

And, suddenly, it wasn't fine at all.

Helena Newbury

50

TEN

Emily

IT STARTED with the pain in my leg. It had been a dull ache when I stepped from the car but now it was heating and blossoming, turning scalding red and sharp-edged. I stopped walking and focused on maintaining my smile: I didn't want the headlines to be *President's daughter bravely battles injury.* I wasn't brave; I was a coward for being scared.

But stopping didn't help. The pain grew and grew, cutting deeper and sending jolts up and down my leg. *What the hell is going on?* I looked down at my leg, expecting to see fresh blood welling from the wounds, but the scars were just the familiar dark circles under my nylons.

Clickclickclickclickclick

I tried to take another step but now it wasn't just the pain that stopped me: I was rooted to the spot, just as I had been when the first shot rang out in the park. I looked ahead of me to the crowd: twenty-deep on each side, held back by flimsy red ropes. Everyone was smiling and cheering but that was irrelevant, like telling someone the water's warm when they can't swim.

I can't move. And it felt as if the whole world was rushing in towards me: photographers and the public, police and cars and barriers and buildings, all sliding inward to press into my mouth and ears and lungs and—

I can't breathe. Something was around my neck, crushing my windpipe invisibly and silently. I couldn't draw air.

I put my hand out to the side, grabbing for something... some*one*. I didn't know who, at the time. But they weren't there.

There was a gentle push on my back. Hudson. I turned to him, eyes huge, and he blinked at me as if to say, *what's the problem?* It wasn't that he didn't look concerned. It was that he didn't look concerned *for me*. It was his first night properly on the job and he wanted everything to go well.

"—*get out,*" I croaked. I couldn't even manage a complete sentence.

He tilted his head to one side and smiled blankly. *Come on,* his expression said, *be a good girl. Play your part.* He put his hand on my back and pushed a little harder.

My feet didn't move. I swayed in place and almost fell.

Hudson frowned and he couldn't stop just a hint of frustration from showing. "It's okay," he said. "We'll be inside in a sec'."

I stared at the gaping black maw of the John F. Kennedy Center. A building wasn't safer. It meant shadows where people could lurk, people who wanted to hurt me. Only the White House was safe.

I spun around to face the motorcade and tried to walk forward, but hit Hudson's strong chest. *"Whoah,"* he said, slightly panicked. "Wait..."

I still couldn't pull in air. My heart was thumping faster and faster and every thunderous beat ratcheted the fear higher and higher in my chest.

The press noticed first. As I cast frantic glances around me, a ripple went through them. Cameras and video cameras swung my way, capturing my pale skin and the dark "O" of my mouth.

I pushed at Hudson's chest, which was like pushing on a brick wall. *I have to go, I have to get out of here,* I wanted to say. But it came out as a hysterical, fractured shriek. *"Go!"* Whose voice was that? It wasn't mine.

Hudson was genuinely panicked, now, and looked around for assistance, unsure of what he should do. That only made my own panic worse. There was one tiny part of me that was still calm: it seemed to bob above the whole scene like a balloon on a string, watching my freak-out with dismay as it tried to claw back control. But any second, I was going to lose that, too. I was sinking into that black, icy fear: it was up to my shoulders, my neck, flooding in through my lips and drowning me—

When I glanced back over my shoulder, Harlan had picked up on what was happening. He looked torn: my dad was moving and he had to stay with my dad *no matter what.* But I was clearly going into full-on meltdown before his eyes. *I'm sorry!* I thought. *I don't know what's happening!*

I tried to sidestep around Hudson but he blocked me as if I was drunk and he was trying to stop me walking into traffic. "Whoah," he said again, and then he spoke for the benefit of his radio. "We have, um....a problem here with Emily." He was flustered enough that he didn't use the Secret Service codeword for me, which is *Liberty*.

"Emily?" My dad's voice. I twisted around and saw that he'd stopped just before the building's doorway. That was bad. That was *really* bad. We'd all been drilled that the President mustn't dawdle on that walk from the car to the building: every second he was exposed put him at risk.

I was putting him at risk. Guilt joined the fear, I was putting everyone at risk because of some stupid... whatever the hell this was. And the press were right there recording it all: not just stills cameras but TV cameras broadcasting all of this live. I needed to snap out of it, *right now*. But I couldn't.

My heart wasn't just racing, now. It was a constant stream of beats, barely discernible. I was beneath the black water, drowning fast. I hadn't gotten air for what felt like hours and the world was going dark around the edges, narrowing down to a tunnel. The pressure was building and building: my chest ached with it, screamed with it.

I ran.

I bolted so fast that I took Hudson by surprise. I shot along the side of the motorcade, searching for a gap between the vehicles where I could race across the street to where my animal brain said it was quieter, safer.

Absolute chaos erupted. The Secret Service had prepared for every possible threat... but not for me to go psycho and try to evade them. Was procedure to evacuate the whole family or just me? And how do you evacuate someone who's trying to escape?

A Secret Service agent the size and shape of a linebacker stepped in front of me and tackled me, wrapping his arms around me and lifting me clear of the ground. I flailed and kicked, catching him in the knee with the point of my shoe, and he gritted his teeth. The crowd, which had been clapping and cheering, grew eerily silent. I could imagine hands going to horrified mouths, lips being bitten... and a thousand camera phones clicking.

Harlan took control. "Liberty to Castle, *go!*" he snapped. *Castle* was the White House.

The White House. Safety.

I was bundled headfirst into the limo. The interior should have been dim but it was being lit up almost continually by the flash of cameras from behind me. I felt the bodyguards pile in alongside me and then we were screeching away from the curb. I looked up through the rear window and saw my dad being bundled into the car behind me. *No!* He was having to leave, too. The whole evening was ruined because of me!

"Emily?" said Hudson. "Emily?"

The darkness at the edges of my vision closed in... and I passed out.

***

Two hours later, I was sitting on the floor of my bedroom with my ear pressed up against the door. Dr. Thorpe, a psychiatrist, had left me in my bed doped up with a sedative but I needed to know what they were saying about me so I'd staggered over to the door to listen.

I could hear my dad's hushed voice in the hallway outside, demanding answers. My mom was there, too. My emergency consultation with Dr. Thorpe should have been private, of course, but things like that go out the window when it's the President asking.

The first thing I heard was *post-traumatic stress disorder*. Which was ridiculous because that was something soldiers got, after being shot in Iraq. I didn't have any right to have something like that. *Just grow up, Emily! Get over it!*

"—not uncommon." Dr. Thorpe was saying. "We can make progress, given time. But we should have started treatment much sooner after the event."

I heard my dad sigh. "We didn't *know*. We thought she was okay."

I closed my eyes as the first hot tears rolled down my face. I wanted to be okay. I wanted to be the dutiful girl I'd always been, on hand for photo opportunities and interviews, supporting him. I was messing everything up.

"—a sedative," said Dr. Thorpe. "She'll sleep now. But she needs to start seeing someone to address this."

A concerned question from my mom, too low to hear.

"Months. It's harder because she's under so much pressure. Everything is harder when you're doing it in public view."

I could imagine my parents nodding understandingly. I couldn't hear their parting words but I could guess at them. *We'll give her as much time as she needs.*

I didn't *want* more time. I wanted this thing out of

me. I wanted *me* back.

I put my head in my arms and wound up falling asleep like that, wet-cheeked and hunched up against the door.

***

When I woke, fourteen hours had passed. It was the first uninterrupted night's sleep I'd had since the shooting. My mind was full of half-remembered nightmares that I'd been too drugged to wake from but at least I was rested. It gave me enough energy to make a decision.

I had to beat this thing.

Therapy might help and I'd try that, too, but I knew myself and I'd watched this thing progress over the last month. The longer I hid away, the worse it was going to get. I had to get out there and face my fears: that's what a President's daughter should do, no matter how much my mom and dad tried to reassure me it was okay. Me being weak weakened *them*.

What I needed was to feel safe. What would make me feel safe?

I ran a deep, hot bath, climbed in and sat there with my knees bent and my arms wrapped around them, staring down into the water. I kept reliving the previous night. Clearly, crowds were a trigger. So were the press and their cameras. But what I kept remembering was that point just before the panic had fully taken hold, when I'd reached out for someone.

I'd reached out for Kian.

That's stupid. I'd met the guy for the sum total of less than ten minutes. I knew almost nothing about him. And yet, at my darkest moment, it was him I'd wanted.

He made me feel safe.

Oh, get real! I pushed the thought away. *Come up with a real solution!*

Medication, maybe. Millions of people were on some pill, for something. There was nothing wrong with it. But I had the horrible feeling that that would just disguise the problem, not fix it. Maybe I'd be able to sleep through the nightmares, as I had the night before, but they'd still be there. I'd still wake up each morning with the sick feeling that I'd died in the night, over and over.

Kian. Even back in the park, as soon as he'd covered me with his body, he'd made me feel safe. And yes, I wasn't denying there was attraction there, too, deep and powerful. But it was more than that. I felt *safe* in the White House because of the thick walls and security but Kian made me feel *protected,* like an animal guarded by her mate.

I squeezed my arms tighter around my knees. This was no time for infatuation. I needed a proper solution. My dad had asked if I'd be more comfortable with a female bodyguard, someone I could talk to. But I'd never had a problem with the men before—I didn't in any way blame Hudson for what had happened, it was all on me. The Secret Service were fine: they looked after me.

But they didn't make me feel *protected.*

Shut up, Emily!

There was only one force on earth that did, right now. Whenever I thought of him, the fear receded a little. I remembered that whiskey-and-rock voice telling me it was going to be okay... and I believed it even now.

Kian O'Harra.

And finally, I just stood up, the water sluicing down my naked body, and said, out loud, "Okay."

If that's what it took for me to get back to being *me,* if that was really the only option, then I'd do it.

I dried off and dressed, went to my computer... and started hunting down Kian O'Harra.

ELEVEN

Kian

I was nursing my fourth drink.

Four is one too many, the tipping point. Three and the memories stay walled up. Four and they start to ooze out. Then I tend to need five to drown them out: sometimes six. And going down that path too often leads to problems.

So normally it's three drinks. But tonight it was four because I was mad. I'd been about to leave the bar when the TV had flicked to a recap of last night's clusterfuck outside the concert. I'd watched as the Secret Service agents tried to calm Emily down and then finally bundled her into the car, watched by about a million people. It wasn't that they'd reacted particularly badly, given that they'd been taken by surprise. It was that they'd been taken by surprise at all. Why couldn't they see that something was wrong the second she climbed out of the limo? *I'd* seen it written all over her face. Hell, why was she even *at* an event like that? Clearly she wasn't ready. I imagined how terrified she must have been, to bolt like that, and my guts twisted.

Hence the fourth drink. It helped me slide away from a sensation I didn't want to ever feel again: the feeling of watching someone you care about get hurt.

Stupid. I barely knew her.

So why hadn't I been able to get her out of my head since the park?

I lived a pretty simple life. I got up—usually not before noon—met the asshole who thought he needed protection, stayed by his side all evening and saw him back to his five-star hotel room and then went down to the bar. Sometimes it was DC and sometimes it was New York and sometimes it was even Sao Paulo or Paris or London. But five-star hotels are pretty much five-star hotels the world over. So are their bars and so are the women I found in them. Female executives traveling on business: single, lonely, with no time to date outside work and terrified of dating someone inside work and risking "complicating things." Sex with me was *un*complicated. They knew they'd never see me again, that I wouldn't show up at their corporate headquarters and embarrass them. There was never any pretense that it was anything other than a one night thing. We hooked up, had fun and I was gone long before the sun rose. That had always done me just fine until this last month.

Now, though, I couldn't stop thinking about soft, mahogany hair. About a body that was just the right combination of hard and soft with a rounded ass my palms had caressed a million times in my mind. I only had to think of those soft pink lips and I was instantly hard. All of which at least kind of made sense: Emily was hot as hell.

What didn't make sense was that I kept thinking about her energy, too, that spark that lit up rooms. I wanted to see her smile again. I wanted to see her laugh. I wanted to *make* her laugh. When I'd seen her on TV, outside the concert, she'd looked not just deathly afraid but *different,* as if the life had been sucked right out of her. That bothered me on a much deeper level, one that I hadn't felt in years. One I hadn't thought I even still possessed.

It killed me that she'd been hurt. Not just the physical wound: that would heal. But the damage I could see all too clearly when I watched her freeze, turn and finally run. I recognized that sort of damage.

I was intimately familiar with it.

And the fact it had happened to someone as sweet and good as Emily tore me apart. I'd failed her. If I'd gotten to her sooner, if I'd been able to get her out of the park instead of being forced to take cover....

I downed the fourth drink and got a fifth. But I still clocked the Secret Service agent as soon as he walked in. I didn't recognize him but I knew the suit, the coat, the earpiece. Then his buddy joined him and they came over to my table.

"I've already given a statement," I told them. "More than one. The cops, the FBI, you guys... how many times do you want me to go through it?"

"That's not why we're here, sir," said the first one. The *sir* confused me because they were Secret Service and they must have known who I used to be... and what happened to me. I looked closer and... *yep*, their faces were carefully neutral but I could see the barely-contained sneers in their eyes. They hated me, as I'd expected. The fact they were being polite must mean they were here under orders....

No way.

"She's outside, sir," confirmed the second one.

Part of me wanted to tell them where to go, just to piss them off. But the chance to see her again easily overrode my ego. I slowly stood and followed them to the parking lot.

Three black SUVs were there. They searched me and confiscated my gun: I glared at them but didn't argue. And then they opened the rear door of the center SUV and there she was, sitting in the middle of that huge backseat looking even smaller and more vulnerable than I remembered her.

"Hi," said Emily.

TWELVE

Kian

I SLID ONTO THE SEAT next to her and the agent outside slammed the door. The driver stayed in place up front, in case we needed to get out of there quickly, but he was behind a layer of glass and couldn't hear us. Outside, the agents faced outward, watching for threats... but they glanced over their shoulders to let me know *I* was being watched, too.

"Ma'am," I said cautiously.

"You're not on duty now," she said. "Emily."

Emily. I wanted to say it. I wanted to whisper it, pant it, growl it. But down that road lay disaster. I just nodded.

"I never got a chance to thank you," she said. Her hands were twisting together in her lap, her fingers never still. Even in a bulletproof SUV, surrounded by agents, she was scared witless. How hard had it been for her to come all the way out here, to this dive of a place?

"Not necessary," I told her. I didn't say *I'm glad*

you're okay because she wasn't. Clearly, she wasn't.

I'd seen it on TV but I'd hoped it had just been momentary. Now, in the flesh, I could see the change in her. That energy I liked so much had gone, the light cruelly extinguished. She looked more fragile. And she didn't light up the room, anymore. She *hid,* even when you were looking right at her.

That didn't change her beauty but it changed how I reacted to it. Before, she'd been so damn pretty it had hurt. That face, that body... they brought out an animal need in me to grab her and kiss her harder than I'd ever kissed anyone, tear that white blouse off her button by button and then start working my way all the way up those long legs with my lips. But I liked her way too much to make her a one night stand and I couldn't offer anything else... not anymore. So it had hurt, knowing that I could never have her.

Now, though, it was different. Now, it was goddamn heartbreaking. The fear was owning her, draining the life from her and making her shy away from everyone. I hadn't kidded myself she could be mine... but the way she was spiraling downward, she wasn't going to get to be happy with *anyone,* even the asshole oil tycoon I'd imagined her with.

It wasn't fair. She'd done nothing wrong. She hadn't asked to be born into this life and these risks.

I knew I was staring at her, losing myself in those soft green eyes. But I couldn't stop. I figured this was probably the last time I'd ever see her and part of me wanted to just selfishly drink in as much of her as I could.

Meanwhile, she was staring right back at me. I could feel her fear easing, like when you pet a nervous animal and it slowly stills. Except I wasn't touching her. I wasn't doing a damn thing except being near her. And the longer we looked at each other, the more I could feel a different kind of tension building. Part of me wanted to warn her off, to tell her that she had no idea what she was getting into.

Part of me just wanted to dive across that seat, push her back on the upholstery and *own* her.

"How did you find me, anyway?" I asked. "How'd you know I'd be *here?*"

She swallowed. "I didn't. The agents asked at your apartment building. Then we went around the bars people suggested. This is the fourth we've tried."

She must have been cruising around the neighborhood for a full hour, all while scared out of her mind. However strong of a hold the fear had on her, she wasn't giving up easily. "All just to say thank you?" I asked, deliberately gruff.

"No. Not just to say thank you." She looked right into my eyes and something passed between us. We both *knew,* in that second. We glimpsed the future: tangled sheets and clothes torn off, kisses so deep and goddamn desperate you don't want to stop to come up for air. It was like looking down into a ravine. The sensible thing would be to turn around and walk away from the edge; the sensible thing would have been to get out of the car.

Neither of us moved. I've never felt so helplessly drawn to anyone my entire life. I watched as she finally dropped her gaze, the car so quiet I could hear every breath she took, and I knew she felt the exact same way.

"I need protection," she said. And lifted her gaze to see my reaction.

She was right. Unlike all those assholes I'd been

67

guarding, she actually *did* need someone. Not just from the physical danger, although that was definitely true. From the fear. She was sinking fast into a blackness I'd seen claim too many good people—a blackness that claimed *me,* in a different way. She didn't just need *safety,* she needed protection and she needed it on a deep, base level, the only level that could counteract the fear.

I understood that, because my need to protect her was just as basic, just as primal. And I knew that I couldn't.

I could look after assholes in suits all day long because I didn't care about them. I'd do my job, even take a bullet for them if I had to, but I didn't feel anything for them. That was the way it had to be. I'd made that decision a long time ago, learning twice that caring for someone brought nothing but pain. I wasn't going to make that mistake a third time. And I knew that being around Emily for any length of time was going to end with me caring way, way too much for her.

"You've got the Secret Service," I told her. "That's their job." Then, despite the bitter taste rising in my mouth, I managed to add, "They're the best in the world."

"I don't want the Secret Service," she said. "I want *you.*"

Those final three words, in that wonderfully soft voice, almost burned through what was left of my self control. I could almost feel the fabric of her skirt under my palms: I'd grab her and pull her along the seat towards me so she flopped down on her back, mahogany hair streaming down over the edge of the seat like a waterfall. I'd hunker down atop her, one leg sliding between her thighs, making her gasp into my mouth as she felt the hard bulge at my groin. Then those soft lips would be under mine and—

Maybe I'd hear that gorgeous voice whoop and holler after all.

I forced the sound of her screaming her orgasm out of my head. "There are rules about this stuff," I told her. "The President's family is guarded by the Secret Service. I'm just a private contractor."

She twisted a little more in her seat so that she was facing me more fully. That meant crossing her legs and the hem of her skirt rose a half-inch or so. Damn it, how could she manage to be so innocent and earnest *and* sexy as hell?

Her next words cleared all those thoughts from my mind. "But you used to be Secret Service."

I think my mouth actually dropped open. "You dug into my background?" I felt the anger start and not just the usual slow-burning resentment over what happened. This was sharper and fresher, making my face heat.

Shame. I didn't want her knowing. I wanted to be perfect in her eyes, which is so ridiculous it would have been laughable if it hadn't hurt so much.

"I read up on you, yeah," she said, crossing her arms. "I could pull some strings and get you reinstated."

I sat there and stewed for a few seconds. Okay, so she knew. Nothing I could do about it now. And at least it provided a way out of this whole thing. "If you've read up on me, you know they don't *want* me back," I told her. "I got anger management issues."

"You don't *seem* angry." She stared at me with those big, innocent eyes.

"Well, you've never seen me upset."

We locked eyes again and, just to make her drop the whole thing, I let her see just a hint of that anger that burned inside me. Not just the surface stuff from what happened with the Secret Service, but the stuff from deep down inside, the stuff that's so dark and thickly black it has no shape, no detail, just a boiling mass that'll obliterate anything it touches.

I waited for her to back off. It always works. I've had Russian gangsters and Mexican drug lords take a step back when I give them that look. And at first, I thought it had worked on her, too. She shrank back, her eyes growing even bigger, and I felt bad.

But then it all went wrong. She rallied and leaned in towards me again and the look in her eyes was—

No! I don't need your sympathy, dammit!

I closed my eyes and turned away, groping for the door handle. "Answer's no," I growled.

THIRTEEN

Emily

I PUT MY HAND OUT, but hesitated just before I touched him. God, he was so *big,* and right now every muscle was hard under his shirt. I'd gotten him angry and right now he put me in mind of one of the bulls back on my dad's ranch when I was a kid. Once they got riled up, it was really dangerous to go near them.

There was another problem, too. Ever since he'd climbed into the car, I'd been trying to focus, trying to drag my mind away from fantasizing about what it would be like to touch him again. I hadn't admitted to myself, until I saw him, just how deeply those blue eyes and those thick, sculpted forearms had etched themselves into my mind. It was only when I saw him again in the flesh that I realized how much I'd been replaying the memories... and the memories didn't do him justice. He'd seemed big outdoors, at the park, but here in this confined space he seemed *huge.* He was wearing an eggshell-blue shirt, the sleeves rolled up, and the contrast between the blue and the tanned, hard flesh of his arms was amazing. The attraction was so strong it was almost frightening, as if just looking at him short-circuited every rational part of my brain. Did I actually dare to touch him?

He shifted his weight on the seat, about to push the door open and climb out. Did I dare *not* to?

I reached out and brushed my fingertips against his shoulder. He was incredible: so *solid,* powerful muscle bunched and taut under warm skin. I felt him stiffen at my touch...and then he relaxed. Only minutely and he let out a little hiss of frustration as it happened, as if he didn't *want* to relax, as if his body was obeying me despite his wishes. He was fighting it: I'd bought myself a second or two, then he'd be out of the car and gone.

"I can't sleep," I blurted.

He said nothing. He was still gripping the handle and the door was open a half-inch. I could see a couple of Secret Service agents turn towards the car, unsure whether my visitor was about to leave.

"I can't go out," I said. "I'm not just scared: I *can't.* I can't make my feet move to walk towards a crowd. I can't function like this. And it's getting worse."

He was still facing away from me but, if I angled my head just right, I could glimpse his reflection in the door's glass. His jaw was set and I could see that massive chest rise and fall as he drew in angry, shuddering breaths. I knew I should be scared of him, especially when he was in this mood. He could twist around and lash out with one of those big fists and just one hit would be enough to do me serious damage. But I wasn't scared. I don't know why, but I had this deep, unshakeable certainty that he'd never,

ever hurt me.

"I'm sorry I dug into your background," I told him. I meant it. As soon as I'd seen the pain in his eyes, I'd regretted it... and I'd just wanted to take that pain away. "But I needed to know if you could help me. I think you can."

Still he didn't turn around. But in the reflection in the glass, I saw him close his eyes.

"I have nightmares and, when I wake up, I can still feel them. I can feel the knife going in or the bullet hitting me or the rope they're using to strangle me." I swallowed. "Sometimes, they do worse things. I wake up and I can still feel the guy on top of me—"

He suddenly snapped around to face me, eyes open, and gave me a look of pure, murderous rage that made the hint I'd seen before seem like nothing. It was so fierce, so uncontrolled and base, I felt it as a scalding heat against my skin. But again, it didn't feel frightening because it didn't feel like it was *me* he was mad at. It was like walking into a nuclear blast, gale-force winds made of fire that would annihilate everything in their path... but the energy was directed around me, slamming into the faceless men who pursued me and turning them to ash. The mere idea of someone hurting me, violating me, even in a dream, was enough to make him want to kill.

And that was exactly what I needed. It was the first time since the park that I hadn't felt totally alone. I stared right back at him as all that rage flooded around me and prayed that he understood.

Kian let out a long, slow breath as his anger cooled, his eyes never leaving mine. And just for a second, I saw it in his gaze: he *did* understand.

But then he pushed open the door, bathing me in

night air that felt shockingly cold. He was out of the car so fast I barely had time to react. I lunged across the seat after him, already missing the closeness.

"Okay," he muttered, already turning to walk away.

"Okay?" I echoed.

"Talk to the Secret Service," he said without turning around. "If you can get me reinstated, I'll do it." He wouldn't look at me, wouldn't let me see his expression.

I swallowed. "Thank you, Kian."

He took a deep breath. "Ma'am."

And he was gone.

FOURTEEN

Kian

What the hell am I doing?

It was dawn. I'd gotten the call the night before, just one day after Emily had sought me out, telling me to report for duty that morning at eight. I needed to get going if I was going to make it on time. But....

But I looked at the guy staring back at me from the mirror and just shook my head grimly. I hadn't been right for the Secret Service back then. I sure as hell wasn't now. None of it fitted: not the big, muscled body, not the tattoos I'd picked up in the Marines, not the gleam of resentful anger in my eyes, like a burner turned to low. I couldn't even imagine taking orders again. Not from *them*.

In the Marines, it had been different. I'd respected my captain and I'd had no problem obeying him. They'd known how to use my anger: I'd always been the first one through the door, the one they didn't so much *send in* as *unleash*. In the Secret Service, there'd been too many damn rules... but even that had been bearable. I'd been good at my job and that had bought me some slack.

Until that day at the hotel when I suddenly went, in their eyes, from hero to criminal.

And now I was meant to take orders from them again, after they'd chewed me up and spat me out?

I closed my eyes and sighed. I'd call them. I'd call them and tell them the whole thing was off. They'd be relieved. I'd been able to hear it in the guy's voice when he called: they were going along with this under duress. They'd be relieved, I'd be relieved...

... and Emily would be unprotected. She'd have the Secret Service, but not that close, personal protection she needed to feel safe. The nightmares would continue. She'd turn into even more of a recluse. That light in her eyes would fade to nothing.

I growled and thumped the wall with my fist, then stomped through to the bathroom. When I'd showered, I rooted through my closet and dug out the black suit I'd used to wear. It was still wrapped in plastic: I hadn't touched it in a year. When I pulled on the white shirt, I felt like a kid forced into their Sunday finest for church. The black tie made it even worse.

I took another look at myself in the mirror, then ran a hand through my hair. It was long enough to be soft and tousled, not like the clean buzz-cut the other agents sported. I drew my thumb down my cheek, feeling my stubble. That was wrong, too. *Aw, the hell with it.*

I fastened on my holster, checked my handgun and slid it in, then pulled on my suit jacket. It was tight across my shoulders: I must have packed on a little more muscle, since I left. I shook my head at my reflection. I looked like a criminal who'd jumped a Secret Service guy and taken his clothes. *This is nuts!*

But I didn't have a choice. Not if I wanted to save her.

I stalked out of my apartment and headed for the subway before I could come to my senses.

***

At the White House, the guard at the guard post looked me up and down and radioed for confirmation, *twice,* before he let me in. To be fair, I probably would have done the same.

Waiting for me in the Secret Service command room was Miller, the head of the White House detail. I'd never been assigned to the White House—my job had been to guard foreign dignitaries—so we'd never met. But I knew the type right away: the close-cropped hair, speckled with gray, the perfect suit and shiny shoes; the disapproving look he gave me. Smaller than me but fit: the sort of guy who hit the ground every morning doing a hundred push-ups just because he felt that he should. He was made for the job as surely as if he'd popped out of his mom with his Secret Service earpiece already in his ear.

"Before we start, I want to make something perfectly clear," he told me. "You've been temporarily reinstated as a courtesy to the President and to Miss Matthews. Don't get the idea that any of us here actually like the idea."

I nodded silently.

"Your job will be to guard Miss Matthews. Her codename is *Liberty.*"

"Liberty?" It suited her.

Miller continued as if I hadn't spoken. "The President is *Lone Star*. The First Lady is *Lark*. You'll pull one eight-hour shift per day: whichever one coincides with her leaving the White House. You will stay by her side and *you will follow orders*. Are we clear?"

"Crystal." His barely-concealed contempt for me was really starting to get to me but I wasn't going to give him the satisfaction of letting it show.

He picked up a file as thick as my fist and shoved it at me. "You'll need to get up to speed on procedure: read and inwardly digest." He slapped a radio and earpiece down on top of the file. "Wear this. Now wait while I get you your service weapon."

I shook my head and patted the bulge under my jacket. "I have my own gun."

Miller shook his head. "Not on my team. Hand it over."

My gun was a Desert Eagle: big and dumb and all about brute force. We'd always gotten on very well. It had saved my life more times than I could count, including at the park. I raised my eyebrows: *really?*

Miller just glared back at me and held out his hand.

I had to take a deep, calming breath. I drew my gun out but hung onto it for a second. I loved everything about that gun, from its worn handgrips to the little chip in the side of the barrel where some guy had caught it with a samurai sword.

For Emily.

I laid it in his hand, secretly loving the way his arm dipped a little under the unexpected weight. He glowered down at it in distaste and then locked it away in a gun safe, returning with a plain black SIG Sauer. It felt like a toy in my big hand but I sighed and holstered it. "Anything else I should know?" I asked. I lifted the file he'd given me. "Aside from memorizing the rulebook?"

He just stared at me.

It took me a few seconds to realize what he was waiting for. *Aw, hell. Really?!* "Anything else I should know... *sir?*"

"Since you're guarding Miss Matthews... you should be aware that she had a tracking chip implanted under her skin when her father took office, in case of kidnapping."

"You can track where she is? Via satellite?"

He shook his head. "It doesn't have that sort of power: the chip's only the size of a grain of rice. But if she was taken, we can set up roadblocks and make sure she doesn't pass them, or sweep the city with a low-flying helicopter and zero in on her that way." He fixed me with a look. "Obviously, this isn't public knowledge."

I'd just about had it with this guy. I wanted to slam a fist right up under his jaw and send him halfway to the ceiling. I knew how to keep a damn secret. I'd had security clearance the whole time I was with the Secret Service.

But, of course, he knew that. He was making sure I knew that I was no longer trusted. The reputation I'd built up when I was here was a distant memory: I was going to have to build it up all over again. *What the hell am I doing back here,* I wondered.

Then I thought of that fading light in Emily's eyes. The way she'd seemed smaller, more fragile, than she had in the park. She needed help... and if I didn't save her, who would?

"Yes sir," I grated. "Understood."

Miller turned on his heel. "Come on," he snapped. "There's someone else who wants to meet you."

I fell in behind him. The first few rooms we passed through were used by the Secret Service and, at first, I assumed we were going to meet someone else from the detail. Maybe they'd buddied me up with someone so they could keep an eye on me.

But then we were into the main part of the White House, with its softly-carpeted hallways and hushed conversation. I'd only ever visited a few times when some dignitary I'd been guarding had an appointment there. I hadn't thought it would affect me but... it did. There's something about the place, the power that throbs through every room. I'm just about the most cynical person in the world but even I could feel the hairs on the back of my neck standing up. We started to pass by guys I recognized as senators and lobbyists. All of them did a double-take when they saw me: the differences between Miller and myself were obvious.

And then it got weird. We entered the West Wing. I glanced around uncertainly. *He* must be around here, somewhere. We might even run into him. I straightened up—I didn't mean to, it was just an unconscious reaction. *Don't be stupid. We probably won't even—*

We stopped outside the Oval Office. I turned to Miller and blinked but he didn't give me a chance to speak, just knocked twice and then opened the door. Inside was a sort of anteroom: wood paneling and an elderly but very intimidating lady behind a desk. She picked up a phone. "Mr. President," she said, the disapproval clear in her voice, "Special Agent O'Harra is here to see you."

Special Agent O'Harra was something I hadn't heard in a long time. Normally, that alone would have been enough to make me reel. But the *Mr. President* part made that seem insignificant. *Wait! Are we— We're not seriously going to—*

The lady put down the phone and nodded us towards a door. Miller led the way and I followed dumbly behind him, still playing emotional catch-up.

We walked into the room, Miller stepped out of the way and....

I'd always disliked politicians. I'd always thought of them as a bunch of privileged rich guys sitting smugly round a table, carving up the world. So I wasn't ready for what I felt, what had been building inside me ever since we'd entered the West Wing.

I stared at the man sitting behind the desk and... I was in awe. I'm a big guy but, in his presence, I suddenly felt small.

"Well," said the President. "So this is him."

I tried to speak but my mouth had gone desert-dry, so I nodded instead. I'd underestimated how deep it all ran: my time in the Marines; every time I'd sung *The Star Spangled Banner* or looked up at the flag.

He wasn't a politician. He was the President of the United States of America.

I glanced across at Miller and caught him smirking, as if my reaction was entirely predictable. I suddenly wished I'd shaved.

The President strolled out from behind his desk, straightening his jacket with a little tug. Like his daughter, Jake Matthews still had a lot of Texan in him: he hadn't tried to smooth out what some saw as rough edges. Squint and you could still see the ranch owner and oil man. He folded his arms and leaned back against his desk. "My daughter tells me you're the one guy she trusts."

I swallowed. There was something about the way he said it: just a hint of suspicion. He was a master of reading people: could he read something in me? Did he know just how much I wanted to take Emily, push her up against a wall and kiss the hell out of her? I couldn't speak. I settled for nodding again.

"And people at the Secret Service tell me you're the one guy she shouldn't," said the President. He gave me a look I suspected he reserved for hostile dictators. "Can I trust you, Mr. O'Harra?"

I finally found my voice. "Yes sir, Mr. President."

He glanced at Miller. "Miller here has already registered his protest." He paused. "Several times." He let the tension in the room build for several seconds before continuing. "You were in the Corps?"

"Yes sir."

"And you were *good*. But you left after four years. Why?"

I closed my eyes: only for a split-second, but it felt like it lasted a lifetime. Stinging sand in my face, the wetness of blood and the sound of their screams in my ears.

"I lost some men, Mr. President."

His gaze softened just a little. He'd served himself, long ago: Army, if I remembered right. Then, as quickly as it had appeared, the softness was gone. "And then you joined the Secret Service... and you refused to do things by the book."

"Three counts of insubordination," muttered Miller. "And the third one—"

"The third one would have been assault, if the

ambassador had pressed charges," said the President. "You should be in jail, O'Harra, not protecting anyone. Least of all my daughter."

I couldn't meet his gaze any longer. I stood there staring at the floor with the heat rising in my face. It was useless to try to explain. I'd tried that enough times when it happened and it had gotten me nowhere. Clearly, this wasn't going to happen after all. I waited for him to order me out: I actually lifted the file I was holding, ready to give it back to Miller.

But the order never came. I slowly lifted my eyes and found he was still staring at me.

"My daughter doesn't eat," he said. "She doesn't sleep. She won't—*can't*—leave the building. She thinks you can help her. Can you?"

"Yes sir, Mr. President," I said. "I believe I can."

The President gave me a long, appraising look. "Then I don't care what you did," he said at last. He nodded at the door. "Go to work."

Suddenly, the heat of shame was gone, replaced by cool, clean air that filled my lungs. All of the resentment Miller had stirred up faded away. "Yes sir, Mr. President."

I walked out of the Oval Office about an inch taller than when I'd walked in. It lasted ten paces, until Miller stopped me in the hallway. "The President is desperate," he told me. "I have to go along with this; I don't have to like it. Maybe you got away with things on your old detail but this is the White House and I don't need a loose cannon on my team. One mistake, O'Harra, one screw up and I'll personally kick your ass out the door and all the way down Pennsylvania Avenue. You are *not* going to embarrass the Secret Service again."

I felt my hands tighten into fists but I knew that was what he wanted. "Yes sir," I said. "Understood."

"Go to the residence," he almost spat. "And for God's sake, learn how to use a razor!"

I stalked away, only stopping to stash the file he'd given me in my locker and put on my radio. Moments later, I'd reached the residence. And there, right at the end of the hall....

I slowed to a stop as I reached Emily's door. I'd been mad as hell when I left Miller but, suddenly, all the rage was draining out of me, to be replaced by something even stronger. It was as if I could feel her presence oozing through the thick oak of the door: a subtle hint of her perfume, an aura of soft femininity.

I stopped. My hand was already raised to knock but, all of a sudden, I was as nervous as some kid arriving to pick up his prom date. How did she do that to me?

I knocked. A second later, she opened the door wide and—

It wasn't how it had been in the car. Maybe it was because we were alone, this time, or maybe it was the quiet of the hallway but it felt much more intense— way too intense to deny. A good foot or so separated us and yet it felt as if we were already touching. I was immersed in that aura that surrounded her, the sweet warmth of her bathing me. And I could feel her responding, too, shifting her weight from foot to foot, her eyes stroking over my arms, my chest, my face. This thing we'd started... it was like a physical presence between us, the air pulsing with it.

"You scrub up well," she said at last.

I inclined my head. "Reporting for duty, Ma'am," I said. Inside, I was asking myself what the hell I thought I was doing. This was a bad, bad idea. I'd sworn I'd never let myself care about anyone. But she needed me: I could see how scared she was and it made my chest ache. That feeling that I had to protect her, combined with the attraction... I could feel it tugging at me, drawing me towards her... and it was only going to get worse.

"Well, you'd better come in, then," she said. And stepped back out of the way.

I knew, then, what was different. It wasn't just that we were alone or that it was quiet. It was that I was standing on the threshold of her private space: the one room where the press couldn't follow. And she was inviting me in.

I took a deep breath... and stepped inside.

FIFTEEN

Emily

Holy hell, he gets better looking every time I see him.

I stepped back from the door, praying he couldn't see how he was affecting me. I could feel his gaze on me, leaving a trail of heat as it passed over my face, my neck, my breasts... either he wasn't bothering to hide it or he couldn't and both of those options made me heady. I'd never had a guy want me like that—not in such a direct way. Washington guys played mind games. Kian didn't.

At least *I* wasn't that obvious. I tried to stop looking at the smooth curve of his pecs under that snow-white shirt. *He doesn't know,* I reassured myself. *He totally doesn't know.*

I had a sudden stab of worry as he closed the door behind him. Was that what this was really about? Had I really tracked him down and gotten him reinstated because I was—I weakened and admitted it—*ferociously* attracted to him?

I took a deep breath and looked at him, pushing the feelings away, and... *no*. It wasn't just that. I could already feel the fear easing, the black waters retreating like a tide.

It was real: he made me feel safe. I took another slow, deep breath and it felt *good*. It felt as if I could really fill my lungs for the first time in days—I hadn't realized how tight my chest had been. I luxuriated in the feeling... and then noticed that Kian's eyes had dropped to my breasts and were following their slow rise and fall. I turned away, blushing, and pulled my cardigan a little tighter around me... but a wave of heat was rippling down to my groin and I felt oddly proud.

"Kian," I said to break the silence. I tried to pronounce it like he did: *Key-an*. "Is that Irish?"

"Yes Ma'am. Born over here, but my dad's Irish."

I turned around just in time to see a flicker of pain at the mention of his dad. It made me curious... but I didn't know him nearly well enough. Not yet. So I said, "Are you really going to call me *ma'am* the whole time?"

"Yes ma'am." He looked down at my leg, my injured calf visible beneath my green skirt. "How's the leg?"

I looked down at it. "It's okay. Not too bad as long as I don't walk far... and I haven't been doing much of that, of late. It stiffens up, sometimes..." I looked up at him... and found he was still gazing at my legs. He seemed to be having trouble taking his eyes off them. Part of me wanted to be righteously offended but... it didn't feel lecherous or creepy, as it would have if some stranger in the street had stared. Coming from Kian, it felt... *honest*. Good, clean, absolutely filthy red-hot desire... aimed at me. Maybe that would be normal for some women, but I'm nothing special. I didn't understand why he was so into me... but the fact he was sent a deep, warm glow through me.

He finally looked up and met my eyes. He didn't look the slightest bit guilty that he'd been savoring my legs. There was another one of those silences, the ones that built and built until I wanted to just hurl myself against him. *"Anyway,"* I said to break it, "at least it made some people happy."

He frowned, confused.

"My leg," I said. "Me getting shot. It made some people happy."

"Who?"

"Commenters, on the internet." He frowned deeper, not understanding, and I sighed. "It's nothing. Morons sitting in their mom's basement. They post... you know. Mean stuff." I shrugged and looked at the floor. I hadn't been looking for sympathy. "It's no big deal."

"Mean stuff?"

I shrugged again. "Death threats."

He took a step towards me. "Death threats? People send you *death threats?"*

"They're not serious. The Secret Service look into anything that's a viable threat to my life. Most of them are just... you know. Wishing that I'd die in horrible ways." I looked up at him and tried to smile. "You can relax, they're just idiots. They're not dangerous."

And then I saw his expression and realized he wasn't worried: he was angry. "What do they say?" he asked, his voice a low, dangerous growl.

No one had ever really talked to me about it before. The Secret Service were only interested in investigating the viable threats, not the other 99% that were simple outpourings of hate. And no one had ever seemed interested in how it affected *me.* "Just... you know... *I hope you fucking die,*" I told him. "Or, when we went on the trip to Africa, it was *I hope you get gang-raped and get AIDS and die.* Or—"

His hand gripped my arm. I could feel the tension in him—he was almost shaking in rage. When I looked up into his eyes, it was as if he wanted to kill every single one of them. "You... shouldn't read that stuff," he said tightly. He was having to force each word out past his anger.

I swallowed. "I know. But it's like picking at a scab, y'know? Sometimes, I can't help myself." I searched his face in wonder. No one had ever looked so... *indignant* about it. It was as if he honestly believed I didn't deserve it, as if I shouldn't just accept that it came with the territory. I felt this tight knot of emotion rise up inside and I wasn't sure how to deal with it. So I looked away.

After a few seconds, he said "You should be exercising that leg. It'll help. Didn't they give you exercises to do?"

I nodded, glad of the change of subject. "Yeah, but..." I bit my lip guiltily.

"I was the same. Never seemed to get around to it. But you should do it."

"You were hurt?"

He tapped the right side of his chest. "Got hit by some shrapnel just here. The doctors kept telling me to exercise it as it healed, but that just reminded me of it, so I kept finding excuses."

He looked at me and I nodded. That sounded familiar.

"Wish I had, though," he said. "Would have got my strength back a lot sooner. C'mon: what are you supposed to do?"

"Calf raises," I said. And I showed him, going up on my toes and then slowly back down again. I had to hang onto the back of a chair for support but, like everything else in the White House, the chair was an antique and wobbly as hell. I lurched sideways.

"Here," he said, slipping off his jacket and offering his shoulder. "Hang onto me."

I swallowed. On the outside, he was still all crisp white shirt and professionalism, but the sunlight from the windows was streaming through the thin fabric and silhouetting the body beneath. I could see the dark ink of the tattoos on his arms and the shadows between each ridge of his abs. The bad underneath the good. As he turned to toss his jacket on the bed, I could see one more tattoo, small and circular, right between his shoulder blades. I squinted, but I couldn't make out what it was.

He turned back to me and I put a hand on his shoulder. I'd touched him before, in the park and in the car, but I'd never held onto him like this. It was like grabbing hold of a sun-warmed cliff, solid and infinitely strong: I knew that, even if I lifted my feet off the ground and dangled, he wouldn't move an inch.

I rose slowly up onto my toes. Our eyes were locked on each other and, as I rose, our faces came closer and closer. His gaze tracked me all the way up... and down. *Three. I'll do three.*

On the second one I found myself moving slower. And... was it my imagination, or had we drawn closer together? *Up... and down.*

On the third one I knew it wasn't my imagination. Our bodies were definitely closer, the tips of my breasts almost brushing his chest as I rose higher and higher. I was going so slowly, now, that I was barely moving. When I reached the top of the exercise, our lips were only inches apart....

There was a loud knock at the door.

SIXTEEN

Kian

WE FLEW APART, but not fast enough. The door opened wide and standing there, staring at us, was a woman I'd only ever seen in photos. Her hair was smooth, glossy black with only a hint of silver. Her face was barely lined, her gray jacket and suit pants immaculate.

Roberta Matthews. The First Lady.

She took in the scene in a split second and I saw her lips purse in disapproval. "It's time for your meeting with Senator Giggs," she told Emily. Then she turned to me. "Perhaps you'd like to accompany her, Mr. O'Harra." She stressed the *Mister* and I got the message loud and clear: I was the hired help and I needed to keep my hands the hell off her daughter.

I grabbed my jacket and pulled it on while Emily checked herself in her dresser mirror. What had just happened—or nearly happened—hung in the air, but there was no way we could talk about it with her mother standing right there in the doorway. When we walked past Roberta and down the hallway, she didn't follow... but I could feel her gaze burning into the back of my neck the whole way.

In theory, we could now talk. But whatever moment we'd been having had passed and now it was awkward. Had I really nearly kissed her? I hadn't meant for anything to happen, when I told her to hold onto me. But, dammit, those soft pink lips had just looked so good... suddenly, it had been the only thing in my head.

What the hell am I doing? I'd been in her room all of ten minutes and already I was losing control. But I couldn't help it: this girl had gotten right under my skin.

"So who's Giggs?" I asked to break the silence. There were getting to be a lot of silences, whenever we were alone. The quiet seemed to press in on us, pushing us together, unless we said something to defuse it.

Emily shrugged. "Just a senator. Kind of an ass, actually. But..." She trailed off, distracted. She was glancing around, checking the shadows.

I realized that even in the White House, she didn't feel completely safe. She was slowing down the further we got from her bedroom. I'd seen similar things with buddies who'd returned from combat with PTSD: scared to leave their apartments, they'd turned into near-hermits, not living, just *existing*. I didn't want that to be her future.

I wasn't going to *let* that be her future.

I put a gentle hand on her arm. It wasn't meant to be a sexual touch, just a brush of my fingertips on her forearm to reassure her I was there. And it worked: I felt some of the tension in her body ease. But at the same time, the contact was addictive. I wanted to grip her arm tight, pull her face-to-face with me and—

"But what?" I asked, trying to keep my voice level. "What were you going to say?"

She picked up the pace a little and focused on the conversation again. "But there's a good chance Giggs is going to be President, one day. That's why my mom gets me to say hi whenever he comes by the White House."

I blinked. She'd said it so matter-of-factly, like it was *normal*. "You mean... wait, she's setting you up to...?"

"It's not like that," she said unconvincingly. "She's not meaning I should marry him. I mean... not necessarily."

I stopped in my tracks and just gaped at her.

"What?" she asked, looking back at me with genuine confusion.

"So you're just going to wind up with some guy your mom picks out for you... and then, what, you form a dynasty?"

"No! I'm just... you know." She sighed in frustration. "I'm the President's daughter. There are things that are expected of me."

I started walking again and we fell silent. I was fuming, remembering now how much I hated this whole system. Hadn't she given up enough for her father? The constant press intrusion, being hated and threatened by those bastards on the internet and now this? She was so determined to do her part, to make everyone else happy: didn't she deserve to be happy herself?

It wasn't just that, though. Much as I wanted to pretend I was just concerned for her, something much more powerful was fueling my anger: I didn't want to think of her snuggling up to Senator Giggs. Or any senator. Or anyone else at all.

We reached the library and Emily turned and gave me a quick smile. "OK, this is it."

She opened the door and started to step through. I followed... and she suddenly stopped and turned in surprise as she heard me behind her. "Oh! Um... you can wait outside."

We stared at one another. She flushed and I stood there feeling like a klutz. I'd forgotten, for a second, what I was. Of course she wouldn't want me there for a private meeting. But was that because it would be inappropriate... or because things were going to get romantic? I glanced over her shoulder and caught a glimpse of Senator Giggs: forties and in good shape, with dark hair... irritatingly good-looking.

"I'll only be ten minutes or so," said Emily apologetically.

I nodded and stepped back. She closed the door.

Dammit, what was wrong with me? I *knew* I couldn't be with her. It wasn't just her mom, her dad and Miller because, frankly, screw them. It wasn't even the massive gulf between us in money and power. If they were the only things stopping me, I would have already picked her right up off her feet, rammed her against a wall and kissed the hell out of her.

The problem was me. I wouldn't—*couldn't*—let myself get close to someone again. That only left sex: and that didn't feel right, with Emily. She deserved more than that.

I couldn't be with her. So what right did I have to get angry over who she saw?

I realized I'd started to pace. I forced myself to stand still outside the library door, facing away from it with my hands behind my back.

What if she has a boyfriend? I'd never considered that. My stomach lurched. I liked her and I was pretty sure she liked me but she must know as well as I did that we could never work, and that left her available. Even if she was just being polite and flirting with Giggs a little to please her mom, she might have some guy she really *did* like. What if I had to drive them places? My hands formed into fists. What if they expected me to sit in the front seat while, in the back seat, they giggled and kissed and—

Behind me, in the library, I heard a faint sound. My mind went into overdrive. Had that been Emily's high-heeled shoe, knocking against the carpet? Was she just crossing her legs or—

Was Giggs on top of her, with her stretched out on the leather couch, heels kicking the floor in ecstasy? Everyone knew what these senators were like, drunk on power and into kinky sex... fucking the President's daughter in the White House library would be right up their alley. And power was an aphrodisiac... Giggs *was* good-looking. So what if he was *kind of an ass:* maybe she was into arrogant assholes? Maybe she was lying there, skirt pulled up around her hips, panties pushed aside, biting her lip to keep from screaming, her body quaking with pleasure as he plunged into her again and again—

Emily opened the door and I had to stumble aside to let her through. She took one look at my face and asked, "What's eating you?"

I coughed. "Nothing, ma'am." I cast a suspicious look through the doorway. Giggs was standing there looking longingly at Emily but neither of them had any clothes askew. I relaxed... a little. Then I remembered that this was just my first morning. *This is going to be unbearable.*

We started walking back towards the residence. After a dozen paces, I couldn't take it anymore: I had to know if she was seeing someone. "This event tonight, the reception... you're sure you want to go?"

I saw her face pale at the mention of it, but she nodded. "I figure the longer I leave it before I try again, the worse it'll be." She looked up at me. "Right?"

I nodded. "Right." Once again, I was thrown by how brave she was. It wasn't just the fear itself she was struggling against: she must know that, after what had happened at her last public appearance, the press would be out in force and salivating at the thought of another scene. They *wanted* her to freak out again. No other PTSD sufferer had to put up with *that*.

I left it another few paces so that it didn't sound too obvious and then threw in, "Will you be attending on your own, ma'am?" There. Nice and subtle.

She shook her head. "No. My dad will be there. My mom's got a separate event on."

Dammit. "I meant..."—I tried to sound nonchalant, but I'm not good at nonchalant—"is there anybody special that you'll be—that you might want to—"

She stopped and spun around to face me. "Are you trying to ask if I've got a boyfriend?" she asked incredulously.

We stared at each other. I almost dropped the whole thing, feeling like a street urchin who's been caught trying to chat up the princess. But... her eyes didn't look horrified or embarrassed. There was something else there, something I didn't understand.

The hell with it. "I need to know for... security purposes. Ma'am." And I straightened up and looked her right in the eye.

"Am I interrupting something?"

Shit. We both spun to face the voice.

Kerrigan. The Vice President. I'd seen him on TV but he looked even younger in real life. And, like Senator Giggs, he was annoyingly good-looking. He didn't look to be in bad shape, either: he still carried some of the muscle from his Army days.

I coughed. "No sir, Mr. Vice-President." Had he heard what we'd been talking about? Could he see what had been going on? What was with this place, anyway, with everyone creeping around and walking in on people? Everyone was sneaky and silent, here—I felt like a bull in a roomful of prowling cats.

"Was there something you wanted?" asked Emily. I blinked at her, surprised: I'd never seen her be anything but polite to anyone, but she sounded downright cold.

"I just wanted to say thank you to Mr. O'Harra," said Kerrigan, slapping me on the back. "You did a great thing, in the park. I can see that, even if no one else around here can. You have my complete confidence."

I swallowed. It was the first wholly positive thing anyone but Emily had said to me. After Miller and the President and the First Lady, it should have been a welcome relief but... something felt off about it. He was saying all the right words but there was something missing, some human warmth that just wasn't there. "Thank you, sir," I said.

"We should be going," Emily told him—if anything,

her voice managed to ice up another few degrees. She was walking almost before she'd finished speaking and I had to move fast to catch up. Kerrigan didn't complain, but I could feel him watching us as we left.

When we'd turned the next corner and were out of his sight, she glanced across at me... and suddenly, all that tension between us was back, the air thick with it. And now, studying her expression, I saw what that look in her eyes was: she wasn't horrified I'd asked, she was... *bitter.* "If you want to know if I've got a boyfriend," she asked, "why don't you just turn on a TV? My whole private life is public property."

"I don't watch that stuff," I said truthfully. We came to a stop outside her bedroom door. "And I don't think it should be."

Her expression slowly softened. "No," she said. "I don't have a boyfriend."

Relief. But now we were into another of those loaded silences. She walked into her bedroom and I followed, which only made it worse. Now we were alone again, in private...my hands tingled with the need to just grab her shoulders and spin her around to face me and—

Don't let it happen. DO NOT let it happen. "Why were you so frosty with the VP?" I asked to break the silence.

She shook her head. "I hate him." Then she turned to me... and hesitated. I frowned: I'd expected her to just say *he's a douche* or something, but this felt like something more. Then she bit her lip and I got it: *this is the first time she's told anyone about it.* She'd chosen me to trust and that felt really good.

She took a deep breath. "He's trying to turn the country into a police state."

"The Guardian Act?" I hadn't really been following it. I don't have a lot of time for politics. "It's just some extra security: military guys to back up the police. *Police state's* a little strong."

She shook her head and sighed. "This is the problem. It *sounds* harmless. By the time anyone sees what he's really doing, it'll be too late. It's not going to be just a handful of extra guys on patrol whenever there's a big football game on. We're talking about a huge military presence, *permanently,* right across the US. *Tens of thousands* of soldiers."

I frowned. "C'mon, he *wants* that many but he won't *get* that many. The Army couldn't spare—"

She huffed. "When Kerrigan talks about the military, he doesn't mean the armed forces. He means private military contractors: *his own* private military contractors, from his old company!"

"*Rexortech?*" My stomach twisted. Some private military contractors were great—ex-military guys who'd done their time and then moved into the private sector. But I'd run into Rexortech's people a few times in Iraq and they were very, very different: little more than thugs with guns. Rexortech were known for taking almost anyone who applied, stuffing them into a uniform and handing them a rifle. And the results, at least in my experience, had been about what you'd expect: I'd heard reports of unlawful killings, corruption, even rapes and connections with human traffickers. The idea of those guys on US streets, with authority over citizens, made me want to throw up.

I stood there, my face probably turning a nasty shade of green, while she laid out the rest: the facial recognition cameras and the legal changes in the bill that would allow unlimited detention and interrogation of "suspects." It would take billions of dollars in manpower, surveillance tech and computers... and of course Rexortech would be the lead contractor. When he quit office, Kerrigan could return to being CEO... and he'd immediately be one of the richest men on the planet.

As she filled me in, I saw some of Emily's old spark return. It was the first time I'd seen her really fired up about something since the park and it felt amazing. She was still terrified, but she cared so much about this she was able to push back the fear, if only for a moment.

When she'd finished, I wanted to knock my head against a wall: this whole thing had been happening right in front of me, played out on the nightly news, and I'd barely noticed. And the few times I had paid attention, I'd actually thought it sounded like a good idea: anything that made life more difficult for the terrorists was good, right? "I'm an idiot," I muttered grumpily. I felt like a big dumb ox, next to her.

But then Emily's face softened. "You're not an idiot. You're a patriot. Kerrigan's good at playing on that." She held my gaze for a second and I felt a little less dumb. A look passed between us: I was on her side, now, and that felt good.

"What about your dad?" I asked. "I mean, no way is he going to let this come to pass."

She shook her head... but doubtfully. "A month ago, no way. But since the attack, he's been under *a lot* of pressure. The media started off giving both sides, but they're leaning more and more Kerrigan's way. And it's tough for the grassroots protestors to fight: they try to organize a march or a rally and people scream that they're supporting terrorists. Plus, Kerrigan's smart: he's made some powerful political friends. I've heard him talking to senators, promising Rexortech factories in their state if they'll back him."

I tilted my head to one side. "You're eavesdropping on him?"

She flushed and looked at the floor. "Not eavesdropping. Just... you know, it's easy for me to overhear things. I kind of blend into the background, around here. People don't really notice me."

That made a hot pulse of anger stab up inside me. I put a finger under her chin and gently lifted it so that she was looking up at me. "They should," I said quietly.

And then I was looking down into those big green eyes and I felt myself sliding inexorably as I leaned down to kiss her....

SEVENTEEN

Emily

I DREW IN A SHAKY BREATH as Kian leaned down towards me, his big body hulking over me. I tilted my head back, my eyes began to flicker closed—

And then he was drawing back sharply and looking away, refusing to meet my eyes. He took a full step back and cleared his throat. "Will you, um... be needing me before tonight, ma'am?" He asked.

I stood there gaping. Had I just imagined that he'd been about to kiss me? I waited until he finally looked at me: no, I could see it in his eyes. He was giving me a look that sent heat rippling down my body to pool at my groin. He *did* want me. But he was holding back.

And realization hit me, making my cheeks go hot. *What are you doing?! He's your bodyguard!* I looked away as well. "No, Kian."

"Then I'll see you later, ma'am." And he strode over to the door and was gone before I could stop him... or maybe before he could change his mind.

I closed the door and leaned my forehead against it while I tried to make sense of it all. I wanted to scream in frustration. God, he was gorgeous... on a whole different level and in a whole different way to Senator Giggs' bland good looks. *Dangerous.* *Exciting.* And ironically, it was seeing Kian get all worked up about Senator Giggs that had cemented my belief that the dark-haired giant was into me. *Into me* in a way no one ever had been: he permanently looked as if he wanted to rip my clothes off.

And he was *angry.* Thick, dark rage bubbling away just under the surface, always ready to explode. I'd heard about his "outbursts" from Miller: it had been one of the many arguments he gave for not wanting to reinstate him. But now I'd seen Kian's rage for myself and it didn't scare me: I couldn't imagine him ever hurting me. In fact, the thing that seemed to make him angriest of all was when someone threatened me. What I wanted was to help him... *heal* him. I got the feeling that anger came from pain, the same deep scarring that made him keep pulling away from me. Could I ever get to know him well enough that he'd let me in?

Even if I could, it didn't change the fact that he was my bodyguard. If people started to suspect something was going on between us, the Secret Service would kick him out faster than we could blink and I didn't want to see that happen. Already, both my mom and Kerrigan probably had suspicions. We were going to have to start being a *lot* more careful.

Because if Kian wasn't around... he wouldn't be able to protect me. And already, I was addicted to the feeling of safety he gave me. It was like cool, clean air after a solid month of stifling imprisonment.

Whenever he was by my side, especially when he touched me, I felt like the old me again.

And that wasn't all that happened when he touched me. Right alongside that feeling of security there was the constant, electric sexual tension. Just being close to him made it difficult to focus on anything else. I'd never felt anything like it, never felt my whole body thrum to a silent rhythm whenever he was around, longing for him, *aching* for him. There was something about Kian, a raw maleness that the guys I'd known before just didn't have. He looked great in a suit, but he might as well be a spruced-up caveman for all he had in common with the political types I knew. I was used to bullshit and mind games but with Kian there was none of that, just the sense that, if his self-control wavered even a little, he'd throw me down on the nearest available flat surface and—

I slowly turned, pressing my back to the door. To feel safe, I needed him close to me. To avoid screwing things up for both of us, I had to keep him at arm's length.

Maintaining that balance was going to be impossible.

EIGHTEEN

Emily

I DIDN'T SEE HIM for several hours, until it was time to go to the reception. He knocked on my door and I opened it wide. "Okay," I said, checking my purse to see that I had everything. "I think I'm ready. Let's head over to the—" I looked up and broke off. Kian was standing there just staring at me. "What?" I looked down at myself. Had I spilled nail polish all over myself or something? I couldn't see anything wrong. I checked Kian again, but he was still just standing there. "*What?*" I asked again.

He took a deep, slow breath. "Nothing, ma'am." he said. "I just haven't seen you..."—he lifted a hand to indicate me—"like that."

I looked down at myself again and realized it was the first time he'd seen me dressed up for the evening. In the park, I'd been in a summer dress. Since then, I'd been in a blouse and skirt. Now, I was in high heels and a deep green cocktail dress: it wasn't too low cut (there'd be an outcry if the President's daughter was seen in anything the media could call *slutty)* but now I looked at it, it did show quite a lot of leg. And I was beginning to realize Kian had a thing for my legs.

I flushed. No one had ever had a thing about any part of me.

"Okay," I said again. "Let's go." I stepped out into the hallway, Kian followed me and—

We both did it at the same time. I raised my arm to slip it through his and he crooked his elbow to offer a loop and it was only when we were just about to do it that we both froze... looked at each other... and quickly dropped our arms and looked away. I flushed again. *Idiot!* He was my bodyguard, not my date! But it had just felt so right, so natural, with him in the suit and me in the cocktail dress, and him picking me up to go out....

And *he'd* made the same mistake. The implications of that made my chest go tight.

Then we were walking down the hallway, eyes front, not daring even to touch. And that gave the fear a chance to come back.

It started in my stomach, a sensation like falling. A gathering, sickening blackness that swallowed me up from the inside, draining my spirit until I felt tiny and weak. Down at the end of the hallway, I saw my dad and the Secret Service detail gathering and I felt my steps slow. One of the agents glanced at me and spoke in a low voice to Miller, who was going to be heading up the detail tonight. Miller gave me a reassuring smile. In fact, all of them did. Everyone was being so *nice* and understanding but I knew that all of them were on edge after how I'd freaked out last time. None of them wanted to get reprimanded because the President's daughter went loco again and they handled it badly. I could feel the pressure piling up and up: I didn't want to let anyone down. "They must hate me," I muttered under my breath.

Kian put his hand on my arm, slowing me to a stop. He waited until I looked at him before he spoke. "No one hates you," he said sternly. "Everyone understands. They'll take care of you. This is what they *do*."

I gave him a weak smile. He sounded so sincere... and I knew it must have taken a lot for him to say that, given the differences between him and the Secret Service. But as I looked at Miller, quietly giving his agents a last-minute pep talk, I didn't feel any better. It still felt as though they were movers, discussing how best to transport a fragile grand piano. They cared about getting the job done right, but they didn't care about *me*.

As if he'd read my mind, Kian leaned close. "I'll be there too."

And the fear retreated just enough for me to breathe.

This time, my dad rode in one limo with Harlan and the rest of his detail while I rode in a second one with Kian, Miller and the rest of mine. I figured this was so they could whisk me away more easily if anything went wrong: after last time, they probably had all sorts of contingency plans for if I freaked out. Knowing they'd gone to all that trouble only made me feel worse.

I *had* to get through this.

We settled into our seats, Kian beside me, and we pulled away. As we left the safety of the White House and slid into the dark streets of DC, I felt my heart begin to speed up. It felt like setting off from a safe port across a bottomless black ocean. I looked down at my hands, knitting together in my lap. I willed them to keep still but I couldn't stop. I glanced down at Kian's massive hands, gently resting on his powerful legs. What I really needed was for him to hold my hand. But that would be totally inappropriate and, when I checked Miller, he was looking right at us and giving Kian a look of open disdain—

Warm, strong fingers captured my left hand and squeezed. I looked down and saw my hand in Kian's, then glanced up disbelievingly into his eyes.

He just nodded at me, as if to say, *I got you.*

I glanced at Miller again. He was staring down at our joined hands. As I watched, he lifted his eyes and gave Kian a *what the hell do you think you're doing?* look.

Or he tried to. Because when I looked up at Kian again, he was still looking at me, ignoring Miller completely. That's when I knew he'd do whatever it took to take care of me. I squeezed his hand and he squeezed back. I could feel his strength flowing into me, forcing back the fear.

But when the limo purred to a stop, my panic went into high gear. Each sound pushed me a little further towards the edge: the slamming of doors as my dad got out of his limo; the rising cheers of the crowd as they saw their president; the click-click-click of cameras. I could feel it all pressing in on the outside of the limo, the outside world so big and powerful and deadly that I swore I felt the car shift on its suspension.

The door of our limo opened. That huge, dark ocean of fear swept in: the noise, the camera flashes, the *people.* So many strangers. It felt like freezing water rising around me, filling my mouth and ears, drowning me. I wanted to slam that door and cling to my seat all the way home... and instead, I was going to have to go out there. *I was going to have to go out there!*

Miller climbed out and did a last-minute check of the scene, then leaned in again and nodded to me. My turn. My eyes bugged out. *Out there?!*

"I can't," I whispered.

I'm not sure if I meant it for myself or Kian, but it didn't matter. He put his big, warm hands on my shoulders, cupping them, and said. "I'll be right here with you, Emily."

I knew I was meant to breathe—that was supposed to help—but when I sucked in air it didn't seem to contain any oxygen. I stared at the scene outside: faces and camera flashes and noise and—

I felt Kian's hands on my shoulders—not forcing me, not pushing me... it was almost as if they were magnets and he was drawing me up out of my seat, me the puppet and him the puppeteer. "We're going to do it together," he whispered in my ear. "I'm going to have a hand on you the whole time and I promise I won't leave you. Okay?"

I took another deep huff of air and this one contained a faint trace of oxygen. I felt myself nod.

"One," he told me, guiding me towards the door. My legs felt like wax and I almost stumbled. But he was like a warm lantern casting a glow around both of us, pushing back the darkness. As long as I stayed within that circle of light, I was safe.

"Two," he said. Just a hint of Irish in his voice, shining like silver. It only came out when he was really under pressure.

"Three." He said it with so much finality, so much confidence, that I believed we could do it.

I stepped out of the limo.

NINETEEN

Kian

MY CHEST TIGHTENED up at how brave she was being. I could see how terrified she was and I knew that asking her to step out of that limo was like sending a wounded soldier right back into a war zone. That's why I hadn't asked: I'd told her how it was going to be. I had to help her beat this thing. But when I saw the crowd, even I was taken aback.

When I'd guarded foreign dignitaries, it had been about looking for the assassin, the lone shooter. The public doesn't care at all about foreign ambassadors and minor royals from far-off nations, so I'd never had to cope with crowds like this. But I knew from Iraq how dangerous a big group of people can be. Get enough people in one place and they stop acting like individuals: a pack mentality takes over and they operate like one massive creature. That's how riots start and stampedes happen: panic and anger spread instantly and the mood can shift in a heartbeat.

The crowd was restrained by waist-high metal barriers and, if they tried to get over them, by a line of Secret Service agents. But even armed as they were, they weren't going to be able to stop a rampaging mob of thousands if things went wrong.

It wasn't a hostile crowd. People were cheering and waving as the President slowed to greet them and there'd been a big wave of applause as Emily and I emerged. But they were *hungry*. Every single one of them wanted a piece of her—they felt like they deserved that, they were entitled. It was like being next to a tank of piranha eager to gnaw you to the bone.

We began to move along the red carpet, my hand on her back. God, she looked even smaller and more fragile in the middle of all this noise. Ahead of us, the President was just entering the building. Miller was walking backwards a few feet ahead of us, watching us closely. Emily took slow, cautious steps, as if she thought the ground might disappear under her feet at any instant. And the whole time, on either side of us, the crowd *roared*.

I wanted to get her inside as fast as possible. I heard the sigh of disappointment sweep through the throng as they saw us make a beeline straight for the building and I ignored them. But Emily slowed, gazed wide-eyed at the crowd... and stopped. "No," she said.

I had to lean close and put my mouth almost to her ear so that she could hear me over the noise. "It's okay," I told her. "You don't have to."

She looked at the crowd again. Her face had gone ghostly white with fear, but her jaw was set in a way I recognized from her father. "Some of them have been waiting for hours."

And she looked down at her feet for a second. I realized then just how frightened she was: she was having to will herself to walk forward.

Step by shaky step, she moved closer to the barriers. The crowd noise doubled as she approached, until talking was impossible and even thinking was difficult. I put my hands on her shoulders again. I didn't give a shit if someone thought it was inappropriate—I wanted to communicate with her not to get too close. I scanned back and forth along the crowd, looking for any possible threat.

At this range, the crowd broke up into individuals again: guys who wanted her, girls who wanted to be her. Hands stretched out, desperate to touch her, even if it was just a brush of her dress, but I made sure she stayed just beyond their reach, in case someone grabbed her and dragged her forward, or whipped out a knife or a syringe. I was getting madder and madder: these people were meant to be her fans, but they were so selfish: it was like they felt they owned her. Couldn't they see how scared she was? She was physically shaking with fear: I knew that she couldn't even hear what they were saying to her over the roar, but she was nodding and smiling, doing her best to satisfy them. *God, she's so brave....*

Suddenly, a guy about her age hurled himself forward over the shoulders of the people in front of him, as if he was crowd-surfing. "Fuckin' *bitch!*" he spat, his voice slurred with alcohol. A big hand, weighted with rings, reached for her, and his arms were long enough that he was in range.

All of my anger welled up inside me. I slammed my fist into his jaw with all my strength, and he flew backward. The crowd opened up, shying away from his drunkenness, and he crashed down hard on the sidewalk. As I drew Emily away, he staggered to his feet holding his jaw. "You sonofabitch!" he groaned. "I'll sue!"

I barely heard him. I grabbed Emily's shoulders and twisted us around so that I was between her and the guy, then gently pressed her forward towards the doors. But she stood stock still, her body rigid under my hands. I knew she was back in the park. Another few seconds and she was going to bolt. That idiot in the crowd had ruined everything.

I gently rubbed her shoulders. "I'm here," I said in her ear. "I'm right here. And I won't let anyone hurt you."

I could see Miller glaring at me, absolutely livid— either about me hitting that guy or touching Emily. *Fuck him.*

I felt Emily twist under my hands, looking back at the open door of the limo, ready to run. I squeezed her shoulders a little, lending her strength....

...and felt her take a deep, shuddering breath. She turned back towards the building and walked forward. I was so, so proud of her.

Seconds later, we were inside, the doors closed and the roar of the crowd dropped to a distant rumble. Emily turned to me to say something, but, before she could, Miller was pushing me away. He waved another agent over to escort Emily further into the building. She looked at me, concern in her eyes, but I nodded that she should go with him. I'd known this was coming.

As soon as she was out of earshot, Miller launched into his tirade. He'd obviously been saving it for the second we were out of view of the press. "Are you out of your mind, hitting a civilian?" he snapped.

"He was a threat," I growled.

"You punched him! You sent him *flying through the air!* And what's with all the touching?" He glanced at Emily's retreating back.

"I'm protecting her!"

"So am I!" He snapped. "It's my job to protect her. *From everyone!*" Shit. I could see in his eyes that he suspected something was going on. And his message was clear: it wasn't just *inappropriate;* he didn't think I was good enough for her. He didn't want a scumbag like me tainting the President's daughter.

The old, familiar anger returned, as hot and dark as ever. "Fuck you," I blurted. "*Sir.*"

We glared at each other until he finally turned away and stormed off.

I marched off to find Emily. Every time my shoes hit the carpet, my resolve hardened a little more. *This whole thing was a bad idea.* I was going to tell Emily I was done. I couldn't do this, not with pencil-pushers like Miller in charge. I didn't do *the rules* or *procedure* or going easy on the people who were trying to hurt her. If they tried to touch her, *damn right* they were going to get punched.

I entered the final anteroom before the big hall where the reception was going on. It wasn't really a room, just a gap between two sets of double doors. With both doors closed to muffle any outside noise, it was almost completely dark between them. On the far side, I could hear the President's rich Texas accent as he toasted the assembled guests. I put my palms on the doors, about to push them angrily open—

A soft, female hand landed on my chest, halting me. I smelled Emily's perfume. She'd been waiting there for me in the darkness.

"Thank you," she whispered. "Thank you for hitting him. I'm sorry you got in trouble."

And all the anger just melted away. It was as if cool, healing *peace* was throbbing out of her palm and into my body. "That's okay, ma'am," I said at last, trying to keep my voice gruff.

I felt her hesitate for a second—I imagined her biting her lip—and then there was a sudden rustle of fabric as she went up on tiptoe and... her lips pressed against my cheek, that soft mahogany hair like silk against my neck. Then she was gone, pushing through the doors, and I was standing there blinking in the sudden light, looking out at the packed hall.

I got my feet moving and followed behind her, every inch the professional bodyguard. When she reached her table, I drew out her chair and then stood behind her, watching for threats. It was only after a few minutes had passed and I was sure no one could make the connection that I lifted my fingers to my cheek and brushed the tingling spot where she'd kissed me.

Okay, then. I stared at Emily, unable to take my eyes off of her. I wouldn't quit. Somehow, for her, I'd make this work.

TWENTY

Kian

THE NEXT MORNING, standing in front of the mirror, I made a decision. If I was going to do this, I was going to do it *right*. Miller was looking for any excuse to fire me and, if he did, I wouldn't be able to protect her.

So I was going to take away all his excuses.

I lathered up my face and then, for the first time I could remember, I shaved completely clean. When I was done, I blinked at myself. I looked... well, not exactly *good* or *wholesome, but*, once I put on a shirt and covered up my tattoos, I could just about pass for a Secret Service agent. I tried to neaten my hair up a little, but it settled straight back into *tousled:* misbehaving seemed to be grown into it right along with that coal-black Irish color, so I gave up.

When I got to the White House, I retrieved the file Miller had given me from my locker and started reading. Whenever Emily didn't need me, I'd be in the Secret Service ready room, trying to memorize radio procedures and codenames. Each time Miller glanced in and saw me reading, he looked surprised and a little cynical, but he didn't say anything.

Two weeks passed. I mostly worked the day shift, because that was when she needed me most, but if she had to go out at night I'd work a double and make sure I was there right up until she turned in for the night. I took Emily out in public four more times: a fundraiser, a gallery opening, a charity event for disabled kids and a horse race. Each time, I kept a hand on her back or on her shoulder and, each time, she seemed to be able to push the fear back a little more. She was still a long way from being back to her old self: sometimes she'd just freeze and I knew she was flashing back to the park. Once, she bolted and I had to race after her, gripping her by the shoulders and telling her it was okay. But each time, with the right word in her ear, she slowly came back to herself and was able to carry on.

That was difficult, those words in her ear. Leaning close to her, smelling her perfume, feeling that soft hair blow across my face and tickle my nose... all I wanted to do was to bury my face in her neck and kiss all the way down it to her shoulder, then on down her body. I wanted to wrap my arm around her waist, pick her up and press her against me and never let go. Instead, I had to tell her it was okay... and then draw back again and be just her bodyguard.

It was almost unbearable. Whenever there was someone around, we had to pretend there was nothing between us. But it was even harder when it was just the two of us, in her bedroom or in an elevator, when there was nothing to hold me back... except the certainty that I would destroy her, if I gave in and kissed her. Once wouldn't be enough and what else could I offer her: a *relationship? Me?* Even if that was remotely plausible, given our stations in life, I didn't dare open myself up to her: I was too afraid of the pain that would follow, if I lost her. I couldn't give Emily anything long term. And I wasn't going to use her and leave her—she was worth more than that.

Already, I was worried by how much I'd come to care about her. And every day, it grew worse: whenever we walked together, we both unconsciously veered inward until our hips and shoulders were brushing. Each time I touched her, to guide her or reassure her I was there, I found it harder to lift my hand away again.

And then came Air Force One.

She was dozing in one of the huge, comfortable seats as we descended towards Andrews Air Force Base. One of the quirks of being on the President's own plane is that they don't have rules about having to be seated for take-off and landing, so I was standing as I watched over her. She was in too shallow a sleep for the nightmares to take hold, a tiny smile on her face as her soft breaths blew strands of hair back and forth in front of her lips. She murmured something in her sleep and, unable to resist, I leaned close.

She murmured it again: *Kian.*

I took a long, shuddering breath and stared at her, our faces only inches apart. Her lips were right there, softly pink and perfect. As I watched, they parted a third time, showing gleaming white teeth and that quick pink tongue. The temptation to kiss her awake was like a physical force, pushing my head down towards her....

I straightened up, folded my hands behind my back and looked away. Seconds later, the wheels hit the runway and she woke.

Every day was like tiptoeing along a knife edge. I knew it wasn't just me: I'd catch her looking at me in mirrors, or we'd get too close and *she'd* start to lean in and then catch herself. The tension between us was spiraling upward, unstoppable....

And then, one day in mid-October, everything moved into high gear.

TWENTY-ONE

Kian

My morning started off weird and got weirder.

I'd finally started to get used to rising early and I'd gotten into a routine of stopping off at a cafe on my way to the White House for steak, eggs and coffee. For the first time in my life, I was taking an interest in politics: I'd browse through the *Post* while I ate and read about which senators were fighting today. As Emily had said, a lot of the media were siding with Kerrigan. A few columnists were trying to raise the alarm but most were pressuring the President to back The Guardian Act. *Idiots!*

A guy sat down next to me, uninvited. "Hey," he said. "Buddy. Will you take a look at this?"

I frowned, expecting to be hit with some sob story and a plea for loose change, but he didn't look like he was homeless. He was a big guy, in a faded hooded top and a baseball cap, and he was showing me a crossword puzzle. "Eight down," he said, pointing. "I'm stuck."

I sighed. *Do I look like the kind of guy who does crossword puzzles?* I looked at the clue and then shook my head. "I got no idea," I told him, turning away. "Sorry."

When I got to the White House, things got even weirder. We'd been invaded by techies: guys in overalls climbing up stepladders, threading bundles of cable into the ceiling spaces and routing them under the floorboards. Twice, I nearly tripped over someone. By the time I reached Emily's bedroom, I was running late and I was in such a hurry I just went straight in without knocking.

I stopped two steps inside the room. She was topless, her bra in her hands, her mouth falling open as she turned her head to gape at me.

I staggered backwards out of the door, grabbed the handle and slammed it closed, then stood there staring at it, my heart thumping. I couldn't see the dark oak in front of me. I relived the moment over and over in my mind. She'd been side on to me, the morning light filtering through the drapes to bathe her soft, tan skin. Her breasts, as pert and ripe as I'd always imagined them, had swayed with her intake of breath as she'd seen me, her brown hair falling to brush across her rose nipples—

Emily, now in a blouse, pulled open the door. "Don't you *knock?*" Like me, she was red-faced.

"Yeah," I said, looking down at my feet. "Sorry."

Nipples rose pink nipples with the most gorgeous areolae I'd ever seen— I tried to push the image out of my head but it was impossible.

She stepped back from the door and I entered. When she'd closed the door behind me, I stood there awkwardly, desperately trying to think of something to say. I couldn't think of anything except the memory of the soft curve of her naked stomach and how it would feel to kiss all the way down to her navel.

"What's with all the techies?" I managed at last.

She sighed and crossed her arms, which made her breasts bulge against her wrists in a way that made me catch my breath. "It's Kerrigan," she told me. "They're from Rexortech. He's refitting the entire White House communications and security system—*for free*. You'll be getting a new radio, at some point. My dad had to wave it through—his opponents would have crucified him if he'd turned down millions of dollars worth of free tech and spent taxpayer's money instead. But now Kerrigan's company can use it as marketing: *We guard the White House!* He wanted to bring in Rexortech guys as well, have them walking the halls alongside the Secret Service, but my dad nixed the idea."

As before, talking about Kerrigan had lit the old fire in her eyes. "The guy's an asshole," I said. "Don't let him get to you. He's VP: he doesn't have any real power."

"He's not going to stop here," she told me grumpily, turning away and pacing. "His guys are putting up cameras all over the city. On the streets, in hospitals and stores. *Everywhere.* DC's going to be a model for how he wants the whole country to be."

I nodded. "I hear you. I get it."

She whirled to face me. "No you *don't!*" she snapped. "No one does!" She sighed and rubbed her eyes. "Sorry. I was up late." She nodded towards her desk. "Look... I've never liked the Guardian Act, or Kerrigan. And maybe, at first, part of it was that I was trying to distract myself from the fear—I needed something concrete to fight. But it's more than that, now. I've been looking into Rexortech. Something's not right."

I moved over to her desk, frowning. Printouts were stacked a foot deep, highlighted, annotated and covered in Post-It notes. "What *is* all this?" I asked.

"Their accounts." When I twisted to stare at her, aghast, she gave me a look. "I didn't steal them! I bought a single share in the company a few weeks ago. As a shareholder, I'm allowed to examine the accounts. And there's weird stuff in there. There's still opposition to the bill, enough that it could still fail. But Rexortech is gearing up and making acquisitions as if they're *sure* it's going to pass."

I stared at her, horrified. "You shouldn't be doing this! I agree, Kerrigan's an asshole, but if anyone finds out you're investigating him, if you so much as *hint* that he's involved in something shady... he's the *Vice President!* The press will crucify you if you're wrong!"

"Somebody has to do something!"

"But not *you!*" Concern for her was fueling my anger. My head spun as I imagined the field day the press would have humiliating her. She'd be paraded on national TV, forced to make apology after apology.... "You're the one who's always saying you're the President's daughter and things are expected of you. Think how it'll look if this gets out!"

I glared down at her and she glared back up at me, her jaw set. I loved her stubborn streak. I loved that she was so *good*, so determined to stop someone evil. But, dammit, couldn't she see I just wanted to protect her from everything... even herself? And did she have to look so damn kissable when she was mad?

I looked away. I was frustrated, turned on, and a

hair's-breadth away from doing something stupid.

"Is there anything else you want to lecture me on?" she asked in a strained voice. When I looked back at her, she was still staring up at me... but now the anger was mixed with something else. Like me, she was teetering between rage and lust, both of them fueling each other. All I had to do was lean in and kiss her....

It took all the willpower I had. "No, ma'am," I said. I withdrew, shutting the door behind me... and let out a long breath. Her naked breasts and then our first fight, all in the space of a few minutes. This was getting out of control. Unless I could find a way to back off a little, we were either going to dive on each other or kill each other.

And then Miller found me and told me the First Family was taking a trip to Camp David. A few days in the country, away from the prying eyes of the press.

And I was going with them.

Helena Newbury

TWENTY-TWO

Emily

I BRUSHED MY HAND down the stallion's side, sweeping my palm over his rich, tan coat and reveling in his warmth. I'd been standing there stroking him for ten full minutes and every pass of my hand made me feel better. Rudy stood much taller than me, his whole body packed with muscle. He'd been a police horse, many years ago, trained to keep his footing no matter how much a crowd was pushing and shoving at him. He gave a very relaxing ride as long as you didn't try to stop him eating daisies.

Big, powerful, protective and stubborn. He reminded me of someone.

I finally looked across at Kian. "How are you doing?" I asked. I was trying to sound grumpy because I still hadn't completely forgiven him for our fight, but I was cheering up despite my best efforts. "Have you bonded yet?"

Kian was standing beside a beautiful white mare named Snowdrop. She was enthusiastically eating apple chunks out of his palm and he was gaping at her and trying to look unconcerned each time she turned her head and snorted in his ear. I tried not to laugh. "I didn't realize what a city boy you were."

"I forgot you were a cowgirl," he grumbled.

I put one foot into the stirrups and pushed myself up onto Rudy. When my ass landed in the saddle, it was right at Kian's eye height and the way he stared at the tight denim made a wave of heat roll through me. I kept thinking back to how he'd walked in on me topless, his eyes roving over my breasts for what felt like hours before he'd backed out of the room. That night, I'd brought myself to an arching, thrashing orgasm playing out a scenario where he'd kicked the door shut behind him, grabbed my semi-naked body and tossed me on the bed.

"Come on," I said, trying to keep my voice level. "Saddle up."

I swear I didn't mean anything by it. I meant, literally, *time to get on the horse.* But he glanced up and met my eyes just as I said it and I was sitting there with my legs wide....

There was so much tension between us, now, that *everything* was coming out sexual. I flushed and looked away. A moment—and a bit of uncertain jumping—later, he managed to swing himself up into Snowdrop's saddle. She gave a snort and shuffled back and forth a little. Kian clutched at the reins. He didn't look scared, exactly, but he definitely wasn't in his element. And that was sort of endearing in itself. It was the first time I'd seen him anything but stoic and unflappable.

And I'd seen something else. As he'd settled himself in the saddle, the hem of his plaid shirt had been trapped under his ass for a second, pulling the shirt down at the back of his neck. In the second before he fixed it, I'd gotten a glimpse at that tiny tattoo between his shoulder blades: a shamrock. It seemed weird that he'd have something so tiny there, given how much smooth tan muscle was available as a blank canvas. It was almost as if that was a statement in itself: as if it was so important, he didn't want anything else to obscure it.

"We'll keep it slow," I told him. And clucked my tongue to get Rudy moving. The horses moved off down the winding forest path that surrounded Camp David, with me in the lead.

Horses were the best thing about Camp David. There weren't stables on site, but there were enough quiet paths to ride on and a local riding school had been more than happy to lend us Rudy and Snowdrop for the day. My dad had raised an eyebrow when I'd asked if we could get *two* horses. "I need a bodyguard with me everywhere I go, right?" I'd countered. "What do you want him to do: drive alongside *really, really slowly?*"

He'd given in pretty easily: the truth was, I knew he'd probably take Rudy out himself at some point. You can take the man out of Texas, but you can't take the Texas out of the man. The same went for me. Riding reminded me of home: happy days spent riding, hiking and shooting guns with my dad. I was noticing things I hadn't even realized I'd been missing, like the rustle of trees and the birdsong. The fear was still present, but it felt like it had been held back at the perimeter of the camp. I could feel the outside world and its constant threats just beyond the trees, but as long as I didn't focus on it, I felt as if I could escape it for a few days. It was the happiest I'd been since the attack.

Plus, it was a chance to spend a couple of hours alone with Kian.

Was that selfish? *Wrong?* I knew nothing was going to happen. He wouldn't let it; I wouldn't let it. But I wanted to be near him and it not be about protecting me, for once. It honestly wasn't about lusting after him.

I glanced over my shoulder. The forest was so close on either side that we were in a green tunnel, with shafts of sunlight lancing down between the branches. Kian was trying—and failing—to look relaxed as he bounced up and down atop Snowdrop. It was difficult to look at him like that, sitting high in the saddle with his plaid shirt stretched tight over his chest (I'd insisted he lose the suit for once) and *not* think about him on top of me, with me lying back in the long grass as he smoothed those big hands over my breasts...

Okay, it was a little bit about lusting after him. But mainly, I wanted to get to know him better. I was hoping that being alone would give him a chance to relax... and maybe lower his defenses a little.

Ten minutes into the ride, he coaxed Snowdrop to come almost alongside Rudy and said, "I'm sorry I gave you a hard time about Kerrigan. I just didn't want you to get in trouble." He kept his eyes straight ahead as he said it, too embarrassed to look at me. But right at the end, he glanced my way and I saw the concern in his eyes. He really was just worried about me.

And there was something else: he hadn't finished with *ma'am.* Each occasion when he'd missed it off was lovingly transcribed in flowery, girlish script in my mind. I hated that I did it, but I did: I couldn't help it. Each time he forgot to say *ma'am,* I could kid myself that he wasn't my bodyguard, that maybe something could happen. And pride of place in my little mental book of *The Utterances of Kian*, in purple ink and silver glitter, was the time he'd called me *Emily.*

"That's okay," I said. "You were right. It would be really bad for my dad if it got out that I don't trust the VP. I just didn't like feeling like... you thought I was the little rich girl playing Nancy Drew."

He coaxed Snowdrop on a little so that she was right up alongside Rudy. "I didn't think that," he said, and there was just a hint of Irish silver edging the roughness of his voice. It made me unconsciously press myself down into my saddle a little. Our eyes met and, like a switch had been thrown, all the nervous, wonderful tension between us was back, rising and swirling in the air around us, drawing us together.

My eyes flicked down to his lips. I was still getting used to the new, clean-shaven Kian: without the stubble, those gorgeous lips seemed to stand out even more, rugged and very, very kissable. It was utterly quiet and there was no one in sight. The horses were practically touching: all we had to do was lean towards each other....

And then Kian was blinking in surprise as Snowdrop passed by Rudy, taking the lead. He'd sped the horse up to catch me, but, "Um... how do you slow it down?" he asked with fake nonchalance.

I tried to tell him, as Snowdrop began to trot off into the distance, but then I heard him mutter, "Slow. *Slow down. Slow, you daft feckin' mare!*" and I started laughing too hard to speak. I tossed the reins, Rudy gamely sped up and I caught them a little way down the path and showed Kian how to slow down.

A half mile further on, he was getting the hang of it. And while he was focused on riding, I threw in, "So... why *did* you leave the Secret Service?"

I'd meant it to sound casual but I've never been good at this stuff. I'm not a diplomat like my dad or a master manipulator like my mom. It came out loaded with curiosity and Kian gave me a look that told me he was onto me. I felt my face flush. I went red *a lot* around this guy.

"You didn't read it in my file?" he asked after a moment.

He didn't say "ma'am" again. "Nope. I just saw there was trouble and you left," I said. "I wanted to hear it from you."

He stayed silent as we passed the next tree and the next. Four trees, five. *Say something!* I could see his body tensing up, that famous anger coming back. I just wasn't sure whether it was me he was angry at. At last, he ran his hand down his cheek and over his jaw. I wondered if it felt weird, to feel the smooth skin after so long with stubble.

"We were in New York," he said. He faced front as he talked, eyes on the path ahead. "A group of ambassadors were over for a UN conference. I was assigned one from some tiny country in central Europe you've never heard of. Pretty typical day: take him to the UN building, pick him up, take him out on the town, keep him safe while he gets wasted on five hundred dollar bottles of brandy... I get him back to his hotel and into his room. But a half hour later, a woman shows up." Kian sighed. "He'd arranged an escort, sometime earlier that day, probably slipped some cash to the concierge at the hotel. Pretty little thing. Black hair. About your age. I don't like it, but she promises she'll be very discreet and he whisks her into his room."

I was watching him intently, but he didn't look at me. He kept his eyes firmly forward and, as Rudy pulled ahead a little I suddenly saw why it was: the rage was boiling away inside him and, with his body motionless, it was escaping in the only way it could: as a bitter, hate-filled stare. He wasn't looking at me because he didn't want to turn that look on me.

"I give it ten minutes," he said. His voice was strangled, now. "Then another five. I'm pacing the hallway outside his door because I can *feel* something's wrong, but..."—I saw his knuckles turn white where he gripped the reins—"...but I knew if I burst in on them, he'd go to my boss and I'd get torn into. We'd all had it drilled into us that the ambassadors had to be kept happy, no matter what. So I *waited*."

His whole body had gone hard as rock—he was almost shaking with anger and it was agonizing to watch because I knew the anger was directed at himself.

"Then, after maybe twenty minutes, I hear a noise. A sob. I don't bother pounding on the door: I kick it in and run in there and she's..."—he swallowed—"she's on the bed, naked, with him on top of her and his belt around her throat. Her lips are turning blue. Tears are running down her face and she's got... *marks* on her breasts. Cuts. I don't know what he used, a knife, I guess. And instead of looking shocked that he's been caught, the ambassador looks angry that I've interrupted. He honestly doesn't think he's doing anything wrong."

Rudy started to slow to a stop because my hands had gone slack on the reins. Snowdrop noticed and started to slow as well. I barely noticed: I just sat there gaping at Kian.

"Before I know what I'm doing, I've pulled him off her and I'm hitting him. Over and over. The woman gets the belt off her neck and starts pulling her clothes on. By the time the other Secret Service agents hear the noise, she's long gone." He drew a deep breath and let it out. When he spoke again, he sounded tired. "I don't hurt him all that badly. Fractured jaw, black eye... nothing like what he deserves. There's a lot of blood, though, because I split his lip, so it looks worse. They rush him off to hospital and I'm taken into custody."

"*You?*"

The horses had stopped. He finally turned and looked at me. The rage was still there in his eyes, but I knew it wasn't directed at me. "The ambassador swears there was no escort. The concierge swears he knows nothing. The hotel clams up: they don't want people to think that sort of thing is going on there. I looked for the escort but I couldn't find her: probably, her madam had convinced her not to talk to the cops so she never pressed charges. So we're left with an ambassador who says I broke in and assaulted him."

"And they *believed him?!* But there must have been evidence—"

"There was. Blood on the sheets. Mascara on the pillow where the woman had cried her heart out. But everyone knows the ambassador has diplomatic immunity: he's not going to face any charges no matter what happens. No one wants an international incident. Easier to keep it simple. They kick me out, the ambassador doesn't press assault charges and it all goes away."

I blinked at him, my eyes suddenly wet.

He shook his head. "I should have gone straight in," he muttered. "Five minutes, *one* minute... I should never have let her go in there."

Now I got why he didn't trust the Secret Service, why the rules drove him crazy. It wasn't just that they'd wronged him. It was *guilt*. Guilt that he'd let the rules hold him back, that night, if only for a little while.

I couldn't think of anything to say. I just wanted to wrap myself around that huge, strong body and give him an enormous hug. But before I could, he'd turned away and managed to coax Snowdrop into walking on.

I sat there in silence watching his retreating back for long seconds before I finally worked out what to say. "Kian?" I called after him.

He turned to look over his shoulder. "Ma'am?"

"I'm glad you came back."

He held my gaze and I saw a little of the pain and anger fade away. "So am I, ma'am," he said at last.

TWENTY-THREE

Kian

WHEN WE'D FINISHED THE RIDE, Emily showed me how to tie up the horses and brush them down. Standing there brushing a horse was about the furthest thing I could imagine from my normal life. No danger. Nothing to protect her from—not even the press. Being out of my suit for the first time in weeks made it feel even more like a vacation. And Emily looked so goddamn gorgeous... the perfect Texan cowgirl: tight blue jeans that hugged that soft rump perfectly, red and white plaid shirt, the breeze plucking at the collar to show glimpses of smooth tan cleavage.... She'd left her hair long and loose and the shafts of sunlight made it sparkle and shine every time one hit her. She was breathtaking.

My hand tightened on the wooden brush handle. Breathtaking and *not mine*. It was getting more and more difficult to remember that. It felt like we were on some romantic weekend away together. It wasn't just the lust, anymore: it wasn't just that I'd been watching that perfect ass bounce up and down in the saddle for mile after mile, or the fact there were *far* too many moss-covered trees in this forest and every one of them made me think of pushing her up against one and having her stand there, clutching at a branch above her head, while I stripped off her jeans, pushed her thighs apart and went to work with my lips and tongue. I'd started to feel things. I'd told her about what happened in New York, something I'd never planned on doing. We were getting too close, just like I'd been afraid of. But how could I pull away when it felt this good?

We thanked the guy from the riding school and headed back to the main house. Less than an hour later, I got a rude awakening.

Emily was swimming laps in the big, kidney-shaped pool and I was keeping an eye on her from the poolside. Standing there in the warm sun, watching her lithe body cut through the water was just about the best way I could think of to spend an afternoon. Or at least the best that involved her keeping her swimsuit on.

So maybe I was looking too hard, being too obvious. Maybe I was *gazing* when I should have been just watching.

My first warning was when a shadow fell across me. "Mr. O'Harra," said a female voice. "Could I get your help with this?"

I looked around and saw the First Lady standing less than six feet away, giving me a *I know exactly what you're looking at* look. As always, her dress and hair were perfect: she looked as if she'd just stepped out of a catalog and I was standing there in casual clothes, looking as if I was slacking off. *Dammit!* How did they all creep around so silently? Was everyone in DC ninja-trained? "Sure," I said, and followed her.

She led me over to a huge barbecue that looked like it dated from Roosevelt's era. It was wedged into a corner of the porch. "Can you get this out onto the middle of the deck for me?" she asked.

The thing looked as if it weighed more than I did: it hailed from an era where things were built from cast iron and girders. But I was all too happy to bend over and wrap my arms around it: it gave me an excuse to not look her in the eye. "No problem, ma'am." I started to grunt and heave it away from the wall.

Out of the corner of my eye, I saw the First Lady turn and look at her daughter, now doing backstroke in the pool. I looked, too. The surface of the water was lapping lazily over the black, glossy hillocks her breasts formed in her swimsuit.

"She's lovely, isn't she?" asked the First Lady in a carefully neutral tone.

I focused on the barbecue. "Yes, ma'am." What else was I supposed to say?

"I'm glad you're helping her," said the First Lady. "She seems happier. Stronger." She watched as I began to haul the barbecue along the deck. "I expect your services won't be required much longer."

The edge in her voice sent cold shooting right up my spine, followed by a stab of anger at the threat of us being split apart. "I guess that's up to Em—Miss Matthews, ma'am."

She said nothing for a moment, but I could feel her cold gaze on me. I tried to concentrate on heaving the barbecue towards the center of the deck.

"I hope she can see clearly," said the First Lady at last. "You know how women can get attached. Even infatuated. The wrong sort of man can seem like the right sort of man."

The barbecue slid into position and there was nothing else I could do to avoid it: I straightened up and looked her in the eye. When she spoke again, she didn't sound unkind, so much as worried. "I'd hate to see you thrown out of the Secret Service a second time, Mr. O'Harra." She crossed her arms. "My husband will do anything to protect Emily: even hire you. But *I'll* do anything to protect her, too. Remember that." She glanced down at the barbecue. "Thank you," she said, dismissing me.

I turned away and headed across the deck. Up until she'd come over, I'd been enjoying the feel of the sun beating down on me. Now the warmth was no longer there: I felt as if I'd been dunked into a bath of ice water. How could I have been so stupid? Of course she'd have noticed the way I looked at Emily and the way she looked at me. I'd been far too lax about things: the horse riding had probably been the final straw. Now I was damn close to being fired and, if that happened, I'd never see her again.

I'd have to get some distance between us. I'd have to make sure I was nothing but absolutely, one hundred percent professes—

At that second, Emily climbed out of the pool right in front of me. Her one-piece black swimsuit left her tan shoulders bare and revealed a mouthwatering scoop of glistening cleavage at the front, little jewels of water trickling down her skin. She looked up at me with those lush green eyes and there was just a hint of a smile on her lips. She knew I was looking at her and, dammit, she was letting me know she liked it.

I felt the First Lady's eyes on me from the other

side of the pool. I tore my eyes away from Emily and strode away, not stopping until I'd turned a corner and was out of sight. *Shit!* I didn't give a damn about breaking the rules or what her mom thought was best for her but I couldn't risk getting fired. Being close to her like this was unbearable... but not seeing her at all would be unthinkable. *What the hell am I going to do?*

TWENTY-FOUR

Emily

I DIDN'T KNOW what time it was. Late enough that Camp David was quiet and still but dawn must have still been a long way off because, when I opened my eyes, my bedroom was black.

I lay there half-awake in the darkness, wondering what had woken me. I strained my ears. A noise from outside? I couldn't hear anything now.

Then my eyes adjusted enough to make out shadowy shapes in the gloom. The dresser, the closet... and a shape that shouldn't be there, standing near the end of my bed. A huge, tall shape.

A man.

He started towards me, his feet silent on the thick carpet. I filled my lungs to scream... then froze. *It's Kian!* Finally, he'd stopped holding back. He'd come to me in the night like some fairytale prince. I was going to get the kiss I'd been aching for and then he'd climb silently into my bed and—

I started to grin, my heart thumping with

anticipation. Then a cloud cleared the moon outside and I glimpsed the man's face.

It wasn't Kian. It was the man from the park, the one who'd pointed a gun at my head.

I opened my mouth to scream, but now I'd missed my chance: a hand slapped down across it, sealing tight against my lips. I sucked in a panicked breath through my nostrils as he rammed my head back down on the pillow. My cries were muffled and pathetic—I wasn't sure they'd even carry through the heavy oak door. *Where was Kian?*

I lashed out with my hands, clawing at him, but suddenly my hands were caught. I could make out another man, now, on the other side of the bed, and then I was being rolled on my side and my hands were drawn painfully behind my back, my wrists cinched together and bound brutally tight. Even as I remembered to kick, someone grabbed my ankles and they were tied, too. The hand was removed and my mouth was stuffed full of cloth. I felt the tape pressed across my cheeks, trapping strands of hair against my skin and sticking to my lips, and however hard I screamed it came out as just a muffled grunt.

Then they picked me up, wrapping their arms under my back and knees, and carried me across the room. I could feel a breeze blowing through the drapes: somehow, they'd got the glass doors that led onto the deck open. Why weren't the alarms going off? Where was the Secret Service? *Where was Kian?!*

I squirmed and thrashed, trying to see where they were taking me, but the moon had gone behind the clouds again and all I could catch were glimpses of grass and trees. Then I was dumped into the trunk of a car and the lid closed, plunging me into total darkness. Seconds later, I was speeding away from Camp David, heading God-knows where, and no one even knew I was missing!

Very faintly, over the road noise, I could hear the men talking. They were discussing how I deserved everything that was about to happen to me: because of what my dad had done. Because of what America had done. Because I was rich. Because I was a woman. *I'm not those things,* I wanted to scream. *I'm just me!*

As the car slowed to a stop, I could hear more men outside, gathering around. Discussing every horrifying thing they were going to do to me. I started to scream, wanting to drown them out, but their voices just rose in excitement, louder and louder until—

"Emily!"

Spread her and tie her and cut her and—

"Emily!"

My eyes opened and I saw the same bedroom as before... but this time the lamp by my bed was on and the man leaning over me was blessedly, wonderfully familiar. Kian had one hand on my shoulder—he must have been shaking me awake—and he was staring down at me, my fear reflected in his eyes.

I realized my wrists weren't bound. I flung my arms around him, pulling him close and just *clinging.* I had to keep opening my eyes and looking over his shoulder at the room to reassure myself that the intruders weren't there.

"It's okay," he whispered. "It's okay."

I pressed my cheek to his, feeling his warmth. It was late enough in the night that his stubble started to grow back and the scratch of it was gloriously real and reassuring, pushing the last of the nightmare away. I felt my breathing start to slow

149

down.

It sank in that I was pressing my whole upper body against him, from my cheek all the way down to my waist, and that I wasn't wearing a bra under my nightshirt. Every time I took a breath, my breasts pressed a little more firmly against his chest. Every time he took a breath, those hard pecs crushed against me.

I loosened my arms and fell back onto the bed. The sheets were damp with sweat and the covers were half off the bed where I'd been thrashing around. We gazed at each other as I calmed myself. It had been so vivid, I actually had to rub my wrists to get rid of the feeling of the bindings around them. "You... heard me?" I whispered.

He nodded. He hadn't moved since I let go of him, so he was still hunkered over the bed, our faces only a foot apart. "You screamed," he whispered. There was a jagged edge to the word, as if the thought of anyone making me scream, even in a dream, made him want to kill them.

I winced and glanced at the half-open door to the hallway. "Did I wake anyone else?"

He shook his head. "I don't think so." He half-stood, backed up a little and gently pushed the door closed with his foot, then knelt beside my bed and put his face close to mine again. "I was right outside."

I looked at the door again. "You were sleeping right outside my door?" I whispered.

"*Standing* right outside your door," he whispered.

My eyes widened. He'd already been on duty all day. It should have been some other agent on the night shift. But....

But he didn't trust anyone else to watch me, away

from the White House. My heart swelled.

"Just in case, ma'am," he whispered. This time, he sounded a little sheepish. I wanted to hug him so bad.

"I'm okay," I whispered. I think I was trying to reassure myself as much as him. "Just a nightmare. I'm used to them."

He blinked, then looked aghast. "It's like that every"—he realized his voice had risen and had to force it back to a whisper—"every *night?*"

I nodded. "But I'm okay in the day—I mean, I'm not *okay*, but I'm getting better."

"That's because I'm there in the day," he whispered.

He was right. The nightmares had subtly changed, since he'd started to guard me. Before that, I'd been alone, but now it was specific: the nightmares always opened with *him not being there*—I lost the source of my safety. "But they're only nightmares," I whispered angrily. "They can't hurt me." I felt stupid. I was a grown woman. I shouldn't be scared by nightmares.

Then I saw the look he was giving me: a very firm *stop being silly* look. He moved a little closer to the bed and I felt myself gulp: it didn't matter that I was lying there in a complete mess, with my hair stuck to my forehead with sweat and the sheets twisted around me—just having him so close felt amazing. *God, I am so ridiculously smitten with this guy.*

"I've known guys twice your size wake up screaming, *crying,* from nightmares," he told me. "Don't pretend it's okay. Not with me."

"You mean soldiers? When you were in the Marines?" I asked.

He nodded.

"That's different," I said. "They got shot."

"*You* got shot."

"They were in a Warzone." It felt ridiculous to be arguing in whispers, but I didn't dare raise my voice in case we woke someone.

"They were trained for it. You weren't. And that attack in the park came out of the blue." He hunkered closer. "You thought the world was safe and suddenly, it wasn't. Right?"

There was something about the way he said it. It wasn't just that he was right... it was that he spoke from experience. I nodded.

"That's the most damaging thing. You don't feel you can ever relax again. You don't feel you can let your guard down, or it'll happen again."

I drew in my breath. That was it exactly. I hadn't been able to put it into words, but he'd nailed it. "*Yes.*"

We stared at each other. And now I was sure of it: he knew what it was like because he'd been there, too. He'd been scarred like this as well and—I felt a sudden rush of emotion as things slotted into place—this was *it,* this was the cause of that pain that made him keep pulling away from me. "What do you do about it?" I croaked.

He reached down and brushed a few strands of hair off my face. "You talk about it," he said, and I could hear the Irish in his voice more than ever. "With someone you trust. You figure it out... before things set in too deep." He settled himself more comfortably beside the bed. "Tell me," he whispered.

And, slowly, I began. I told him about what happened in the nightmares and how it made me feel. I told him about the men and being taken, about being at the mercy of people who detested me. The light from the lamp wrapped us in a tight little cocoon of warmth, the rest of the room falling off into shadow. It felt like we were the only two people in the world and having to whisper made it more private still: I could say things I didn't dare to speak.

It helped. I don't know why, but it did. Just describing my fears took some of their power away, as if they were strongest when they could shift and change and remain formless. It's like the monster in a horror movie: it's always scarier when you can only glimpse it in the shadows.

"But—" I had a sudden realization and it made me start to choke up. "We can talk about it, but it doesn't go away, does it? It's not just the attack, it's not just PTSD. I'm living this life. I'm the President's daughter. *This is real.* There really are people who want to take me, or kill me."

He put his hand on my cheek, the same way he'd done in the park when he first saved me. I pushed my face against him and his warmth helped to hold back the tears. "Yes," he said at last. "There are people like that. It is real."

I hated him for saying it—part of me wanted him to lie to me. But most of me loved him for giving it to me straight.

"So we should do something that maybe you've never done: we should *plan.* We should think about what would happen if someone *does* take you," he said.

I drew in a shuddering breath and shook my head. I could feel the dark waters of panic swirling around me, threatening to rise. "I don't want to think about that."

"It's okay. I'm here." He leaned on the bed a little, his muscled forearm close to my leg, and the bed creaked under his weight. Somehow, that creak was reassuring. "What would you do?" he whispered, his voice gentle. "What would you do, if they *did* take you, and put you in a car?"

I shook my head. "I don't know. Panic. Scream." My stomach lurched at the thought of it and I turned away from him.

He cupped my chin in that big, warm hand and gently turned me back to face him. "Here's what I want you to do: keep calm. *Listen.* Listen to where they're taking you." He looked right into my eyes. "And know that *I will always find you.* No matter what."

The way he said it made me really believe it. I nodded.

He took something out of his pocket and held it up: a tiny cell phone, from that era when they were getting smaller and smaller, before they swelled into smartphones with huge screens. "I want you to have this," he said.

"I already have a cell phone."

"Have this one too. Just in case. But keep it on *you,* not in your purse."

He put it in my hand. It was the size of a box of matches. I nodded and closed my hand around it.

He cupped my chin a second longer and then slowly drew his hand away. He didn't have to say anything: his eyes said it all. *Better?*

I nodded. I did feel better. Talking about it *had* helped. And it made me wonder: could I help him, too? Could I free him of whatever pain *he* was carrying around?

He caught my questioning look and stared back at me for several seconds. Then he gently shook his head. I remembered what he said about doing it *before things set in too deep.* Did he think it was too late for him?

I felt the idea harden into a promise. I wasn't giving up that easily. He'd helped me; I'd help him.

Kian stood and took a step away from me. I was fine until he put a hand on the door handle, but then a sudden stab of panic shot through me. The idea of closing my eyes in that room, alone, filled me with sick dread. "Kian?" I whispered.

"Ma'am?"

I swallowed. "Can you stay with me? Just until I'm asleep?"

He hesitated for a second, maybe thinking about the consequences if someone realized he was in my room in the dead of night. Then he slowly sat down with his back resting against the door. "Of course, ma'am."

I lay down. And with Kian watching over me, I had the best night's sleep I'd had since the attack.

***

Those few days were idyllic. I could have happily stayed at Camp David for months but, the next evening, we had to get back into the motorcade and head home to DC. I looked back through the rear window of the limo, trying to catch the last glimpses of greenery before the gray city swallowed us up. When I turned around, Kian gave me a reassuring smile: *I'll be there. It'll be okay.* But I could only manage a weak grin in response and the closer we got to DC, the more the feeling of dread increased.

DC was home; the White House was home.

So why did I feel like we were driving right back into danger?

TWENTY-FIVE

Kian

THE DAY AFTER WE RETURNED to DC, Emily had to attend a drinks reception: basically a meet-and-greet hosted by the First Lady where she could thank all the senators and other bigwigs who'd donated to her favorite charity this year.

In theory, it should have been an easy evening: without the President there, everything was a little more scaled down and there were no crowds to worry about. It was peaceful, with a string quartet playing in one corner and flowers everywhere. The doors onto the garden were open and the warm breeze blowing through the room stopped it feeling claustrophobic, even though the guests were almost shoulder-to-shoulder. Emily was nervous in the limo, but once we got inside, she seemed to be okay as long as I kept a gentle hand on her back. She looked fantastic: shining hair cascading down over her shoulders, red cocktail dress slit just high enough to show off her gorgeous long legs.

But as I watched Emily's mom work the room, kissing cheeks and telling everyone how wonderful they looked, my stomach started to churn. This would be Emily's future, if her mom had her way. She'd already lined Emily up with a job at one of her charitable foundations: a nice, safe career that wouldn't rock the boat. Emily would do it to keep everyone happy... and I could imagine the fire in her eyes dying out forever as her life became nothing but fundraisers and photo opportunities. She'd be married off to some senator or CEO, playing second fiddle to them....

My hands tightened into fists. Emily shouldn't be playing second fiddle to *anyone.*

I could see she knew it, too. She'd managed to plaster a big, happy smile on her face as she was introduced to everyone but the smile didn't reach her eyes. Guys lined up to shake her hand or lean in to kiss her cheek and I didn't miss the lust in their eyes or the way they tried to look down her dress, even though many of them were twice her age. I wanted to kill every one of them.

I could see the weight of it all pressing down on Emily: everyone thought she was the luckiest woman in the world: after all, she had *everything*... except the choice to do what she wanted and marry who she chose.

"Emily," called her mom. "Senator Giggs is here."

I caught Emily rolling her eyes. I managed not to laugh, but a warm little bomb went off in my chest. *She doesn't like that asshole after all.*

"Come on," she muttered to me. "Let's get it over with."

She started through the crowd towards the main

doors. I could see Senator Giggs standing there, watching us approach. *We* had to come to *him,* of course. Arrogant jerk.

I was ahead of Emily, shouldering my way through the guests to clear a path for her and not caring whose Martini I spilled. Then I felt it: cool, slender fingers grasping mine, and I automatically closed my hand around hers and squeezed.

She squeezed back, our hands hidden by the guests around us. And when she looked up at me and smiled a nervous smile, dammit if my heart didn't skip about a dozen beats.

Don't. Don't do this. Camp David had been dangerous enough, getting closer and closer and then staying in her room—I'd sat there for hours, long after I needed to, just watching her sleep. And all the while, the First Lady had been one step away from splitting us up forever.

I had to get it into my head that she wasn't mine, could never be mine. But, *damn,* holding her hand felt good.

I faced forward just in time to walk right into a big, tuxedo-clad chest. *Shit!* Edward Kerrigan, the Vice President. I dropped Emily's hand instantly, but the look he gave me told me he knew *exactly* what was going on.

"Sorry, Mr. Vice-President," I said, looking at my feet. "My fault."

He gave me the most openly patronizing look I'd ever seen in my life. It didn't matter that I was a few inches taller, he talked to me like I was a kid he'd caught running in the halls. "Oh, that's all right, Mr. O'Harra. I think we can cut you some slack, given how you've helped Emily." He gave her a wide grin. "So good to see you out and about."

"We were actually just on our way to see someone," said Emily sweetly.

Kerrigan tilted his head to one side, then spoke to me as if Emily wasn't even there. "I'm afraid Emily doesn't share some of my views on law and order. What about you, though? I hear you were a Marine. You must understand the need to stop the bad guys before they act."

He sounded so reasonable. He made it sound like you'd have to be an asshole to disagree with him.

"At that point, sir," I asked, "aren't they still innocent?"

He blinked at me but just about managed to keep his smile together. "I'm surprised at you. We're at war, Mr. O'Harra, even if it's a different kind of war. Terrorists, cyber-terrorists, criminal gangs... they're all a threat to us. And sometimes, the laws that were meant to protect us just get in the way. We have to make a few sacrifices to win the fight. You've been to war. You must have made sacrifices."

The anger started to circle and rise in my chest, uncoiling like a snake. I could smell blood and smoke and feel the sand on my face. If there was one thing I hated, it was politicians turning real deaths into fucking metaphors. "Plenty, sir." I fixed the tuxedo-wearing prick with a cold stare. "But freedom wasn't one of them."

Kerrigan's smile finally collapsed and I stepped around him, leading Emily on. She didn't say anything but, as soon as our hands were hidden by the press of bodies again, she grabbed my hand and squeezed it again.

"Emily!" Senator Giggs did us the courtesy of

walking the last few feet to meet us. He grabbed her waist with both hands and pulled her close, then kissed her on both cheeks. Emily gave me a warning look over his shoulder: *stay!* It was a good thing she did, because my instinct was to pull him off of her and hurl him across the room.

Giggs lowered his voice, but I have good hearing. "I've been thinking about you," he murmured, and my stomach twisted into a tight knot. What if she *was* into him? She kept indicating she wasn't, she kept sending me the clear signal she was into *me,* even if we couldn't do a damn thing about it. But what if she was being realistic, like her mom wanted? What if I was just her fantasy, some guy to flirt with, but she knew she needed to find a guy like *this* asshole to settle down with?

"Do you want to take a walk?" Giggs asked. "The gardens are meant to be really nice."

That knot in my stomach tightened. He was a good-looking SOB and he had money and said all the right things. *Why didn't I take her on a romantic walk in the gardens? Because I'm meant to be just her bodyguard!*

I'd never in my life been jealous of any other guy. I've sure as hell never wanted to be some swanky guy in a suit. I hated this whole political scene. But right then, I was jealous of Giggs because he *fitted*. He could slot right into Emily's life instead of battering clumsily up against it.

I stared at Emily, waiting for her response. She was looking over Giggs' shoulder, maybe looking for a way out of the conversation and I assumed she was about to shake her head.

And then, out of nowhere, she turned back to Giggs

and said, "That sounds lovely. Let's go."

They started walking, heading for the doors that led to the garden, and all I could do was fall in behind them like a faithful dog, the anger expanding to fill me with each step. *I thought she didn't like him! What the hell's going on?*

TWENTY-SIX

Emily

Thirty Seconds Earlier

A romantic walk in the gardens, with Giggs? I couldn't think of anything worse. Now, a few minutes alone in the warm, fragrant darkness with *Kian*....

I was just about to give Giggs a polite *no* and promise to catch up with him later (hopefully, I'd be able to avoid him for the rest of the party). I looked over his shoulder, planning our escape. Kerrigan was close by, talking to someone on his cell phone. He seemed to be barely paying attention to the call, just giving monosyllabic answers to the caller while he carried on making the rounds, slapping people on the shoulders and shaking hands. "Late," I heard him mutter as he passed by us. "I don't know when."

I was pretty sure he was on the phone with his wife—and clearly, she was just an annoyance next to the important business of networking. I hated guys like that.

Then it happened: he fished in his inside jacket pocket and pulled out a *second* phone, one that must have been set to vibrate because I hadn't heard it ring. His smile disappeared and he ended the call with his wife immediately, not even bothering to say goodbye.

Why did he have a second phone? I watched as he answered the call. He'd moved too far away for me to hear what he said, but it looked like *wait*. He was glancing around him, cupping the cell phone to his chest. Someone he didn't want to speak to in public.

That meant it was a call I *had* to hear. I hesitated when I remembered Kian's warning... but if I could listen in discreetly, find out something damaging....

I didn't want to embarrass my dad, or make Kian mad. But I was convinced something shady was going on with Rexortech, Kerrigan and The Guardian Act. I was like a dog with a bone by this point: I *had* to know.

Kerrigan started to move towards the doors that led to the gardens—he was going to find a nice, private place where he could talk openly. If I moved fast, I could follow behind him and listen. But I couldn't just march out there on my own or it would be obvious.

I turned to Giggs. "That sounds lovely," I told him. "Let's go."

Giggs' face lit up. He took my hand and started to lead me through the crowd. Immediately, all I could think about was how different it felt. Kian's grip had felt strong and reassuring, his fingers curled around mine for support, but with just enough quietly confident pressure to let me know I was *his*. Giggs' palm was clammy and he held on too tight, his arm lifted a little so that everyone could see that he was holding my hand. Kian's grip had felt wonderfully possessive; Giggs' made me feel like a possession.

But it was working. We were now close behind Kerrigan and, when he glanced around, he just saw a happy couple off for a stroll in the gardens, not a lone woman intent on listening in. He even gave us a patronizing smirk.

We were almost to the doors when I remembered Kian. *Oh God!* I twisted around to look at him. He was following behind, staring down at our joined hands as if he could laser them apart with his gaze. When he saw me turn, he looked up and met my eyes... and I could see the hurt there.

He didn't know I was just faking. And I couldn't explain, not in front of Giggs.

Worse, we'd reached the doors. Trying to maneuver two of us close enough to Kerrigan to listen was going to be hard enough. Three would be impossible. "I'll be fine," I told Kian. "You wait here."

Kian gave me an angry, disbelieving look. "I'd better come, ma'am."

Giggs put a hand on Kian's chest. "I'll take good care of her."

Kian looked down at the hand as if wondering whether to snap it off at the wrist or the elbow. A few weeks earlier, I don't think he would have been able to restrain himself, but he just bristled and looked to me for a decision.

"It's okay, Kian," I said. It felt as if I was stamping on his heart. "You stay here."

And I led Giggs out into the darkness.

"What's *his* problem?" muttered Giggs.

Shut up, asshole! "He's just a little overprotective," I said.

Giggs glanced back to where Kian stood, the light from the party silhouetting him in the doorway. "You think maybe he has a thing for you?" He chuckled as he said it, to show how ridiculous that would be, and I wanted to slam my purse into his head. The fear was starting to come back, too, slithering in from the edges of my mind as soon as Kian wasn't there to hold it back.

Find Kerrigan. I had to focus on that and do it fast, before I freaked out. My chest was aching at the thought that I'd just trampled all over Kian's feelings, but, if I'd hurt him, I at least wanted it to mean something. I looked all around us and strained my ears. There were a few other people outside, but most of them had stayed close to the building where the light spilled out onto the patio. I couldn't see Kerrigan anywhere and for a moment I thought this whole thing had been in vain.

If it wasn't for the gravel, I wouldn't have found him. Fortunately, the garden's designers had favored gravel paths between the high hedges and Kerrigan's heavy footsteps made plenty of noise. He was heading directly away from the party, into the darkness—as I'd suspected, he wanted somewhere private.

I tugged on Giggs' hand and led him down a path that ran parallel to Kerrigan's. He grinned as he fell into step beside me. *Oh God, now he thinks I'm eager!* I sighed under my breath and hurried onward, trying to go fast but quietly. When I heard Kerrigan stop, I pulled hard on Giggs' hand to bring him to a halt, too. Kerrigan was now only a few feet away, separated by a hedge. I held my breath and strained my ears....

"OK," I heard Kerrigan mutter. "Go ahead. Keep it short."

I stepped back until I was pressed right up against the hedge—fortunately, that took me off the gravel and onto the grass, so I made no noise at all. Now I could hear even better.

But Giggs grinned and stepped forward, too, until we were almost touching. *Oh, great—now he thinks I want to make out.*

"What?" asked Kerrigan. "It's a shitty connection, I can't hear you. Say that—"

And then, just for a second, I caught a break. The guy on the other end raised his voice and the connection cleared up at the same time. Even so, I wouldn't have heard it unless I'd been pressed right up against the hedge. "—next piece of business?" asked the caller.

I went absolutely still. The darkness around me flared into light. Balloons against a brilliant blue sky. I knew that voice. I'd heard it almost every night for the last six weeks. I could see the man standing over me, leveling his gun at my head. *"It's just business."*

Kerrigan was talking to the second shooter from the park.

I couldn't process it, didn't even know how to begin. And then, as I was standing there frozen, Giggs leaned in close to me, his lips coming down to brush mine.

That snapped me back to reality. I twisted to the side and gave a quick, violent shake of my head.

Behind me, Kerrigan said, "Start your planning. Use S32, it's quiet."

Giggs frowned at me, as if telling me not to be foolish. He moved in again to kiss me and I twisted away again, still desperate to avoid making any noise.

"Keep me posted," said Kerrigan. And I heard him

end the call and walk away. I let out a long sigh and turned back to Giggs just in time for him to kiss me.

My arms came up automatically, but my hands just grabbed at empty air: I didn't know what to do. I tried to step back, but I was already right up against the hedge and all I did was scratch my bare shoulders. Giggs' lips were rubbery and wet and, as I opened my mouth to protest, his tongue slid into my mouth.

I shoved him away as hard as I could. "No!" I hissed. I still didn't want to make too much noise: partially because Kerrigan was probably still within earshot and partially because I was scared of making a scene—there's no worse crime, in polite DC society.

Giggs stared at me, confused, then grabbed my waist with both hands and pulled me close. I twisted out of the way of his kiss, but his lips landed on my neck, instead.

This is my fault. I asked him out here. He thought I wanted this. I felt so stupid, so ashamed, that I didn't think to be angry. His lips worked their way down my neck and across the bare skin of my shoulder: wet and slimy and horribly invasive. I squirmed and kicked. "No!" I said insistently. I felt him nudge the shoulder strap of my dress off my shoulder. "No!" I said again, right in his ear.

He drew his head back and this time he looked mad, as if I'd worn out his patience. He actually shook his head at me warningly. "Don't be a bitch, Emily," he chided. And he squeezed my ass with both hands.

And then there was a presence next to us. One with enough strength that just being near it lent some to me. Giggs and I looked around just as Kian's fist connected with Giggs' face.

Giggs flew backward and crashed down on the

gravel path. As Kian marched past me toward him, Giggs reeled and made the mistake of getting to his feet.

So Kian hit him again. This time under the chin. I saw Giggs' feet lift clear of the ground and he went down again, spitting blood and possibly teeth. Kian grabbed the collar of his shirt and hoisted him off the ground. He would have hit him a third time if I hadn't run over and grabbed his arm. "*Stop!*" I told him. "Please."

Kian looked over his shoulder at me. The arm holding Giggs didn't waver an inch—he could have held the guy there all night long if he'd wanted to. There was so much anger in his eyes—the only reason it wasn't terrifying was that he was on my side.

I checked behind me. People were rushing over from the party to see what was going on. I could see three Secret Service agents ramming their way through the growing crowd towards us and my mom was close behind them. "*Please,*" I whispered to Kian.

Kian dropped Giggs to the ground. A Secret Service agent grabbed each of Kian's arms and I saw him tense... but a pleading look from me made him slump and he let them lead him away, resigned to his fate. The third Secret Service agent hauled Giggs off the ground and led him away, too.

My mom ran up to me, shooing everyone else away and bombarding me with questions. But my eyes were on Kian. I had to speak to Miller, or my dad. I had to explain what had happened.

And then, at the back of the crowd, I saw Kerrigan. Everyone else was watching either Kian or Giggs being led away, but his gaze was firmly fixed on me. Then I saw his gaze move from where I was standing to the spot where he'd made his call.

He knows.

TWENTY-SEVEN

Kian

A HALF HOUR LATER, I was back at the White House. I waited in the anteroom outside the Oval Office for another half hour before finally being called in. I braced myself, expecting Miller to be there to formally end my career—I'd already assumed I was fired, but I wasn't looking forward to his gloating at having been proved right about me.

I looked around in surprise when I opened the door and realized Miller wasn't there. The President was standing by the windows, looking out across the Rose Garden with a glass of Scotch in his hand. It swept over me again, even stronger than before. I felt... *awed.* "Mr President?" I asked. "Did you want me to get Miller?"

"He just left," said the President, walking around his desk. "He had a lot to say about you." He rubbed his ear. "Most of it at full volume."

"Are you going to yell at me, sir?"

He didn't reply at first. He came to stand in front

of me and then just looked at me. It felt as if every bad and good thing I'd ever done was being weighed.

"I'm going to thank you," the President said at last. "For hitting that son of a bitch."

"Yes sir. Even though he's a senator?"

"If someone tries to touch my daughter, I don't care if he's the President of France."

"Understood, sir."

We lapsed into silence.

"Miller wants to fire me, sir?" I asked. I had to know where I stood.

"Miller wants you to go to jail," the President corrected. "Luckily for you, you had an advocate."

Emily. I looked into his eyes, but he was unreadable. *Does he know or not?*

He swirled his glass, making the ice clink and rattle. "You're dismissed, Mr. O'Harra."

I backed out of the Oval Office before he could change his mind. And right outside the door was Emily.

TWENTY-EIGHT

Emily

I PRACTICALLY DIVED ON KIAN as he emerged from the Oval Office, then pulled him away down the hallway. "What happened?" I asked. "Are you fired?"

He was looking back in the direction of the Oval Office, frowning suspiciously. "No...."

I felt my shoulders slump in relief. "I'm so sorry. It was my fault. I took him out there and he thought—"

Kian snapped his head around and stared at me. "Wait—*what?*"

"I—You know, I said I'd go on a walk with him and he thought I wanted to make out. It was my fault."

We were still walking. He suddenly grabbed my arm and pulled me up short, then spun me to face him. "Are you *kidding?*" I could hear the Irish in his voice. "'He thought you wanted to make out'... so that makes it *your fault?!*"

I just stood there gaping at him.

"It was *not* your fault. There's no feckin' excuse for

what he did!"

I stared at him. I knew it, I'd been trying to convince myself of it... but that wasn't the same as hearing it from someone else. I finally nodded, a huge lump in my throat. But weirdly, once I couldn't blame myself, the whole thing felt scarier in some ways. If it had been my fault, I could tell myself I'd be smarter next time. But the idea that it was *him,* that that could be lurking behind expensive suits and designer ties everywhere, anywhere....

Kian's hand landed gently on my shoulder, right where Giggs had kissed the skin. The warmth of him felt cleansing, soaking away Giggs's touch. The hand slid smoothly up and cupped my cheek and I felt myself relax into it.

"Come on," he said. "I'm going to show you something."

He took me by the hand and led me to the residence, then straight into my bedroom.

"I want to show you what to do, the next time some bastard doesn't know what 'no' means," he said.

I nodded.

He stood facing me and took each of my hands in his. "Grab him here," he said, planting each of my palms on his hips. I'd felt his hands on me plenty of times but it was almost the first time I'd touched him. I could feel the power of his hip muscles, huge and solid. If my fingertips slid back just an inch, they'd be holding that tight, hard ass I'd admired so many times as he walked ahead of me.

"Bring one leg between mine," he said. He sounded calm and neutral, so I tried to be clinical about it myself. *This doesn't mean anything. He's just teaching me.* I moved my leg between his.

"No," he said. "If you do it right in the middle, between my feet, I can squeeze my legs together and trap you." He demonstrated, closing his legs like a trap. My dress left my lower leg bare and suddenly my calf was pinned between both of his, the heat of him throbbing into me through the thin fabric of his pants. I felt my breath hitch faster in my chest.

He opened his legs again. "Try it again, but this time, press your leg up against one of mine. It makes it harder for me to trap you: I can do it, but I'd have to throw myself off balance."

I slid my leg between his again, but this time I pressed the outside of my thigh tight against the inside of his. Feeling the heat of him there was very different to feeling it against my calf. And as he shifted his weight, I felt the outline of his cock brush against my inner thigh. He was already half-hard and swelling against me.

"Good," he said. His voice wasn't so neutral, now. "Now you need to bring your knee up at just the right angle. *Slowly first!*" He said it so firmly we both laughed and the tension was broken for a second. But as soon as I started to lift my knee, it was back. My dress fell away from my leg as it rose, baring my knee. It moved higher, higher—*that was his cock I just brushed against.* I wobbled—it was difficult to do it slowly, especially in heels—and he grabbed for my shoulders and steadied me, his palms warm against my bare skin.

And then my knee reached his balls. I could feel them resting right on my kneecap, hot and... *heavy.*

"There," he said. His voice was strained and the Irish was the clearest I'd ever heard it. "That's where you need to be."

I nodded as if we were discussing the best way to change a tire.

"Now let's get you bringing your knee up fast. *Not like this!*" We both laughed again, but this time it barely broke the tension at all. We were too close. *Way* too close. It felt like the temperature in the room had shot up ten degrees since he closed the door.

He eased away from me. "Let me see your hardest, fastest knee." He held out his hand, palm down, as a target.

I swung my leg up. My bare knee hit his palm with a soft slapping sound and, as I wobbled around on my standing leg, his fingertips grazed my thigh just above the knee. I let my leg fall back. We must have only been in contact for a split second, but the feel of his hand remained, sending twisting ribbons of electricity all the way up my leg to my groin.

"It needs to be harder," he said. He walked around behind me, almost-but-not-quite touching me. I could feel his breath on the back of my neck. Then his hands were on my hips from behind. I swallowed. "You need to twist from here," he said. "A little step back... then step into it, twisting, and ram your leg up the inside of his thigh and hit right where I showed you." He started to move me, controlling me like a mannequin. "*Back....*" My hips flexed under his hands, his fingertips stroking the crease where my legs joined my body, and I went weak. I stepped back... and my ass pressed against his cock, hot and fully hard now, outlined through his suit pants. I was almost panting, the need to just spin around and kiss him almost overpowering.

"And *forward,*" he murmured in my ear, his hands directing me. His cock nestled right up against my ass

176

as my knee came forward and up.

We stayed there for long seconds, me balanced on one leg and supported by his hands, his body molded to my back. I could feel every slow breath he took.

"You know I didn't want to kiss him," I whispered. "I mean: not at all. I didn't go out there for that. I don't even like him."

I felt his slow nod... and with it, a shift in his body as he relaxed. He *had* been jealous, and hurt.

I lowered my leg and turned to face him, looking up into his eyes. The tension had never been this thick, this heavy in the air. I realized we were breathing in time. I could see the struggle in his eyes: he *did* want me... and he was straining against whatever it was holding him back. I saw his hands flex and then tighten into white-knuckled fists. *He's having to force himself not to grab me.*

Very deliberately, he took a step back. The air that rushed in to fill the gap between us was freezing. His eyes said, *we can't.*

And I felt my own eyes go hot. I turned away before the frustration and hurt could spill over. I knew it was something inside him, or maybe the gulf between us, not *me*... but that didn't stop it feeling like a rejection.

"Why *did* you go out there with him?" Kian asked. His low voice vibrated through me, those slivers of shining Irish making the back of my neck prickle and my breath catch.

"It was Kerrigan," I said.

"*Kerrigan?*"

I took a step away from him—I had to, or I was just going to throw myself at that big, strong chest and wrap my arms around him. I shook off the scarlet fog of lust in my brain—I had to physically shake my head to clear it and even then, when I answered, my voice was strained. "I went out there to listen to him on the phone."

Kian gave me a look.

"He didn't know! Giggs was my... cover." It sounded stupid, now. "It worked! I heard him!"

Kian nodded and crossed his arms. "Okay... what did you hear?"

I looked up into those clear blue eyes and opened my mouth... then hesitated. It sounded ridiculous. He was going to laugh at me... or think I was crazy. That's why I hadn't said anything, until now.

He tilted his head to the side. "*What?*"

I looked at my feet. A second later, he took a pace towards me and I felt his warm finger under my chin, tilting my head back up. His voice was low and serious, but with just enough teasing to make me smile. "If you build up to it like that and then don't tell me, I'm going to take you over my bloody knee."

I stared up at him. He *wasn't* going to laugh at me. He was the one person who wouldn't.

I took a deep breath and let it out. "I heard him talking to a guy, telling him to go ahead with the next piece of business."

"Okay..." said Kian.

"But—and I know this sounds crazy—"

He nodded and waited, his patience helping me through my nerves.

I took a deep breath and then said it in a rush. "The guy he was talking to was the second shooter from the park."

I watched him go through a whole range of emotions. Incredulity. Disbelief. *Fear...* for me. He finally put his big hands on my shoulders and said, "You're *sure?*"

I nodded. Saying it out loud had made me even more certain. "I've heard that voice over and over in my head, ever since the attack. *Definitely* him."

Kian turned away and ran a hand through his hair. He took a few slow breaths as he gazed around the room. "Fuck," he said at last.

"That was my reaction, too."

Kian rubbed his chin, then scowled. I got the feeling he missed his stubble. "You know what this means?"

I shook my head. "Don't say it." It was too big, too shattering. I'd tried to go there in my head several times since the party and I just couldn't—my brain refused to process it. I sat down on my bed, pulled my legs up and hugged my knees.

"Kerrigan's—"

"*Don't.*" I buried my face in my knees. "It's crazy."

"Kerrigan's working with the Brothers of Freedom."

I could feel him looking at me. I lifted my head just enough to look up at him. "I must be wrong," I said. "It must have been some guy with a really similar voice."

He stared right back at me. "*Are* you wrong?"

I thought about it... *willed* it not to be true. But the certainty was iron-hard, had been since the second I'd heard the voice again. "... no," I said in a small voice. Saying that one word was like casting a spell. The temperature seemed to drop by several degrees—goosebumps stood out on my bare arms.

The White House didn't feel safe, anymore. Kerrigan had brought the danger right inside.

Kian let out a long breath and leaned against my closet. "*Fuck,*" he said again. He stared off into space as he worked through the implications.

I was growing colder and colder. I'd never felt so alone in my life. "What are we going to do?" I asked. And then realized I'd said *we* when I meant *I.*

Kian looked right at me and I suddenly realized it was *we* after all. A little glow of warmth bloomed into life right in the center of my chest. "We need to go to your dad," he said. "Right now."

I shook my head. "We don't have any evidence. You're the one who warned me about causing an incident and embarrassing my dad."

"That was when we were talking about Kerrigan wanting to turn America into a police state. That's politics: this is actual *crime.* Jesus, we're talking *treason* here, he's involved with terrorists! And if they're planning something else...."

I shook my head again. "*No.* Listen to what we're saying. Its nuts."

He hunkered down so that he was at my eye level. "Truth is, if we follow this thing to the logical conclusion, it's worse." He took a deep breath. "The guys at the park—they weren't militia thugs, they were ex-military. The sort of guys Rexortech has thousands of. And the attack in the park gave Kerrigan exactly the excuse he needed to push the Guardian Act. Put it all together: I don't think Kerrigan's just working with the Brothers of Freedom; I think he *set them up.*"

I stared at him. I knew it made sense, but I didn't want to believe it, not even of Kerrigan.

The Vice President was responsible for the attack in the park. For six deaths. For me getting shot.

"We *can't* go to my dad," I said. "We *can't.* Not

without any evidence."

"Emily...."

"No!" I was so worked up, it didn't even hit me that he'd called me *Emily*. "Put yourself in my position. Everybody already thinks I'm crazy—"

"They don't."

"They *do!* Think about how this'll look: messed up woman accuses the VP of treason. No one'll believe it and—" I broke off and swallowed, choking back a sob. "What if I *am* wrong? What if it wasn't his voice, what if it's just my mind playing tricks on me?"

He sat down beside me on the bed, the mattress sinking under his muscled bulk. I'd leaned forward, my hair falling over my face like a curtain, but suddenly his big, warm hand was there, fingers sliding between the strands and pushing it back. "I don't believe that," he said softly. He left his hand there, palm nestled against my cheek, and I could feel his strength throbbing into me.

"I wake up," I whispered, "*every night* clutching at my throat because I felt it cut, or grabbing at my chest because I felt the bullet go through, or—" Tears sprang to my eyes. "Or I'm curled into a ball because I've just lived through them stripping me and—"

His hand slid from my cheek. He wrapped his arm around my back and hugged me into his side. His whole body had tensed with anger, every muscle rock hard. I leaned across him, resting the back of my head against his chest. "I think I *am* crazy," I whispered. "You've helped me cope. But I don't know if I can trust myself anymore. We need proof. I need to *know* I'm right before we tell anyone."

I felt his nod. "Okay," he said at last. "How do we get proof?"

"He told them to use *S32*. Like it was a place." I shook my head. "I've got this feeling... I recognize that from somewhere but I don't know where. It's been going round and round in my head. I'll keep thinking about it."

He nodded again. "We've got one thing on our side: Kerrigan doesn't know anyone suspects."

Shit.

He must have felt me tense up because he pushed me back so that he could look at me. "What?"

"When you beat up Giggs... Kerrigan heard all the noise and came to look."

"You think he knows you heard?"

I slowly nodded. "Maybe."

Kian put his hands on my shoulders again. This time, he gave them a squeeze. When he spoke, his voice was more scared than I'd ever heard it—scared not for him but for me. "You have to be *very, very* careful. Don't go near Kerrigan. No more digging into stuff on your own."

"You think he'd hurt me?" As soon as I'd said it, realization hit and I closed my eyes. Of course he would. If I was right about all this, he'd already plotted to have me killed at the park. That whole brutal attack, just to scare the public into accepting the goddamn Guardian Act. My stomach suddenly twisted. Kerrigan had already gotten most of the country on his side—how much worse would it have been if I'd been killed along with the six others? The President's daughter, slain by terrorists... a big public funeral... there would have been *outrage.* And my dad, grief-stricken, would have gotten behind the bill himself.

That's why Kerrigan had targeted me. It was the

one way he could get my dad on his side, the only way he could guarantee his bill got passed. It would have worked, if Kian hadn't been there.

I opened my eyes and nodded to Kian that I understood. I could see the pain in his eyes: like he'd trade places with me in a heartbeat if he could. "I'll stay away from Kerrigan," I said.

Kian nodded and rose, then turned to face me. "It's late," he said. "I should go."

I checked my phone and it was after midnight—I'd lost track of time. "You should go," I agreed. And then, for some reason, I stood up and took a step towards him. I was almost touching him, chin already lifting, when I realized I'd been moving instinctively to kiss him goodbye. That's how strong it was, between us: I couldn't bear to just let him go.

He looked down at me, those big blue eyes infinitely sad. And he shook his head. *We can't.*

'You do... *like* me?" I asked, a lump in my throat.

His eyes widened, as if aghast that I'd doubt it. "Jesus!" He looked away for a second and I could see him fighting with it, the words difficult to say after so many weeks spent bottling them up. Then he looked right at me. "*Yes!*" he blurted. "I'm so into you it would scare you, if you knew how much."

I bit my lip. "Then tell me why," I whispered. "I know it's not just the job. I know it's something that happened to you. Tell me."

He held my gaze for a moment, then shook his head and looked away. "Doesn't matter what it was," The Irish was thick in his voice, now.

"It *does!*"

"It doesn't!" He took my hands and squeezed, then sighed. "I'm not someone who can do..."—he indicated me and him—"*this.*" And he turned, pulling roughly away from me, and opened the door.

"I don't want you to go," I said. I wrapped my arms around me, suddenly cold.

He hesitated on the threshold. "I'll be right outside the door," he said. And he was gone.

I leaned against the door and stared at the white-painted wood, not seeing it. I saw *him,* outside, standing there staring back at me, hands folded behind his back.

The feelings were too strong, out of control. *This can't go on.*

I was right. The next day, those feelings exploded.

TWENTY-NINE

Kian

Fuck. I strode down the hallway towards the residence, slamming my feet down as if each step was a curse screamed at the top of my lungs. But no matter how hard I stamped, the soft carpet absorbed the noise. I was powerless.

It was the next day and I'd spent all morning in a Secret Service briefing with Miller. The President was due to give a speech at the Museum of Natural History that night: not a big event, but it still needed a lot of planning. Miller didn't bother to hide his anger at having been overruled by the President—he wanted me *gone* for hitting a senator and he let me know it, treating me like an idiot pupil for the entire three hour briefing: *have you got that, O'Harra? O'Harra, is that clear?* And instead of taking a swing at him, I'd had to suck it up and stay calm. I was on my last warning and Emily needed me now more than ever.

Emily.

I hadn't been able to get her out of my head since

that first day I met her, but now it was much, much worse. It wasn't just the raw, hot lust anymore: Camp David and her nightmare and now being the only one she'd told about Kerrigan... we were getting closer and closer. She was opening up to me and part of me wanted her to, even as the rest of me screamed that I was being a moron, because I couldn't do the same for her.

I'd dreamed from the start of grabbing her and kissing her, tearing her clothes off and burying myself deep inside her. That, I understood. But *this...* I was addicted to listening to her voice, smelling her scent, I was addicted to just *looking* at her, drinking her in in big thirsty gulps from the second she opened her bedroom door to the second it closed. I wanted to *be* with her, had crazy dreams of running away together, not just keeping her safe but being happy together. As if I was a regular guy, who could have all that.

More than anything else, I wanted to be that guy. Not some rich guy who could shower her with millions, not the sort of guy her mom wanted her to marry. Just a regular, *unfucked* guy who could have a life with her. The rage had started the instant I'd left her room, a slow twisting that I knew would build and build. I'd barely slept and then had to suffer Miller's patronizing briefing. Now the anger was spinning at hurricane speed, a white-hot monster that was slowly shredding what was left of my self control. Walking it off was *not* working.

I thought of those big green eyes looking up at me, begging me to stay. I thought of the feel of her against me when we'd sat on her bed. I thought of the silk of her hair between my fingertips.

I'd never felt this way about *any* woman. But it

always came back to the same thing: I couldn't have her. I wanted to scream, but this was the White House: I couldn't do so much as a growl. *Goddammit!*

I couldn't go to her in this state: I'd do something stupid. I veered off and went to the little break room at the entrance to the residence, where agents can grab a coffee. I grabbed a mug, put it under the spout, mashed the button for *black coffee* and listened to the grind and hiss and—

I grabbed the mug and hurled it at the wall. There was an almighty crash as it shattered. Shards of white bone china printed with the black Secret Service logo rained down. The coffee machine hissed angrily as it shot coffee into the drip tray.

I heard a Secret Service agent run in behind me. "What the *fuck?*" he asked.

I turned and glared at him. "I dropped a mug," I said in a voice that told him not to argue.

He backed out of the room.

Fuck. I was almost panting with anger, completely out of control. The rage was spinning so fast that everything was a blur. *What the hell am I going to do?* I couldn't be near her anymore. If I so much as saw her, let alone touched her, I'd be lost. But what was I meant to do: call in sick? She needed me.

I marched down the hallway towards her room. A couple of other agents were coming the other way, but they sidestepped and pressed themselves back against the wall as I stormed past. And then I was at her door. I reached for the handle. Jesus, my hand was shaking.

I can't do this.

I have to do this.

I closed my eyes and took a deep breath. *You've done it before:* when she'd emerged from the pool at

Camp David, her skin slippery-wet; when I'd felt her lithe hips under my palms, teaching her self-defense; when she'd stood there in that red dress in the garden, wide-eyed as I'd torn Senator Giggs away from her, and I'd just wanted to kiss the hell out of her....

I opened my eyes. I could do this. It wouldn't be so bad: it was the middle of the day, we weren't going to *do* anything, she might not even need anything right now and I could go away and calm down—

I knocked and heard her soft Texas voice tell me to come in. I opened the door wide, looking at the floor as I entered to give me an extra few seconds to get myself together, and—

I looked up to find her standing there half-naked.

She was in a shimmering blue evening gown, on at the front, but the back was unzipped all the way down to the top of her ass. She was facing away from me and all I could focus on was the long, elegant curve of her naked back.

There was a single thread of my self-control left, hair-thin but strong. The sight of her back made it glow red hot like an overloaded wire. "I... *knocked*," I growled.

"It's okay." I finally looked up into her face. She was looking back over her shoulder at me and I could see it in her eyes: she was as desperate as I was.

Step away. Leave the room.

"I can't get the zipper," she said, turning to show me. "I need both hands to hold the damn thing up." She showed me the loose fabric that formed the front of the thing. She was right: if she let go, the whole thing was just going to fall around her hips. And she wasn't wearing a bra....

I stepped closer. She lifted her hair up out of the

way, exposing the bare skin of her neck. Suddenly, I could smell her, that scent that drove me crazy, warm skin and the wind whipping across huge, open plains. She smelled like freedom, tempting me from my prison. My head spun. The rage—at my situation, at myself—super-heated my lust.

I looked down at the zipper. Now I was closer, I could see right down inside the dress. I could see the white lace waistband of her panties. The thread of self control glowed hotter, turning white.

I grabbed the tiny zipper between finger and thumb, feeling like a giant trying to dress a doll. The damn thing wouldn't move. I stepped closer still and now my lips were inches from her bare neck. I jerked the zipper again. "It's stuck," I said. It was a struggle to get the words out. And I was so close to her, each angry little explosion of air blew across the nape of her neck. I could see the tiny hairs there standing up as she stiffened, her elegant back flexing. God, she was beautiful.

"Try undoing it a little, then go back up," she said. Her own voice sounded as tight as mine, but that was impossible: she couldn't be as turned on as I was because I was ready to melt through the floor.

I saw now that the zipper wasn't all the way undone—not quite. It started about two inches lower, right over her ass.

I gently pulled it downward. It stuck at first but then came free, rasping right down to its stop, and now—

Now I could see her ass: the cheeks firm beneath their covering of tight white cotton. I took two long breaths, staring at that ass. I wasn't sure my hand was ever going to obey my instructions to move, but, eventually, it did. The zipper rose... but the dress started to lift and bunch. I'd have to hold it in place.

I swallowed and tried to grab the fabric over her ass, but it was tight, outlining every glorious curve of her. The backs of my fingers had to stroke across that firm flesh once, twice, before I finally got some of the cloth trapped and I heard her breathing hitch each time. My self-control was almost melted through, now, only seconds to go. I held the dress there and tugged the zipper upward and the dress came together all... the way... to the top.

I let go and stepped back, barely able to breathe. There. I'd done it. I'd held back.

"Thanks," she said. And turned around.

Until that second, I hadn't seen the front. A low vee-shaped neckline left the tops of her breasts exposed, tan and ripe and, as she let her hair fall down her back and her green eyes looked up at me—

The thread of my self-control snapped clean in two.

She saw it in my eyes a split second before it happened. Her mouth had just enough time to open in shock, her eyes open wide.

And then I was kissing her.

THIRTY

Emily

I'D BEEN WANTING HIM TO KISS ME for so long that, at first, I couldn't believe it was actually happening. *This isn't real. He's going to pull away—*

And then his lips met mine and there was absolutely no doubt. *None.* His kiss had weeks of pent-up longing behind it. I could *feel* every time he'd looked at me and held back, every hour he'd stood outside my door, every step we'd taken side-by-side. It had all been stretching back a bowstring, loading it with power, and now all of it was unleashed. This wasn't going to stop. Neither of us could have stopped it even if we'd wanted to.

Kian's lips were savage on mine. That full, soft lower lip was as dreamily perfect as I'd always imagined it, stroking at me, brushing me in a way that sent tremors right down my body. But at the same time it was fast and urgent, his head twisting to follow mine, our lips slowly parting, panting into each other's mouths. It was raw, burning lust and deep emotion twisted into one. Knowing how much he wanted me sent a rush of heat straight down to my groin; knowing how much he *needed* me made every bit of tight, aching worry in my chest detonate and form a warm, swelling glow.

I rocked back on my heels... would have fallen if he hadn't slipped his arm around my waist. The kiss moved and changed, every new touch of his lips awakening new nerve endings, filling me up with pink, sweet pleasure shot through with crackling lust. I grabbed for him, found his shoulders and clung on. Somewhere in the distance I thought, *so* this *is what kissing's meant to be like.*

I was panting, gasping for breath between each frantic kiss, but it wasn't air I needed. I was breathing pure Kian, now, pure essence of Irishman, straight from the source, and I couldn't get enough. My fingers dug into his shoulders through his suit, pulling him closer. I wanted to merge with him, wanted him in me in every possible way.

He bent me backwards over his arm, pressing closer, the hardness of his chest stroking the softness of my breasts, and I went weak. His other hand suddenly slid into my hair, fingers running through it again and again like it was the best thing he'd ever felt, and every touch of his fingertips against my scalp sent new ripples of pleasure through me. The kiss was changing again: he was taking control, showing me how he wanted me. A new tremor went through me as I felt his lips begin to push at mine, forcing them to open, and his tongue teased their edges. I felt myself melting: I'd never felt so gloriously soft, so vulnerable, so damn *feminine* as when that hard tongue stroked my lips. I actually went light-headed. My whole body went momentarily limp as I just opened and welcomed him in. I hadn't known, until that second, that swooning was actually a thing.

His tongue invaded me, exploring me and then finding my own tongue and drawing it into the dance. I was sinking lower and lower over his arm and then, suddenly, he swept me up and lifted me, one arm under my ass and the other under my shoulders. He twisted us and I felt my hair fly out to the side. I could feel the distant vibration of footsteps as he walked us across the room, but they were hazy: everything was soft, hot pleasure wrapped around the hard rhythm of the kiss. I was addicted to him, drunk on him. I wanted it to never stop.

Then I was falling. His lips broke from mine, my hands slipped from his shoulders and I felt my hair fly upwards as I dropped. I landed on my back on the bed, arms and legs flung wide, hair spread across the pillow like a dark halo. Panting, open-mouthed, I opened my eyes and searched for him.

I found him at the side of the bed, standing over me. Looking up at him like that, he seemed even bigger and, when I saw what he was doing, I gulped and my heart sped up a gear.

He was staring right into my eyes... and undressing. Quickly. Carelessly. He stripped off his suit jacket and tossed it away, then unstrapped his holster and pulled off his tie. Next, the shirt, button by button, that snow-white facade of goodness stripped away to reveal the badness beneath.

I lay there panting, his gaze like a laser on me, heating me up in deep, powerful waves that rippled out from my groin. I could see in his eyes every filthy thing he wanted to do to me and I wanted it all.

His chest appeared first: twin slabs of tan hardness, so wide and full. Then, as he undid button after button, his abs came into view. I'd known he was hard, there: I'd caught enough glimpses of him when the sun shone just right through the thin fabric or the wind blew it against his body to know that much. But I wasn't ready for how ripped he was: a deep centerline running all the way down between... *wow*. I'd heard of washboard abs but this was like... my fingers actually itched with the need to stroke his torso, riding the smooth rise and fall of those hard ridges. And his arms... now I could see the thick swells of his biceps and his military tattoos for the first time. His past, written in dark lines of ink across tan muscle. I wanted to touch him there; I wanted to touch him everywhere.

He didn't stop looking at me. Not as he kicked off his shoes and pulled off his socks. Not as he drew his belt through its loops and tossed it aside. Then he was unfastening his pants, shucking them down around his muscled hips and letting them fall to the floor—

I swallowed as I got my first look at the bulge under his jockey shorts: thick and long and pushing out the stretchy fabric in a way that made it impossible not to stare at it. God, I could actually make out the blunt-arrow shape of the head, so... *thick*.

I realized I was pressing my thighs together.

He saw and his cock visibly twitched. He focused on that one part of me and I felt the molten heat at the juncture of my thighs turn to slick wetness. I was pinned to the bed by his gaze and it was getting hard to resist the temptation to reach down and play with myself just to relieve the throbbing ache there. Part of me was still shell-shocked, not really believing it was finally happening. *Things like this don't happen to me,* I thought. I was the original good girl: I was the President's daughter, for God's sake. *I don't lie here on a bed in the middle of the day while some guy—*

He stepped closer, his thumbs hooked in the waistband of his jockey shorts... and pushed.

He was standing right next to the bed, now, so when his cock sprang free it hung over me. I stared up at it, my breathing growing ragged. The shaft was the same smooth tan as his body, the head a rich purple-pink, glossy and firm as a plum. Kian took a long, slow breath himself. I was looking up at him at such an angle that I could see his cock and his face, all without moving my eyes. I could see him staring at me and I could see what I was doing to him. And he could see me looking up at him and see me slowly grinding my thighs together, helpless now to resist the need for friction. We were in a feedback loop, his cock rising and stiffening as he stared down at my slow writhing, me getting wetter as I watched him getting harder.

"This is you, Emily," he said in a low growl. "This is what you do to me."

I swallowed and said nothing. I was torn between wanting him to climb onto the bed and wanting to hear more.

"I've wanted you since I first saw you." The Irish was thick in his voice now, the words fireballs dipped in silver that seared into my mind. "One second after you spoke to me, I was wondering what it'd be like to kiss you. Two seconds, I was thinking about what it'd be like to fuck you."

His eyes blazed down my body. My dress might as

well have not been there: I could feel each tiny millimeter of skin throb as his gaze passed. *Face. Throat. Chest.* My nipples tightened as he gazed at my breasts. *Stomach. Groin.* My hips lifted as if drawn by an invisible thread and then my ass ground hard into the bed.

Kian put one knee on the bed, the mattress sinking under his weight. My stomach flip-flopped. This was happening, really happening. My eyes kept flicking between his erect cock and the sculpted thighs either side of it: so much power, ready to drive that cock inexorably into me....

"Turn onto your stomach," he ordered. "I'm taking that dress off you."

My head was swimming. I turned over, my head to the side. In the mirror, I saw him swing one leg over me and kneel astride my legs. Then he leaned forward, one hand extended to my neck... I gasped as I felt his fingers brush my hair out of the way. His lips met the nape of my neck in a slow kiss and I squeezed my eyes shut, just relishing it. Then I felt the neck of my dress pull tight at the front and the metallic rasp as the zipper came down all... the way... to the bottom. His lips followed, tracing a path of fire down my back, so many kisses that his lips barely left my skin.

Then his hands were sliding under the fabric on either side of my torso, just below my breasts. His thumbs stroked across my back for a second as if he couldn't resist touching me. Then he was lifting me up off the bed and the upper half of the dress was slithering down my arms and off....

He turned me over and lowered me again. There was something about the way he did it: so effortless, his hands so big, that sent a stab of heat straight down to my groin. Then I was on my back again, staring up at him. It was the first time he'd seen my breasts, except for that tiny glimpse when he'd walked in on me, and I could feel them throbbing, aching in their sudden nudity, my nipples puckering and tightening as the cool air hit them. That sudden, momentary panic: *what if he doesn't like me?*

The look on his face as he gazed down at me blasted that thought away. I heard his breathing quicken, saw his whole magnificent body tense as he feasted his eyes. Then his head was coming down and—*Oh God!*—I arched my back as his hot mouth enveloped me, tongue lashing across my nipple. My hands grabbed for his head, burying themselves in that thick, black Irish hair. Streamers of scarlet pleasure sparked down from my breast to my groin, feeding into the slowly spinning core that was building there. He took possession of my other breast with his hand, rolling and kneading it with just the right pressure while his thumb teased the nipple. Meanwhile, his tongue never stopped, expert and quick as it teased my slickened flesh. I began to pant and thrash, moving in rhythm with him, the pleasure spinning faster and faster.

I'd never been good at talking during sex. Growing up as a Senator's daughter will do that to you: I was a good girl, even in the bedroom. But now, as Kian's mouth and fingers teased me closer and closer to the edge, I found my voice. I tangled my fingers into his hair and gently pushed him back. "Please," I gasped. One word was all I could manage, but he got the message. I wanted—*needed*—him.

My dress was still on my lower half. He grabbed the top of it and I lifted my hips and shimmied as he pulled it down my legs and off, tossing it into a corner and leaving me in just panties and heels. Kian took a moment to run his hands languorously up and down my legs, trailing his fingertips along my skin as if he couldn't get enough of them. The satisfied smile on his face said it all: he'd been wanting to do that for a long, long time. Every stroke of those warm palms and strong fingers sent pleasure rippling through me, all of it spiraling inward towards my groin. And the longer he did it, the more his whole muscled body seemed to harden with arousal, everything becoming tight and primed, even his breathing growing strained, until at last he couldn't wait any longer....

I gasped as he suddenly hooked his fingers into my panties and slipped them off. I lay there naked, every inch of me exposed to him, getting wetter and wetter as he knelt there just looking at me. Without ever taking his eyes from me, he felt in his discarded pants for a condom and rolled it on. I swallowed as he nudged my knees apart and began to lower himself atop me, one hand at the base of his cock to guide it—

Footsteps outside my door.

I heard them just as Kian's hands slapped down on the bed either side of my shoulders, tanned, hard, and thick with muscle. I grabbed at his forearms and looked towards the door in horror. I suddenly remembered we were in the White House, in the middle of the day.

Kian didn't stop, didn't seem to even care. He pushed forward, his body so hard, so *big* as it moved up between my thighs. Over his shoulder, I saw his ass tighten and dimple as his hips came forward... and then I gasped as the tip of his cock caressed my folds.

The footsteps stopped outside my bedroom door.

Right outside. My chest tightened with panic as someone coughed. Were they about to come in? My eyes flicked between Kian and the door, about to tell him to stop—

Then he eased forward and I felt myself open, silk around iron, and suddenly I didn't care anymore. I could feel every millimeter of him, could feel myself stretching deliciously around his girth... my eyes fluttered closed and my hands dropped from his arms to fall to the bed, clutching at the sheets.

Low voices outside, one Secret Service agent muttering to another. Probably wondering where Kian was. *He's in here,* a crazy voice inside my head wanted to yell. *He's....*

...slidingdeeperandOhGod—

I arched my back, breasts pillowing against Kian's chest, and quickly brought my hand to my face, biting one knuckle between my teeth to keep from crying out. It *felt... so... good!* I panted hard through my nose as he went deeper, his hard, muscled ass driving between my thighs maybe ten feet from where the two agents were standing. My knees sank outwards, my shoes scraping along the comforter as I drew my feet in. I wrapped my arms around his muscled back as he drew back and thrust deeper, every inch setting off new waves of pleasure. And then suddenly my head lifted off the pillow and my eyes opened wide as he filled me completely.

We stayed like that for several seconds, his hard body covering mine, his thighs holding mine wide apart. Then he slowly began to thrust and the pleasure I could see in his eyes mirrored my own. I'd never seen a man so turned on before, never seen such intensity as he stared down at me, our gazes locked as his hips rose and fell. He was brutal and gentle, a hard thrust in that made me gasp, then a silken withdrawal that made me tremble. I glanced in the mirror again and my heart thundered in my chest at the sight of his muscled body between my thighs, his ass rising and falling. I felt my climax building, the pleasure tightening its hold on me, making me claw my way along his back, making my feet come up off the bed and scrabble at his legs. *God, I'm out of control!* The pleasure was whirling faster, faster—*too soon—*

He could read me perfectly. He slowed down and sank onto his elbows so that we were in contact all the way from groin to chest. For a second, we just panted and stared into each other's eyes. Only when my breathing slowed a little did he start to move again.

This time it was even better. His hard chest slid across my breasts with each thrust, stroking nipples that were as hard as pebbles. The base of his cock ground against my clit, giving the pleasure a new core to wrap itself around. When he rooted himself in me, his chest came so high I could stretch up and tongue the hard slab of his pec, flicking my tongue over the dime-sized nipple, and he groaned low in his throat in pleasure. He grabbed my hands and pushed them down to the bed, interlacing his fingers in mine, then nudged my head to the side so that he could whisper in my ear, his words molten silver that soaked straight down inside me. *"I'm fucking crazy for you. Every inch of you. Every scrap of you. Every atom of you. I'm not going to let anyone hurt you, but right now I'm going to make you mine."*

I writhed under him as he began to speed up, squeezing his hands harder and harder. His raw strength made the bed start to move—a slow rocking at first, but then the headboard started to bang against the wall. I remembered the two agents outside my door but then he sped up again and I didn't care anymore. My world contracted to just my hands in his, palms wet with sweat, my calves hooked tight around the hard muscles of his thighs and the effortless, tight pump of him into me, my climax whirling and contracting, drawing all the pleasure inward.

He began to slam into me, his breath coming in pants—he was getting close, too. I couldn't stay silent any longer: I let out a high little cry of pleasure each time he filled me and a panting sigh each time he left me. I could feel myself beginning to clench and spasm around him, the climax rushing towards me and—

He put his lips to my ear and said, out loud, "You're mine, Emily."

And then he buried himself in me and we were both rocketing over the edge, my body tightening around him as the orgasm ripped through me, him leaning down to kiss my panting mouth as he shot and shot inside me.

THIRTY-ONE

Kian

SHE LAY ON ME UTTERLY NAKED, using my chest as a pillow, and it was the best thing in the world. I watched, mesmerized, as her head rose and fell with each breath I took. I started stroking her hair, from the soft, glossy strands on the top of her scalp to the strands at the back of her neck that were plastered to her by sweat. Then on down her body, over her shoulders and down that long, sinuous back that had tempted me over the edge, right down as far as my arm would stretch, almost down to her ass. And then I'd bring my hand all the way back up and do it all over again, and I was instantly addicted. I could have stroked her like that for weeks.

I could feel my rage subsiding: after years, I'd finally found the cure, at least for a little while. It had never been like that before: sex had always seemed empty, just a physical release. *That* hadn't been just sex. That had been goddamn spiritual. Something in her had cleansed me of all my anger and now, running my palm over her tan skin again and again, I didn't think it was possible to ever be angry again.

There was a nagging doubt, somewhere deep inside that told me all my troubles hadn't gone away, that I might just have ruined everything. Wasn't this *exactly* what I swore I wouldn't do, because I couldn't give her a proper relationship?

I took that doubt and crushed it. I wasn't going to let it spoil this.

Emily began to smooth her hand in slow, lazy circles over my chest. At first, it was relaxing. Then, as her hand slid lower, it started to take on a whole different mood. When she reached the tight tangle of hair above my cock, I looked down at her in shock, even as my cock rose in response. "Damn... *already?*"

She looked up at me and the look of guilt mixed with timid lust was the hottest thing I'd ever seen. "Sorry," she said.

"Don't *apologize.* I just thought you were all... y'know... sweet and innocent."

"I am!" She blushed. "I think I'm just... making up for lost time."

Her hand reached the base of my cock and it strained upward, achingly hard. It wasn't just where she was touching me, it was *her*... her smell, her voice, her soft skin... everything about her turned me on. "It's not like I'm complaining," I clarified, rolling us over so that I was on top. I looked down at her breasts and grinned. Then I grinned again when I heard footsteps in the corridor outside, enjoying the way she tensed and held her breath until we heard them recede. "Come on. Let's break some more rules."

She started to smile... and suddenly went stock-still.

"...what?" I asked, worried. "What did I say?"

She shot off the bed, sliding from under me before I could stop her, and ran across the room. I flipped myself over onto my back and gaped after her. "What are you...*What?*"

Emily had reached her desk and was now bending over it, rooting through papers. I kept trying to form a coherent question in my head but, every time I managed to get a sentence together, she'd move a little, her ass would wiggle or her breasts would sway, and I'd forget what I was going to say and have to start all over again. She seemed blissfully unaware of the effect her body had on me. Didn't she realize how gorgeous she was? Suddenly, she grabbed a piece of paper and straightened up. "*Ha!*"

"Ha... *what?*"

"I *knew* I'd heard S32 before." She hurried back to the bed and almost dived onto it next to me, shoving the piece of paper in my face. "See?"

I couldn't tear my eyes away from her breasts—they were still bouncing to a stop. I shook my head. "No," I said in a voice thick with lust.

She blushed, finally aware of her nakedness, and pointedly covered her breasts with one arm. I reluctantly focused on the page. A report from the Environmental Protection Agency. "What am I looking at?"

"A few years back, Rexortech was storing chemicals in an old warehouse. Nasty stuff, the things you use to make printed circuit boards. They weren't careful enough and some of the chemicals started leaking out. Nothing really major—it didn't contaminate the water table or anything but the EPA went ballistic and shut the place down until they cleaned it up. Except cleaning it up would cost more than just buying a new warehouse, so Rexortech fought it. And they've been back and forth in the courts ever since. Meanwhile, the warehouse is still sealed up and supposedly out of use."

"So?"

"Look at what the EPA calls the building." She pointed.

South Side Unit 32 (S32)

"It would be quiet," I said. "If they wanted a place to meet and plan things...." I checked the address. "I'll go take a look."

"Now?"

I got up, hunted for my jockey shorts and then saw them across the room. "The sooner we get some evidence, the sooner we can go to your dad." I padded naked across the room, grabbing clothes as I went. "We don't need much. If there's even a hint of the Brothers of Freedom in a building owned by Kerrigan's old company, that shows you were right."

Emily got up and walked over to me as I pulled on my suit pants. "Be careful."

"Always." I grabbed my shirt and started to pull it on. Truth was, I was eager to get going. This whole time, Emily had been doing the investigating and I'd had to take a back seat. Now it was my turn. With luck, I might even get the chance to beat the crap out of the guys who'd tried to kill her.

But then she got right in front of me and pushed in close, sliding her hands under my open shirt and across my chest. *Closer,* so her nipples stroked me and my cock was nestled against her warm thigh. Suddenly, I just wanted to stay right the hell there, with my woman.

I'd never had that urge before. Usually I'm gone while the sheets are still warm. *Damn.* How did guys with girlfriends do this?

Was she my *girlfriend* now?

I leaned down, she tilted her head back, and we kissed, fitting together as naturally as if we'd done it a thousand times instead of just once. It felt *right.* Maybe it was because we'd both done it a million times in our minds. And if there's such a thing as a girlfriend kiss, not a lover's kiss, then this was it. Soft and gentle but heavy with promises: a *see you later,* not a *goodbye.* I closed my eyes and I didn't want to open them when it was over. When I *did* open them, the look she was giving me made me want to just hurl her right back onto the bed and start all over again. I had to force myself to look away and start buttoning my shirt. "I'll be back in a couple of hours," I said. "Well before we leave for your dad's speech."

She glanced at herself in the mirror. "I better make myself look presentable," she said, running a hand through her sweat-damp hair.

"You look amazing," I growled.

"I don't look like the President's daughter." She glanced down at her naked body.

I strapped on my holster, pulled on my suit jacket and then walked over and gave her another kiss. "Maybe you don't have to be the President's daughter all the time."

She gave me a shy little smile, then kissed me again. And I headed for the door before that wonderful body made me change my mind.

THIRTY-TWO

Kian

The warehouse was way over the other side of the city and I had to crawl there through DC traffic. But that couldn't dampen my mood and neither could the storm clouds on the horizon. I had a big, stupid grin plastered across my face like a teenager who's just lost their virginity.

Eventually, though, my hormones started to calm down and the doubts started to creep back. It was just a sense of unease, at first, but it thickened and chilled until I felt like I was itching inside my own skin. *Shit*. What had I done? What the hell was going to happen now? Was she expecting us to be together, an actual couple? That idea would last about three seconds once the President and the First Lady found out about it, not to mention Miller.

Sure, she was a grown woman and could make her own decisions but between them her folks could bring a lot of pressure to bear. She was still a princess in a gilded cage: it wasn't like I could just sneak into the

White House every time I wanted to see her. And if I let her leave the safety of the residence and run off with me, I'd be putting her in very real danger. All those bulletproof windows and Secret Service agents were there for a reason: no matter what happened with us, she'd always be the President's daughter.

And that wasn't even the real problem: the real problem was me. I didn't know if I could open myself up again, after having been ripped apart twice.

The warehouse was all closed up, the doors chained and sealed with EPA stickers. For a moment, I thought maybe Emily was wrong after all.

Then I spotted the small door at the back. The chain on that one wasn't rusty like the others but shiny and new. And unlocked. There were three SUVs parked outside and, when I crept up to the door, I could hear the murmur of voices inside. *Shit.*

I crept inside. The first thing I noticed was the smell. It pushed right up my nostrils, burning them from the inside until I wanted to sneeze and gag. Some sort of chemical and not the sort it's healthy to be around. The floor was wet with it and, as my eyes adjusted to the gloom, I realized I was surrounded by towering racks of chemical drums, many of them leaking. *No wonder the EPA closed this place.*

The voices were coming from the far end of the warehouse. I crouched low and crept between the racks of drums, trying not to make a sound. At last, I leaned around a corner and saw them: six men, standing around a table looking at some sort of map. All of them looked like they were ex-military: I could see it in their posture, in the way they listened to their leader. And the man at the head of the table, giving the orders, was the second shooter from the park.

Emily had been right.

I couldn't make out what they were saying. I had to get closer. I crept out from behind the drums, hidden only by the shadows. One noise and I was dead. I sneaked closer, closer... and suddenly stopped, my heart in my mouth. My leg was a half-inch away from knocking into an open shipping crate, full of gleaming assault rifles. Another crate contained grenades. It looked like it had all come straight from Rexortech—no doubt supplies that were meant to be heading to our troops in Iraq or Afghanistan but had been "lost" along the way. They were planning another attack and a much bigger one than the park.

I was close enough now to hear parts of the conversation. "If that happens, what then?" asked one guy.

I only caught the end of the second shooter's response. "—Isabella," he said.

Who's Isabella?

Then I caught some luck. "Who's going to lead the teams?" a long-haired man asked.

An older guy spoke up. "I'll take the south side team." He nodded at the second shooter. "Powell will take the north team. We go as soon as we get final confirmation."

Powell. I took a long, slow breath in. Finally, the leader had a name. Now if I could just get close enough to get a look at the map...

My foot landed in a puddle of chemicals, invisible in the darkness. The splash echoed around the steel walls.

Immediately all six men drew guns. Torches stabbed out into the gloom, searching for me and, as I scrambled back behind the drums, one of them picked me out.

"*There!*" yelled someone. A flurry of shots rang out, some of them hissing inches past my head. I threw myself to the floor behind a stack of drums.

"You see who it was?" a voice asked in the darkness.

"O'Harra." Powell's voice, and he didn't hide his disgust. "The guy from the park."

I drew my gun, wishing I still had my Desert Eagle instead of the toy Miller had left me with. But even with it, I'd still be ridiculously outnumbered. I could already hear them fanning out: they were going to surround me.

It went against my instincts—I was just itching to go to work on that bastard Powell with my fists—but I had to run or I wouldn't be able to warn anyone about what I'd seen.

I took a deep breath and sprinted for the door at the end of the warehouse. Immediately, the air came alive with gunfire and not just the staccato bangs of handguns: I could hear the roar of an assault rifle, too. Bullets split the air to either side of me, one of them plucking at my suit jacket. *Shit!* They'd started to run, pounding across the wet floor towards me. I might be able to stay ahead until I reached the door but then I'd be a sitting duck while I hauled it open....

In desperation, I grabbed at the nearest rack of chemical drums and pulled. It was one of the really tall ones, rising thirty feet up into the darkness. It was already rusted and decaying, weakened by years of corrosive, leaking chemicals. With my weight hanging from edge, it sagged... and tipped.

There was a yell from behind me as the men chasing me pulled up short. A second later, the first heavy chemical drum slammed into the concrete, followed by another and another, the sound deafening in the huge, echoey space. It became a cascade, drums bouncing and rolling, each one big and heavy enough to shatter a leg or crush a spine, and some of them were bursting as they hit, spewing their toxic contents. Powell and his men were forced to back off and hug the walls, some of them climbing the racks to avoid the chemicals. I staggered to the door and pulled it open.

The last thing I saw, as I glanced back into the warehouse, was Powell's glaring face. A chill went through me: he'd recognized me. He probably knew I was Emily's bodyguard, now... and with Kerrigan already suspicious about Emily, they'd no doubt put two and two together. I was a threat to them... and so was she. They were going to come after her.

I ran.

THIRTY-THREE

Emily

AFTER KIAN LEFT, I took an epic shower, letting the water sluice over me and soak its heat into my bones. Lying with him on the bed, I hadn't fully appreciated the workout he'd given me. It was only when I walked—*staggered*—to the shower that I felt the pleasant ache between my thighs and the floppiness in my limbs where I'd clung and arched and writhed against him. I couldn't stop grinning. *God, is it going to be like that every time?*

Every time. As I shampooed my hair, a worm of fear started to twist in my stomach. What *was* going to happen now? Some things had obviously changed but some hadn't. He was still my bodyguard. And there was still a lot he was holding back from me: he'd pulled away from me for so long that I knew there must be some serious stuff in his history. Things that bad didn't just disappear overnight—I proved that every night when I woke up in a cold sweat. He'd overcome them for now but they could still tear us apart....

I frowned. *The hell they will.* I'd finally found exactly what I'd been searching for, that one safe place I'd needed so bad... even *before* the park, even if I hadn't known it. I wasn't going to give that up, no matter what anyone said and no matter how hard I had to fight for it. He'd said he was crazy for me, despite the fact he'd seen me at my worst, paralyzed with fear and too scared to sleep. I remembered the promise I'd made to myself at Camp David. Whatever he was going through, I'd let him know I was there for him, too.

I rinsed off my hair, toweled myself off and dressed again. It felt weird, putting the same clothes on again after sex. Sex had always been a night time thing, not something you did in the middle of the day with people—

My eyes suddenly whipped to my bedroom door. *With people right outside.* Had anyone heard? There'd definitely been someone there at one point, but we'd been quiet*ish*. Later we definitely *weren't* quiet, plus someone could have seen Kian leave my room.

I bit my lip. There was no way we were going to be able to keep a lid on this thing. Not in the White House. Kerrigan and my mom already had their suspicions. This was coming out, one way or another.

The only thing to do was to get ahead of it, so we could deal with it on our own terms. I had to go to my dad. I had to stand there, look him in the eye and tell him this was happening. That's exactly what I needed to do.

Right after I painted my toenails.

And tidied these papers.

And answered this email.

I managed to put it off for the entire rest of the afternoon, coming up with excuse after excuse, before I finally admitted I was procrastinating. By then, it was nearly time to get into the limos to go to the speech. *Where's Kian? He should have been back by now.* My stomach lurched. What if he'd run into the Brothers of Freedom at the warehouse?

I chewed on it for a few minutes and decided there was nothing I could do about it—not without drawing attention to the fact he'd gone AWOL all afternoon. I had to solve the problems I could solve. I took a deep breath, grabbed my purse and headed for the Oval Office. But when I got there, I was just in time to see my dad hustling his chief of staff inside, probably squeezing in a last-minute meeting before we left. I sighed and wandered on down the hallway, past the Roosevelt room. I turned the corner and—

The Vice President's office was dead ahead of me, just past the next junction. The door was open and I could see Kerrigan inside, tapping out a text message on his phone.

His *second* phone. The little one I'd seen him answer at the party.

My heart started thumping. I had to find out what was in that message: it could be the smoking gun we needed. But there was no way I could see from here and he'd see me if I got any closer.

Kerrigan finished texting and shoved the phone into the inside pocket of his jacket, which was folded over the back of a chair. No way I could get to it... unless I could get him out of his office. Even then, I'd have to hope he didn't take his jacket with him.

I backed silently around the corner and pressed my

back against the wall, trying to come up with a plan. Then I hurried to the Press Secretary's office and leaned in through the open door. Jessica, the Press Secretary, was focused on one of the three computer screens that sat on her desk, her fingers rattling across the keyboard and a pencil clamped between her teeth to help her think. "Hi!" I said. "Did you find the VP yet?"

She looked up, frowned and spat out the pencil, but her fingers kept on typing. "No...."

I did my best surprised face. "Oh! Didn't you need to talk to him about the *Washington Post* story."

As Press Secretary, the one thing that scares Jessica more than anything else in the world is being second to know something. "*What Washington Post* story?"

I was making this up as I went along. I bit my lip and tried to look clueless. "Maybe I got it wrong. Someone said to me the *Post* was doing a piece on the VP tomorrow and you *definitely* needed to talk to him before they went to press... didn't they tell you?"

"Shit!" She grabbed her desk phone. "Mr. Vice President? I need a few minutes. Right now. Yes, *that* urgent. Can you come to me, sir? I want to set up a call with both of us and the *Post*...." Meanwhile she was frantically searching through emails and Post-It notes, trying to find the message she thought she'd missed. I slipped away and retreated towards the residence. Ten seconds later, I heard Kerrigan's footsteps as he stormed along the hallway. I held my breath and sneaked a look as he entered Jessica's office....

He was still in his shirt sleeves. He'd left his jacket in his office. Now I had to hope the phone was still in it.

I waited until he closed the door and then set off down the hallway, walking as fast as I could without drawing attention. With every step, my fear ratcheted a little higher, a tight knot growing in my stomach. How much time did I have before Kerrigan and Jessica realized there *was* no story brewing at the *Post?* Two minutes? Three? I tried to walk faster. *When did this hallway get so damn long?*

I reached the door to the VP's office and then had to hang around outside, trying to look casual, while a couple of staffers sauntered down the hallway, chatting and flirting. I was sweating, now. *What am I doing? I'm not a spy! Come on! COME ON!*

The second they'd passed me, I darted into the VP's office and closed the door just enough to hide me. I rooted through his jacket and... *yes!* The phone was still there. I glanced up at the door, ears straining for any hint of Kerrigan coming back. I started going through the phone's unfamiliar menus. *Messages. Sent Items. There!*

A text message sent just a few minutes ago. *LS CONFIRMED*

I stood there staring at it. What the hell was that? That could be anything! I went to the next message and the one before that, but they were just times and dates—presumably of meetings. I was hoping I'd find some reference to the day of the attack in the park but Kerrigan was smart: either he'd deleted messages after sending or he'd done nearly everything as voice calls.

I heard footsteps coming down the hallway. Hard, angry, male footsteps. *Shit!* I backed out of the messages and dropped the phone back into the jacket pocket, but I was in too much of a panic. The phone missed the pocket, slithered down the jacket's smooth inner lining and bounced across the carpet. *Shit! Shit!* I scrambled for it, grabbed it and shoved it into the pocket, then ran for the door—

I opened it to find Kerrigan standing right outside, our faces a foot apart.

His expression went from shock to puzzlement to anger. He glanced over his shoulder at Jessica's office, figuring it all out. Then he looked past me to his desk. His computer. His jacket.

He looked back to me and those soulless gray eyes flared with rage. "What the *hell* are you doing in here?" he spat. There was no fear at all, no guilt or shame. He was just outraged that I'd mess with his plans. *How dare I?!*

That was when I started to get really scared. For weeks now, he'd been the enemy but I'd always faced him in the safety of a hallway or at a party, surrounded by people. Now his mask of civility had slipped away to reveal the monster inside and we weren't just fighting with words. This was the man who'd plotted to have me killed... and I was alone with him. *What the hell was I thinking?* Kian had made me promise not to put myself at risk and I'd gone ahead and done exactly that.

I made the mistake of backing up a step... and he took a step forward. Too late, I realized I was trapping myself in his office. *No one knows I'm in here!*

He took another step forward, then another and I backed up fast, almost tripping. He was bigger than me, stronger than me and he was *mad...* and I was alone with him, crippled by high heels. I wanted to scream but I couldn't find my voice. Then my ass hit his desk and there was no place left to run.

Kerrigan moved right up against me, dominating my personal space, towering over me. His knees brushed mine and the stink of his cologne filled my nostrils. I shied back from him, bending backwards over the desk, hands scrabbling at the edge, but he kept coming.

And then, over his shoulder, though the half-open door, I saw Harlan, the head of my dad's Secret Service detail, ambling towards the Oval Office. "Harlan!" I squeaked.

To my relief, he heard me and looked towards the office, then frowned and walked closer. Kerrigan heard the footsteps and backed off a pace, but his eyes never left mine.

I straightened up as Harlan pushed the door open the rest of the way. "Miss Matthews?" he asked, puzzled. His eyes went from me to Kerrigan and back. He wasn't stupid: he could tell something was up. "Everything okay?"

Kerrigan had his back to the door so he hadn't had to stop glaring at me. His eyes were the single scariest thing I'd ever seen in my life, scarier even that the second shooter at the park. I couldn't look away. "Fine," I told Harlan in a shaky voice. "I just realized I'd forgotten the time. It must be about time to go... right?"

"Pretty much, ma'am."

I stepped out from between Kerrigan and the desk, and walked quickly over to Harlan and safety. "Let's go, then," I said.

Harlan looked confused and a little concerned, but he nodded and led me away down the hallway. "Mr. Vice-President," he said respectfully as we left.

Kerrigan didn't reply. But when we'd gone a few paces, I knew he'd turned around because I could feel his gaze burning into my back. I stayed close to Harlan, my legs shaking so much they could barely support me.

Minutes later, we climbed into the limos that would take us to the museum... but Kian was still nowhere to be found. I overheard Miller saying that this was *it,* that he'd messed up his final chance. But at the last second, Kian jogged up, out of breath and with his tie askew. Miller looked as if he wanted to disembowel him, but there was no time for yelling: Kian swung himself into our limo and we were off.

The journey gave me a chance to process what had just happened. The text I'd seen wasn't any sort of real evidence, but from the way Kerrigan had reacted, it was clear I was right: something *was* going on. And from Kian's grim expression, he'd found something, too. We couldn't talk in the limo: not with my dad sitting right next to me. I had to get him alone.

When we arrived, Kian grabbed my hand as we stepped out onto the red carpet. It was a fairly low-key event, but the press were still there and a small crowd had gathered. With Kian's help, I'd improved a lot but I still had to focus on breathing slow and steady as I walked past the sea of faces. It was only once we were inside and the doors were closed that my shoulders slumped in relief.

My dad and his Secret Service detail went into a side room to wait. Behind a huge set of double doors lay the main exhibition hall, now filled with important donors sipping cocktails as they waited for the night's star attraction. I could hear the head of the museum beginning the speech that would introduce my dad. I grabbed Kian and pushed him down a hallway and into a quiet corner.

"What happened?" I asked. "Where have you *been?*" Then I just threw my arms around him and hugged him tight, needing to feel him against me. My heart was still racing from what had happened in Kerrigan's office. Kian's arms wrapped around my back, pressing me to him, and I slowly calmed. It was only then that I noticed the sharp smell of chemicals on him. I drew back... and saw the thumb-sized hole a bullet had left near the hem of his suit jacket. "Are you okay?!"

"I'm fine. I found them. The second shooter from the park is leading them—his name's Powell. They were planning something. I don't know what it is but it's happening soon. They were just waiting for confirmation."

I realized I had the other piece of the puzzle. "Kerrigan already sent it. I saw the text message. So it's happening *tonight!*" I told him how I'd sneaked into Kerrigan's office.

His face fell. "Are you *nuts?*" He grabbed my shoulders and pushed me up against the wall, the plaster cool through my dress. "I told you not to take any more risks!"

His anger would have been scary, given his size... except I could see it came from worrying about me. He managed to look mad at me for another second and then melted. "Jesus," he said, shaking his head. His voice was thick with emotion. "Just—"

He suddenly leaned in and kissed me hard, taking me by surprise. My body caught on before my mind did, that familiar ripple of heat shooting straight down my body as my eyes closed and my lips opened. It was desperate, angry... *possessive,* letting me know just how much I meant to him. And it took my breath away.

He broke the kiss and stood there panting down at me, as speechless as I was. "Just...." he said at last, "Just don't do that again."

I'd never heard such fear in his voice: fear that something would happen to me. Fear that he'd lose me. My heart swelled and I nodded dumbly. "The message said *Confirm LS.*" I told him. "What's *LS*? It must be the target, right?"

We stared at each other as we thought. "Something big they could attack, or maybe blow up," said Kian. "*Liberty... Statue?* But why would they write it LS, not SL?"

"Liberty Bell?" I tried. "Lincoln Memorial?" I couldn't think of anything that started with *LS*. Then it hit me and I grabbed Kian's arm. "*Lafayette Square!*" There wouldn't normally be many people there, this time of night, but maybe there was some gathering we didn't know about, or maybe they were just going to blow up the statues to make a point.

Kian nodded. "Come on, we've got to tell your dad." He grabbed my hand and led me down the hallway. "Where is he?"

At that moment, we heard applause coming from beyond the double doors, followed by *Hail to the Chief.* "Shit," I said. "He's just starting his speech."

Kian stopped so suddenly that I staggered as his hand pulled me up short. I turned to look at him and saw his face turning white, his eyes widening in horror.

"*LS,*" he said. "*Lone Star.* They're going to assassinate the President."

THIRTY-FOUR

Emily

KIAN WAS A BIG GUY but he could move *fast* when he had to. He hauled open the big double doors and sprinted through the main exhibition hall. As *Hail to the Chief* played on, he raced down the center aisle between the rows of seats. The crowd turned to look, their applause dying away.

My dad was walking towards the podium, waving, and he'd almost reached it when Kian vaulted up onto the stage. "Get him off the stage!" he yelled. "Get him out of here!"

The Secret Service agents were all frowning at Kian, but they weren't going to take any chances where the President's safety was concerned. Two of them grabbed my dad under the arms and almost carried him off stage and into the side room. A few people in the crowd screamed as the other agents drew their guns.

I raced up the aisle after Kian and made it into the

side room just before the agents slammed the door.

"You have to evacuate, right now," panted Kian. "There's going to be an attempt on the President's life."

I looked around at the agents. I didn't know any of them well: Harlan was outside with the motorcade, so a younger guy called Eric Brannon was the ranking agent inside. I expected him to argue but he didn't— not for a second. He just gave Kian a look as if to say, *you better be right,* then nodded to the other agents. They started to hustle my dad towards the door.

"Wait," said the President. Then, louder, "*Wait!*" He was still carrying plenty of muscle from his army days and he shook off the agents holding him. "What the hell's going on?"

"There's no time!" yelled Kian. "We can talk about it later!"

My dad shook off another agent who was trying to tow him towards the door. "Mr. O'Harra, I have a room full of people waiting for me. This threat— where's it coming from? Why doesn't Miller or anyone else know about it? What is it, an anonymous tip?"

I could see Kian trying to control his anger. I knew it wouldn't end well if both of them started screaming at each other. I grabbed his hand and rubbed my fingers over his knuckles.

Kian closed his eyes for a second and took a deep breath. "Okay," he said. He looked at Agent Brannon. "You guys set up outside this room. Don't let anyone come in."

Brannon stared at him in dismay, aghast that Kian would presume to give him orders. But then a look passed between them: Kian was trying to make him understand that, the sooner he could satisfy the

President, the sooner they could get him to safety. *Work with me, here....*

"Fine," said Brannon. He took half his men back into the main exhibition hall to guard that door. The other half went out into the hallway to guard the other door. That left Kian, my dad and me in the room.

"Now for the love of God," said my dad, "Tell me why you just pulled me off a stage."

"Sir," said Kian, "the Vice-President is behind the Brothers of Freedom. They're ex-military guys, probably hand-picked from Rexortech. The attack in the park was to scare people into backing the Guardian Act. Now he's going to seal the deal by assassinating you. The whole country will be *baying* for more protection: the Act will pass and he'll turn the country into a police state. There'll be no one to stop him because *he'll be president!*"

My dad just stared at him. "You're talking about a *goddamn coup!*"

"Yes sir," said Kian. "I am."

"I've heard Kerrigan talking to the Brothers of Freedom," I said. "I've seen messages he's sent them. It's all true, I swear."

My dad looked between the two of us. Maybe he didn't believe Kian but he sure as hell believed me. "God help us," he muttered. He threw open the doors. "Get me the hell out of here," he barked at Brannon.

"Yes *sir,*" said Brannon, and started giving orders. A tight group of Secret Service agents surrounded my dad, Kian and me and started walking us towards the exit. I let out a long breath. Everything was going to be okay. We'd get back to the White House, Kerrigan would be arrested—

"Sir," said one of the agents to Brannon, "I can't

raise the motorcade."

Brannon tried his radio and shook his head. "I can't get through to the White House."

Then, from just beyond the next door, three loud bangs. *Gunfire!*

THIRTY-FIVE

Kian

IT ONLY TOOK Brannon a split second to react. "This way!" he snapped, turning us around. The rest of the Secret Service agents followed his lead, taking us back towards the main exhibition hall. "Lone Star is moving," Brannon said into his radio. "Evac, main entrance, we need the motorcade. *Does anybody copy?*"

I'd already drawn my gun. With my other hand, I squeezed Emily's hand... but she didn't respond. When I turned to look at her, she'd gone pale, arms and legs stiff as she walked, eyes darting around in panic. I squeezed her hand again and, this time, I got a weak squeeze back in return. God, this must be like every one of her nightmares come to life. It tore me apart to see her like this again and to know it was the same damn people doing it. That primal urge to protect her was stronger than ever. *I'm going to kill every last one of them.*

We raced down the hallway, the President and

Emily in the middle of the group, myself and the other Secret Service agents surrounding them. We'd just reached the door to the exhibition hall when we heard breaking glass and screams from the other side, then more gunfire. We were cut off from both the main and side entrances. "*Shit!*" said Brannon, starting to lose his cool. "Down here!"

I made sure I kept hold of Emily's hand as we moved through the building. Whatever happened, I wasn't going to let anyone separate us. I understood Brannon's plan: to get us away from the two groups of gunmen and towards an emergency exit. But even if we could make it, we'd be horribly exposed once we got outside. We needed the motorcade to be right outside the door so we could run Emily and the President straight inside an armored limo... but for some reason, we couldn't contact them. I tried my own radio: nothing. *Shit!*

More gunfire behind us—closer, this time. They were gaining on us. When we came to the door at the end of the hallway, Brannon left three men behind to guard our backs and closed the door behind them.

We emerged into another exhibition hall, this one filled with a giant dinosaur skeleton. The hall was two stories high, with wide marble staircases up to the second floor. We were halfway across when we heard more gunfire coming from ahead of us. Now we really *were* surrounded. I heard one of the other agents curse. All of us were panting, adrenaline thundering through our veins. This was the worst case scenario: under siege, with the President right in the firing line.

"Oh God," said Emily, her eyes wide with fear. Anybody would have been terrified, but she was desperately trying to hold her PTSD at bay, too. I put my hands on her upper arms and turned her to face me, then looked into her eyes. For a second, it was almost as if she didn't see me. "Emily?" I said in a low voice.

She finally focused on me. She was still there—just.

"It's going to be okay," I told her. "I'm here." I stroked her cheek with my thumb and she nodded, but her breathing was dangerously fast.

Brannon tried his radio again. "I still can't raise anyone. We can't call for backup." He was close to panicking. The poor guy didn't have the experience of Harlan or Miller—he'd probably never seen action before.

Gunfire echoed down the hallway we'd just come through. This time, there were answering shots from the three men Brannon had left behind. But they were outnumbered and outgunned: I remembered the assault rifles I'd seen at the warehouse. Almost immediately, we heard a cry and one of the three handguns stopped firing. *Shit.* Brannon looked at me in fear. I had to take charge.

"Stairs," I said, pointing. "We go up to the second floor."

"We'll be trapped up there!" said Brannon uncertainly. I could see him going through his Secret Service rulebook in his head—nothing had prepared him for this.

"We're trapped *now!*" I snarled at him.

We heard a body hit the floor in the hallway. The gunfire was getting closer. It sounded like there was only one Secret Service agent left firing, now.

"Okay," said Brannon. "Upstairs." He started walking the President that way. I hadn't waited to be told: I already had Emily by the hand and was halfway to the staircase.

That was when the grenade went off.

Everything seemed to happen in slow motion. Emily and I already passed the door that led onward through the museum but the others were right in front of it. The gunmen must have rolled the grenade right up to the doors because they exploded inward in a shower of burnt wood fragments and gray smoke. Almost immediately, gunfire erupted from the smoking doorway. One Secret Service agent went down instantly while the others dived for cover. Brannon pulled the President towards a pillar. I grabbed Emily and pulled her into the shadows beneath the huge marble staircase. We were out of sight, there, relatively safe... but the others weren't.

The Secret Service agents returned fire but there were only three of them left, now. Just as Brannon got the President behind a pillar, the other door was kicked in... and now they were taking fire from both sides. Another agent went down. Now only Brannon and one other agent protected the President.

"Oh Jesus," whispered Emily. She tried to rise from our hiding place. I hauled her grimly back down.

There was nowhere for the others to run but they couldn't stay where they were. They made a last ditch sprint for safety, hustling the President towards an information desk that would provide some cover, but as soon as they came out from behind the pillar, both groups of gunmen opened fire. I held my breath, willing the President forward. Back in college, he'd been a quarterback and he was still fit for his age. Twenty paces would get him to safety. *Ten. Five—*

A bullet hit him in the chest and spun him around, tearing him from Brannon's grip. He slumped to the ground as scarlet spread across his white shirt.

THIRTY-SIX

Kian

NEXT TO ME, Emily opened her mouth to scream. I clamped a hand hard over her mouth and used my other arm to hold her against me so she couldn't run to him.

Brannon and the other agent dragged the President behind the information desk, sat him up against it and used the desk as cover, returning fire from behind it. The three of them were only thirty feet or so away from us, but it was thirty feet of deadly open space. We'd be dead in a heartbeat if we tried to cross it.

The President was still breathing but his cheeks were going pale and he had both hands clutched to the gunshot wound in his chest. He turned his head and looked right at me. Something passed between us. Not just President to bodyguard: father to son.

He knew about Emily and me.

The gunfire stopped for a second as the gunmen

started to advance towards the desk. The President's voice was raspy and weak, but it hadn't lost an ounce of authority. *"Get my daughter out of here,"* he croaked.

I nodded and turned to Emily. She was staring at her dad, barely breathing—she was in shock, or something close to it.

We were still hiding under the stairs. To climb up them, we'd have to wait until the gunmen passed us on their way to the President and then crawl along the length of the room, right out in the open, to reach the bottom of the staircase. We'd have no cover. Our only protection would be that the gunmen would have their backs to us.

I waited until the gunmen passed by us, counting eight of them, all with assault rifles. I took another look at Emily and my guts twisted—she was still almost frozen with fear, just as she'd been in the park. It looked like whatever progress I'd helped her make had been destroyed. I'd just have to pray that she was lucid enough to follow my lead. I held my finger to my lips, pointed to where we needed to go, and waited until she nodded. Then I took a deep breath and started crawling, pushing Emily ahead of me.

There's a feeling you get, when you turn your back on something dangerous. It's your body's alarm system, its way of telling you this is a very, very bad idea. Doesn't matter if it's an enemy soldier, a vicious dog or a schoolyard bully: the hairs on the back of your neck stand up and your whole body tenses, waiting for the sound of the shot or the teeth sinking into your leg or the words that are going to make you feel like shit for the rest of the day.

It was like that but a million times worse. Eight

men were behind us, all with weapons that could kill us in a heartbeat. We wouldn't even have time to react as the bullets tore into us.

If we made a sound, we were dead.

If one of them turned around, we were dead.

If Emily froze up and we got stuck out in the open, we were dead.

We started to crawl, keeping as tight to the staircase as we could, our left shoulders almost brushing it. Shell casings littered the floor and the air was thick with acrid smoke. Emily was just a few steps in front of me: she'd crawl a few steps and then hesitate and I'd have to nudge her foot before she'd continue.

The marble floor was glossy and cool under our hands but my palms were slick with sweat. I'd never been more aware of the spot between my shoulder blades: that's where a bullet would slam into me, *any... second... now—*

Behind us, I could hear the gunmen edging across the floor towards the information desk. Now and again, a shot would ring out and I'd see Emily flinch. From what I could tell, Brannon and the other agent were firing blind over the top of the desk, trying to hold the gunmen back without showing themselves. It would slow them down, but it wouldn't work forever.

I almost ran straight into Emily. She'd stopped dead in front of me and, when I craned to look around her, I saw why.

One of the agents who'd been shot was lying on the ground right beside her. The poor bastard was still alive, just barely, and he was terrified. *Help me,* he mouthed to Emily. *Please!* She stared back at him, aghast.

I checked over my shoulder. No one was looking in our direction but, the way the gunmen were advancing, we probably had less than a minute before they reached the desk and killed the President. Then they'd turn around and see us. We had to move.

I nudged Emily's foot. She shook her head, staring at the stricken agent, silent tears starting to fall from her eyes.

I reached forward, gripped her ankle and squeezed. *I know,* I thought, praying she understood. *But we can't help him..*

I saw her throat move as she swallowed.

She lifted one hand... and moved forward, her hand almost touching the stricken agent. She stayed there for a second, her breathing heavy, and I worried she was about to lose it. But then she lifted the other hand and took another step forward, then another and another. I followed behind her, staying as close as I could. By the time I passed the agent, he was dead.

Seconds later, we came to the bottom of the stairs. I steered Emily around the handrail and then onto the stairs. Now, finally, we were out of sight as long as we stayed low. We crawled up to the second floor.

I didn't stop until we'd passed under an archway and into the next room. Only then did I help Emily to her feet and hug her. Then I grabbed her hand and started to pull her on through the museum. I wanted to put as much distance as I could between us and the gunmen, then try to find a fire escape—

I jerked to a stop. When I turned, I found Emily was rooted to the spot. *Shit.* She'd frozen. Between the gunfire, seeing her dad shot and then that crawl through hell, she'd finally slipped into full-on catatonia—

"No," she said in a low voice.

I blinked and searched her face. Her gaze was focused and there was a grim fire in her eyes I'd barely seen since before the attack in the park. She *hadn't* freaked out. She'd been damn close, downstairs, but she'd somehow pulled through it. She was fighting back against the fear, harder than I would have thought anyone could. "What?" I asked, stunned.

"No," she repeated. "We're not leaving him."

She glanced over her shoulder towards the stairs. Towards her dad.

I shook my head. "We can't. Emily, we can't. I have to get you out of here."

The tears were rolling down her cheeks but it wasn't hysteria: it was anger. "That is *my father down there!*"

I looked between her and the stairs, torn. *Shit!*

"That is the *President of the United States of America,*" she managed through her tears. "You are *sworn to protect him!*"

I felt it all welling up inside me: everything I'd turned my back on when I left the Secret Service. Everything that President Matthews had made me feel again, in the short time I'd known him. But the need to protect Emily... that overrode everything. I made a decision and shook my head, yanking hard on her arm. "I'm saving *you.*"

But she tore her hand out of my grip, choking out the words through her sobs. "It doesn't—It doesn't *matter* about us. If *he* dies, it all comes down. *Kerrigan will be President.*" She pulled her hand tight against her chest so that I couldn't grab it. "I am *not* leaving him!"

We glared at each other. *Goddamn her!* Goddamn

her for being a better person than any of these asshole politicians.

Goddamn her for being right.

I stepped close to her. "Emily... Kerrigan knows you know. Those men... they're not just here to kill your dad. They probably have orders to kill you, or take you and interrogate you."

She nodded, gulping back tears. "I know."

"We can slip away if we go right now. But if I do this, they'll know where we are."

She took a deep, shuddering breath. "I know." She looked me in the eye. "*Please,* Kian."

I closed my eyes for a second... and nodded. "Stay here," I said. "And be ready to run."

She nodded quickly. I crept back through the archway and over to the balcony that overlooked the first floor.

Almost directly below me, the President was still sheltered behind the information desk, clutching his chest. For a second, I wasn't sure if he was alive, but then I saw him glance across at Brannon.

Brannon and the other agent were crouched either side of the President, firing at the approaching gunmen. They'd killed two of them and managed to slow their progress but the men were sneaking ever-closer, three of them approaching down the left side of the room and three down the right. It was only a matter of time.

I checked my gun. Not for the first time, I wished I had my old one instead of the tiny one Miller had insisted I use. I took a deep breath... and started shooting.

The first one was easy—they weren't expecting shots to come from above. I managed to take out one and was lining up the second before they'd even reacted. The second one went down and *now* they saw what was going on and started to fire up at the balcony. Chips of marble exploded a foot from my face.

I ducked back down, crawled to the side and sprang up again. A bullet flew an inch past my face and smacked into the wall behind me. I shot again... and a third gunman went down.

"*Go!*" I yelled to Brannon. "Go, I'll cover you!"

He didn't need telling twice. He threw the President over his shoulders and ran, the other agent and me firing to cover him. A second later, they were through the door and heading back towards the side entrance and the motorcade. I kept firing until my gun clicked empty, giving them as much time as I could... and then I turned and ran. Before I'd even made it off the balcony, I could hear feet pounding up the stairs behind me.

"What do we do?" panted Emily as I grabbed her hand and dragged her deeper into the museum.

"*Run.*"

THIRTY-SEVEN

Emily

RUNNING IN HEELS is almost impossible. Every step meant rolling the dice: would I go sideways on my ankle, would my heel snap off and send me tumbling? Twice, I nearly fell and only Kian's grip on my hand stopped me smacking into the floor. I thought about taking off my shoes, but the floors were polished marble, incredibly slippery, and running on them in nylons would be just as hard.

The lights were off on this floor—everything was meant to be shut down for the night except for the speech downstairs. Luckily, there was enough moonlight shining down through the skylights above to see by. We sprinted through a fossil exhibition, threading our way between glass cases, then underneath a huge skeleton of a blue whale. The moonlight turned the floor into zebra stripes as it shone through the beast's massive ribs.

Kian pulled on my hand, slowing me. We stopped to listen and to get our breath back. And as soon as I stopped, it all started to sink in.

"I should have figured it out sooner," I panted. "I'm so *stupid!* Of course he'd assassinate my dad: it fast-tracks him to the Presidency. I just never thought he'd go that far."

"We *did* figure it out," said Kian, putting a hand on my arm. "We warned him."

"But not in *time!*" The reality of it washed over me and I wanted to throw up. "What if he's dead? *What if he's already dead?*"

He stepped closer and put his hands on my cheeks. The warmth of his palms soaked into me. "Hey! *Hey!* If we hadn't figured it out, he wouldn't have had any warning at all. He's a tough old guy. He'll make it. And the only person to blame is Kerrigan." I sniffed and wiped my eyes. He waited until I looked at him again. "Okay?" he asked.

I nodded reluctantly.

Footsteps behind us. The glare of torchlight. Kian grabbed my arm and pulled me forward, past displays of stuffed alligators and bison and then to the staircase that led up to the third floor. We crept up the stairs and then waited in the shadows at the top to see if they'd follow. A few moments later, the torches went past and we both slumped in relief. But just minutes later, they reappeared and footsteps started to climb the stairs.

We looked at each other. We both knew what that meant: they were going to keep searching the whole building until they found me. Why weren't they in more of a hurry? Surely the police must be screaming to the scene along with more Secret Service? But the streets outside sounded quiet.

I didn't have time to work it out: Kian was leading

me on through the third floor, sprinting through exhibits on coral, plants and insects. When we slowed down again, we were moving through something called *Treasures of the Earth:* rare gemstones and minerals displayed on silk cushions inside glass cases, the moonlight lighting us up with little points of light as it reflected off all the polished, glittering surfaces. Halfway across the huge room, Kian stopped and pulled me down behind one of the cases.

"We're not going to be able to outrun them," he said quietly. "And they'll have blocked the exits by now. They'll keep hunting us until we run out of places to go... and when they catch us, I'm out of ammo. We need to turn this around. I need to hit some fucker and take his gun—then we can fight our way out."

My guts twisted in fear. I had a horrible feeling I knew what he was going to say next.

He took a deep breath. "I need to leave you for a bit."

"*No!*"

"Just for a minute. You'll be safe here. I'm going to circle back and ambush one of them when they come through here, then I'll come straight back."

"No!" I knew I sounded like a petulant child but I didn't care. The fear was suddenly rising, engulfing me, already up to my chin and threatening to pour into my mouth and drown me. *He promised! He said he wouldn't leave me!*

He pulled me close and I flung my arms around him, his big body so strong, so comforting. The fear receded a little, but I knew it would only last as long as I was with him. As long as I clung to him, as long as I pressed my face against his chest and closed my eyes, it felt as if I was protected from all the evil in the world.

"I'm going to be right in the same room," he whispered in my ear. "But I've got to do this. Okay?"

I took a deep breath and steeled myself... then slowly released him. He leaned in and kissed me on the lips. Then he was away, jogging silently back the way we'd come. I craned around the display case, trying to keep him in view, but within seconds he was lost in the shadows. A moment after that, I heard the footsteps of someone entering the room.

I pulled back behind the display case, sitting with my back pressed up against it. For the next few minutes, all I had to go on were the sounds behind me.

I heard heavy boots creeping closer. Just one man—they must have split up to search the museum. The footsteps seemed to die away in the distance... and then turned and came directly towards me. I hugged my knees, trying to make myself as small as possible. The footsteps came closer, entering the *Treasures of the Earth* exhibition. *Where's Kian? Has something gone wrong?*

They came closer still. I could hear the rustle of the man's clothing, now. *Something's gone wrong.* The fear rose up, the darkness giving it power, paranoia filling my brain like chilling fog. *He's left me. I'm all alone.*

Closer. I could hear his breathing. Every hair on the back of my neck was standing up.

Closer. Shit!

I heard two very quick, almost silent steps and then the sound of a punch and one heavy body hitting another. Grunting. Panting. Two more punches. I closed my eyes tight—

And yelped as something hit the floor right next to me. I opened my eyes to see the unconscious body of one of the gunmen. Kian bent over the man and started pulling the assault rifle from his hands. I let out a long breath.

"Okay," muttered Kian. "Now let's get out of here." He lifted me to my feet. "You okay?"

My heart was thumping so hard that I didn't trust my voice, so I nodded.

He look unconvinced and gave my arm a squeeze. "We're nearly out of here. Just hang in there another few minutes, alright?"

I stared at his hand on my arm. I could feel the warm reassurance pumping into me. "Okay," I managed.

He gave a last squeeze and then moved ahead to check in front of us. "There's a fire escape at the back of the building with an exit on each floor. They'll have someone guarding it, but—"

He was maybe ten feet ahead of me when it happened.

Gunfire and explosions erupted all around me: behind me, left side, right side... even in front of me. How was that possible? Had they surrounded us? I felt something hard hit my cheek and closed my eyes on instinct, spinning and crouching, trying to find somewhere safe. But there *was* nowhere safe.

I fell to my knees as the explosions got even louder and closer. I was hit again on my arm and now my cheek was starting to hurt. I managed to work up the courage to open my eyes for a second and finally saw what was happening.

They were behind us, firing. One or more gunmen

must have sneaked up the stairs without us seeing and now they were shooting wildly in our direction. The bullets were shattering the glass display cases, making one after another explode into lethal, jagged shards. I suddenly knew what had hit me and wondered how badly I was hurt.

Ahead of me, I could see Kian firing back at them, crouching down behind a display case and then jumping up again to shoot. Each time he looked my way, he beckoned me forward.

I screamed as another display case shattered. I went full-length on the floor as heavy shards of glass rained down onto my back. If one of them fell on me point-first, I was dead.

"Come on!" yelled Kian. "Stay low!"

I started to crawl... but the floor ahead of me was a sea of broken glass mixed with bits of rock and gemstone. I tried to find a place to put my hand down safely but there wasn't one.

Something cold slid along the side of my neck and hit the floor. I looked to my left and saw a shard of glass the size and shape of a kitchen knife. A few inches to the right and it would have hit me in the neck.

I *had* to move.

I started crawling, using my fingers to knock the shards aside until I had a clear spot to put my hand down in. Then another spot for my other hand. Then crawl forward and try to put my knee in the clear spot. It would have been agonizing enough if I'd been able to go slow, but new glass was still raining down: I had to race. I could feel myself picking up little cuts as I knocked against the sharp edges of shards. Once, I put my knee down and cried out in pain, feeling something tiny and sharp digging into my knee. When I rubbed my knee and it fell into the palm of my hand, I saw it was a diamond. I tossed it away and carried on.

As soon as I was close enough, Kian grabbed a fistful of my dress and lifted me right off the ground, then swung me behind the display case with him. "There's the exit," he said, nodding to a lit-up sign at the end of the room. "We're going to run. Ready?"

I nodded.

"*Run!*"

We ran, with Kian firing behind us to slow down our pursuers. I hit the door first, thumping down on the bar that opened it. I had a sudden fear that it would be locked... but it swung open easily and cool night air washed over me. I stepped out onto a metal fire escape.

Kian caught up, slipped an arm around my waist, and led me down the fire escape, taking the stairs two at a time and catching me when I stumbled. Halfway down, a bullet from below ricocheted off the metal handrail. He leaned over, fired once and there was a scream from the street below.

Seconds later, we were in the street, a cool wind whipping at our clothes. All was quiet. For the first time in what felt like hours, we stopped and slumped side-by-side against a wall, the stone blessedly cool against our overheated, exhausted bodies. "We made it," I panted.

Kian pushed off from the wall and came around in front of me. He opened his arms and I almost fell into them, burying my head in his chest. He stroked my hair as I just... *breathed.* The solid thump of his heart through his shirt made it real: we'd done it, we were alive.

As the adrenaline started to wear off, I began to notice all the places it hurt... and that was *everywhere*. But then Kian's hands slid down my body and he was lifting me off my feet and into his arms, cradling me there. He leaned his head down to me and I met his kiss, lips hesitant and delicate at first and then hot and urgent, reassuring each other that it was okay.

When we finally broke the kiss, I saw something down the street. *"Look!"* I said excitedly, grabbing a fistful of his shirt.

Outside the main entrance to the museum, cones had been used to mark out a space for the motorcade. And the space was now empty. "The motorcade's gone," I whispered. "It would only leave if my dad was on board. *He made it out!"*

Kian's arms tightened around me and I felt that mighty chest expand as he gave a long sigh of relief.

A rumble of thunder made us both look up. Dark storm clouds almost covered the sky. We were in for a massive downpour. "Come on," said Kian. "Let's find some help." He looked around. "Where *is* everybody? Why aren't reinforcements here yet?"

We started forward, with Kian still carrying me. It was only when we passed the main entrance to the museum that he suddenly stopped dead. I followed his gaze and gave a low moan of horror: just inside the building were the bodies of Agent Brannon and the other agent who'd escaped with my dad. They'd gotten him to the motorcade... but they'd died doing it.

I felt Kian's arms tighten around me in anger. "Bastards," he spat. "Nothing we can do for them now." I tore my eyes away and he moved on.

When we turned the corner, my heart lifted. Across the street, a Secret Service SUV waited together with two agents, guns drawn and fear in their eyes. When they saw us, both agents lowered their guns and gawped. One of them spoke into his radio. "I have eyes on Liberty!" he said. "West side! She's with O'Harra!"

Kian jogged towards them. "Are we glad to see you," said Kian as we drew near. "Listen up—"

A screech of tires made us glance to the right. A car was approaching, a man leaning out of the window—

"Get down!" yelled Kian. He set me down and pushed me out of the way, then he was finally able to reach for his gun. But by then, it was too late.

There was a hail of gunfire as the car squealed to a stop beside us. Both Secret Service agents died before they could raise their weapons. I saw Kian fall to the ground but couldn't see where he'd been hit.

I was still sprawled on the ground when they reached me. Hands grabbed me under the arms and lifted me. Men—at least three of them, in black combat gear. And I recognized one of their faces: the second shooter from the park. *Powell.*

I was hauled towards the rear of the car. Kian was lying on the ground, groaning and trying to rise. One of the men kicked him in the head, sending him back down to the ground. Then he put a gun to his head. My heart stopped.

"No!" It was Powell. "Keep to the plan. He lives." The sound of his voice, in person, tapped straight into my nightmares and the fear came shooting up, unstoppable. I felt myself shutting down, the black water pouring down my throat, into my lungs. My legs gave away under me.

They picked me up and rolled me into the trunk of the car. The lid came down.

And everything went black.

THIRTY-EIGHT

Kian

I ROLLED ON THE GROUND and tried to get up, but it took a couple of attempts. One arm was nearly useless—a bullet had clipped it and it hurt like hell. Plus one of the bastards had kicked me in the side of the skull and everything was still woozy.

I got to my feet just in time to see the car carrying Emily speed around the corner. *Shit!* I ran for the SUV, then realized I didn't have the keys. I wasted precious seconds searching the bodies of the two dead agents before I found them.

The DC police pulled up as I started the car. Why were they only arriving *now?* Where had they been all this time? The officers looked at the two dead bodies on the floor, then at me. "Stop right there!" one of them yelled.

Shit. I didn't have time to explain. I had to get after Emily before I lost them. I put my foot down and screeched away. I knew which direction they'd headed in, but that was all.

I roared to the end of the street, skidded around the corner, and then floored it, hoping to see the car in the distance. But traffic was light this time of night: they could be well ahead of me by now.

I felt physically sick with fear. I'm not such an asshole that I won't admit to being scared in my life. I've been scared plenty of times. But I'd never felt fear like this. I'd never felt my whole insides turn cold. I'd never felt like someone had torn something right out of me.

I'd lost her. I'd lost her, without ever fully opening up to her, without ever letting her know all of me. *You feckin' idiot. You stupid, stupid bastard!*

I'd been scared that I'd get to care about her too much. I hadn't realized that I'd reached that point a long time ago.

Just let me get her back, I begged. *I'll do anything. I'll tell her everything about my past. I'll never push her away again. Just let me get her back!*

THIRTY-NINE

Emily

THE SCARIEST THING IN THE WORLD is to open your eyes... and nothing happens. No dawn breaking through the drapes, no clock dimly glowing in the darkness. Just black. You open your eyes and you can't tell you opened them.

I wasn't sure if I'd fainted or not. And if I had passed out, I wasn't sure if it had been seconds or hours. There was nothing to indicate passage of time. There was nothing at all, just thick, suffocating blackness, like the black of sleep where nightmares breed.

Except this time, my nightmare was real. *They've taken you,* my mind chanted. *They've taken you and you're all alone and they're going to hurt you.*

I was way beneath the surface of my fear, now, sinking fast into the black ocean. I didn't even seem to have a body, anymore: I was just a fading ember in the darkness. Next to go was my ability to think: I was too scared to reason or plan, lost in raw animal fear. My mind retreated further and further, screaming a scream that the darkness swallowed up.

I was *gone.*

And then I felt something: a presence. A big, strong, warm somebody who'd always protect me, even when he couldn't be right there with me. I reached out for him....

...and his voice said, *you can do this. You can beat this.*

I didn't want to. When you're really, really scared, it's easier to close your eyes and ears and shut everything out, to go still and quiet because then maybe the monsters won't see you. But that isn't what he'd taught me. He'd taught me to fight against the fear, to do what I had to do.

In my mind, I began to kick and struggle against the blackness, swimming my way towards the surface. It seemed to take forever but, at last, I got my lips above the surface of the black fear and I could breathe. I felt my lungs start to move properly again— they hurt, and I wondered if I'd been panic-breathing and hadn't even realized it. My senses started to come back. I was lying on carpet, but the carpet was moving. A car.

I was in the trunk of a car.

They've got you they've got you—

I clamped down on the voice and focused on the trunk. I was hunched up into a tight little ball on my side and I didn't want to try to rise because I knew I'd hit the ceiling and then I'd freak out again. But as I felt around with my hands and feet, I realized there was room enough to move a little.

Everything tilted and I realized we were going around a corner. I remembered that that was important. My head started to clear. We'd turned *left*. Remember *left*.

The lesson Kian had given me came back to me. My phone was in my purse and that was lying somewhere in the museum, where I'd dropped it during the initial attack. But he'd given me a second phone.... I hauled my dress up my thighs and felt for it in the darkness, then found the tiny slab of metal I'd tucked into the waistband of my panties. I pressed a button and the screen lit up, filling the trunk with light. And at that second, the phone rang.

FORTY

Kian

She answered on the first ring—she must have had it right in her hand. "Emily! Are you still in the car?"

She sounded terrified, but she was managing to breathe. God, this girl was brave. "Yes!"

"Do you know which way you turned?"

"Left. Just one turn. About ten seconds ago."

They'd stayed on the road I was on until just now. I put my foot down and tried to estimate how far I was behind them. "Good girl. Stay with me. Tell me if you turn again."

Her voice cracked. "Please hurry."

I pressed the pedal a little harder against the floor, weaving in and out of traffic. I was going faster than they'd have dared, because I didn't give a shit if the police started chasing me. I passed a side road on my left, then another. *Too soon.* But the next one felt about right. I hauled on the wheel and cut the corner, bouncing across the sidewalk. "I'm getting close," I told her. "Just hang on!"

I cut around a truck and roared on up the road. It led towards an old industrial area—where were they taking her? Why had they taken her at all, instead of killing her? They must want to figure out who she'd told about Kerrigan's plot.

My stomach churned: they were going to interrogate her.

And then, in the distance, I saw tail lights I recognized. I had to come up with a plan—fast. Somehow, I had to stop the car without killing Emily in the process. And I had to do it fast enough that they didn't have time to shoot me.

"Emily?" I said. "I can see you." I heard her gasp of relief. "Listen: I want you to move around so you're facing the rear of the car, okay?"

I heard her moving around. I fastened my seatbelt while she did it. Lightning lit up the clouds and it looked to be only a few miles away. The storm was going to hit us soon.

"Okay," Emily said, sounding panicked.

I was gaining fast on the car, now. "Alright. Now press your back hard against the back wall of the trunk. Really jam yourself against it, so you can't move."

"Okay," she said after a few seconds. "Done." Her voice was tight with fear. "Why?"

I accelerated past the car Emily was in, then pulled in so I was directly ahead of it. "Because you're going to stop very suddenly," I told her.

And I slammed on the brakes.

A lot happened very quickly. My SUV screeched almost to a stop, but didn't have time to stop completely before the car Emily was in rammed into me from behind. Then I was coughing and choking on smoke and a big, soft, white thing filled my vision. It took me a couple of seconds for me to realize the airbag had gone off. For a few seconds, everything was still, the two cars just sitting there hissing steam on the quiet street.

I got my door open and stumbled out of the car. Despite the airbag and the seatbelt, my neck hurt like hell.

The other car was a wreck. They'd piled straight into the back of me and steam was hissing from the hood. The driver and passenger were both dead: neither had had time to put on their belts and they'd slammed straight into the windshield.

The guys in the back had survived, though, and I had to deal with them first, before I risked getting Emily out of the trunk. *Emily!* Was she even alive? She could be lying there, hurt or dying while I wasted time on these—

I felt the rage descend, hot and red and all-powerful. The rage I'd been trying to hold back ever since I took this job, the rage Emily was so good at helping me control.

For once, *for once,* I could let it out.

I marched towards the car. The first guy was just climbing out of the back seat, the rear door open between us. I kicked it as hard as I could and he staggered back, sandwiched between the door and the car body. Before he could get free, I grabbed his collar and hauled him off his feet and over the door, then slammed him into the ground. *That's one.*

Another guy was getting out on the other side. He was out before I could reach him, raising his gun. He probably expected me to duck back behind cover. He wasn't expecting me to lower my head and just charge at him, yelling at the top of my lungs. He shot once and missed. Then my shoulder whumped into his stomach and we landed on the ground with me on top. My fist hit his face before he could recover. *That's two.* But I didn't recognize either of their faces. Where was Powell, the leader? Had he been one of the guys in the front?

I worked it out just in time. I turned around to see him getting out of the rear door, his gun pointed right at me. They'd squeezed three guys into the back seat, not two. "Send backup," I heard him say into his radio. "O'Harra's trying to get the girl back." I dived and rolled. Bullets sprayed the car just behind me.

I grabbed a gun from one of the men I'd knocked out, ducked down at the ruined front of the car and returned fire... but the bastard ducked down behind the trunk, the one place I didn't dare shoot. *Shit!* And it sounded like reinforcements would be arriving any minute. They were going to kill me and take Emily. Take her and—

That's all it took. Imagining what they'd do to her.

I jumped up onto the car's hood, then onto the roof and dived on him. We hit the ground in a tangle of limbs, both of our guns clattering to the ground. We rolled, hands clenched on each other's shirts, both trying to get on top so we could punch. I growled in pain as we rolled over on my injured arm. Powell managed to get in one good punch in the kidneys but then I got on top and hit him across the jaw and he went limp.

I slumped over him, utterly drained. It was difficult to think through the pain in my arm, I was still woozy from the crash and I'd picked up all sorts of cuts and bruises I hadn't even had time to notice until now.

What brought me back to reality was the sharp smell coming from Powell's military fatigues: a tang of mould that made my nose wrinkle. I shook off the pain: I couldn't rest yet. She needed me.

I managed to stand, stumbled around to the rear of the car and fumbled with the trunk release until it popped open. And there looking up at me was the sweetest sight I'd ever seen: Emily, pale-faced and panting in fear, but alive. She flung herself out of the trunk and into my arms and I hugged her, not giving a shit how much my arm hurt. "I am never," I said in her ear, "*ever* going to leave you again."

She clung even tighter to me, tears sliding down her cheeks. "You're goddamn right you're not."

I heard a car in the distance, driving too fast to be just a late-night commuter. "We have to go," I told her. "Right now. They're coming."

Neither car was drivable: we'd have to go on foot. As thunder rolled overhead, I pulled her towards the nearest alley. Hand in hand, we ran into the shadows.

FORTY-ONE

Emily

We threaded our way through alleys for half a block and then, when we were sure there was no one following, we turned onto a street. We'd wound up in a pretty lousy area of DC, not one I'd ever visited. The shops favored security shutters and razor wire and there were a lot of homeless people around. The two of us stood out a mile: Kian was in a suit and I was in an evening dress and heels. At any other time, I would have been nervous but, given what we'd just been through, walking through a scary area of town seemed like nothing. Plus, the thunderous expression on Kian's face probably made any potential muggers think twice.

We'd walked less than a block when a car screeched around the corner, heading straight towards us. It was close enough that I could see the guys inside had guns... and they'd seen us. Kian grabbed my hand and pulled me into an alley, running so fast I could barely keep up. I thought again about taking my heels off but the alley was littered with broken bottles.

Two turns, three, and we finally slowed. Kian kept us moving, though, putting more distance between them and us. "That wasn't a coincidence," he panted. "They were heading straight for us. How did they find us?"

I shook my head. I had no idea.

Until we stepped onto the next main street and I saw it, across the street. I grabbed Kian's hand and pulled him back into the shadows, then pointed.

Kian followed my finger to the white, boxy security camera. It was high on a post where it couldn't be tampered with, but even from here we could see its distinctive red, white and blue logo. *Rexortech*.

"Oh, shit," breathed Kian. Then the full horror of it sank in. "Oh, *shit!*"

I nodded. "DC is Rexortech's testbed city, remember? Those cameras are *all over the city* now. All with facial recognition, all feeding back to Rexortech HQ. He must have someone feeding the info to Powell and his men. Wherever we go, they'll spot us in a couple of seconds."

Kian looked ill. "I've been trying to figure something out," he said. He took his radio off his belt and showed it to me. "Remember how all the radios suddenly stopped working at the museum?"

I nodded.

He rotated the radio to show me the Rexortech logo on the back.

"Oh my God." I thought back to that day when the techies had swarmed all over the White House. "*Everything* is Rexortech. The radios, the phones...."

"Kerrigan's people control it all." Kian shook his

head, sounding almost impressed. "They blocked the radio signals from the Secret Service guys inside the museum. That's why no backup ever showed up: no one outside knew anything was wrong until it was too late." He cast another glance at the camera. "We have to get off the street."

"Why can't we just go to the White House?" I asked. "Call the Secret Service, have someone come and pick us up."

Kian shook his head. "Not yet," he said.

"Why?"

He put his hands gently on my shoulders. "Just let me figure out what's going on first, okay?" He had a look on his face I'd never seen before: not just worry, more like sick fear. As if he really, really hoped he was wrong about something. *What isn't he telling me?*

As we stood there staring at each other, it began to rain: I'd forgotten about the brewing storm. It started as just a few heavy drops but, within seconds, we were in a full-on downpour. The rain was freezing, the sort of big, heavy drops that soak right through your clothes. There was no shelter in the alley so Kian pulled me to his chest and wrapped his suit jacket around me. His warmth was welcome but we were still both quickly soaked.

Kian looked up and down the alley then at the camera, making a decision. "Okay," he said. "Come on." He pulled off his jacket and draped it over our heads as a makeshift umbrella. It would also hide our faces from the surveillance camera.

I fell into step beside him. We slipped arms around each other's waists, our hips brushing, and that made me feel better. "Where are we going?" I asked.

"Somewhere out of sight," he told me.

We turned onto the street and I felt the back of my neck prickle as we passed the camera. I imagined a roomful of operators somewhere scanning the camera feeds, computers flashing up alerts as they locked onto my face. If I looked up, if I stumbled on the wet sidewalk and the jacket slipped from my shoulders....

We walked for three blocks like that. After the first block, it was impossible to get any wetter but we got steadily colder and colder, the chill seeping right to our bones. We finally stopped outside the sleaziest place I've ever seen. Only three of the five neon letters in the *MOTEL* sign were working.

"Wait here," Kian told me, pushing me into a dry spot beneath an overhang. "They might recognize you and I don't want anyone to know you're here." He hurried into the tiny motel office.

It was several minutes before he reappeared with a key. "Sorry," he said. "They weren't used to renting rooms for a whole night."

I made an *eurgh* face and followed him along a passageway, up a rusty metal staircase and to a cheap wooden door. And then, at last, we stepped out of the rain.

I hadn't realized how tired I was until we were safe. The jacket slithered down my back and fell in a wet heap on the carpet and I just collapsed against Kian's chest. He wrapped his arms around me and hugged me tight, resting his chin on the top of my soaked hair. "It's going to be okay," he told me. "It's going to be okay."

But when I shifted position slightly, I felt his body stiffen in pain. I pushed back from him and looked in horror at his wounded arm: he'd been hit by a bullet outside the museum but, like my exhaustion, he'd been blocking out the pain until now.

I helped him peel off his soaked shirt. The rain had made the blood spread into a pink stain right across his left arm. When I got the shirt off, I could see the ragged wound that stretched across his bicep.

"It didn't go in," he said, gritting his teeth. "Just scraped past."

We had no medical supplies so we just had to do the best we could. The room had a coffee maker and I used that to boil some water, then let it cool and washed the wound out as best I could. Then I ripped strips from his shirt and used those as bandages. I could feel his body tensing in pain under my hands but he never once cried out.

When I was done, he turned on the TV and flicked to a 24-hour news channel. He grabbed my hand and held it: I didn't understand why, at first.

Then the picture appeared and I gripped his hand harder than I ever had before.

"—White House still won't release any information on the status of the President," said the anchorwoman. "We know that he was shot, at an event at the Museum of Natural History, and that he was rushed to George Washington hospital where he remains. The First Lady is said to be at the White House. We don't know—" She broke off. "I've just been told that we're going live to the White House for an emergency press conference."

The screen changed to a shot of Jessica standing in the White House Press Briefing Room. She'd aged at least ten years since I'd seen her a few hours ago. She cleared her throat. "I have a short statement," she said. "I won't be taking any questions." She swallowed. I'd never seen her so hesitant, so downright *scared*. "Approximately ten minutes ago, there was an emergency Cabinet meeting. Under Section 4 of the Twenty-fifth Amendment, the powers and duties of the President have been transferred to the Vice-President. The Vice-President is currently at a secure location and will address the nation shortly. That is all."

Jessica turned away but there was an immediate uproar. Every single member of the press corps jumped to their feet. "Jessica! Is the President alive?"

"Has anyone claimed responsibility for the shooting?

"Is a suspect in custody?"

Jessica started to walk off stage.

A man at the back yelled, "Jessica, what about Emily? Where is the President's daughter?"

Jessica looked towards the man and there were tears in her eyes. She shook her head and walked off stage.

As the news channel returned to the studio, I started to shake and couldn't stop.

Edward Kerrigan was now the most powerful man in the world.

FORTY-TWO

Emily

"We—We have to go there." I was babbling, the words flooding out as uncontrollably as my shivers. "We have to go there and tell them, we have to tell everybody—"

"We can't go to the White House," said Kian.

I gaped at him. "We *have to!* We have to tell everyone what happened! *Kerrigan is running the country!*"

He gently placed his hands on my shoulders. "It isn't safe anymore," he said, the emotion making the Irish come through in his voice. "Look." He pointed to the TV.

The shaken anchorwoman was now talking through the implications of Kerrigan becoming President. Over her shoulder, live footage from the White House Press Briefing Room showed Jessica being escorted off stage... by two guys in Rexortech uniforms.

"This is what I was afraid of," said Kian. "Kerrigan

can do anything he likes now. And the first thing he's done is to put his own people into the White House—he'll say it's additional security, to back up the Secret Service. No one's going to question it, after what happened at the museum. Those guys will be loyal to him and they're just *waiting* for us to show our faces. We're the only ones who know what Kerrigan's done. He wants us both dead."

Now I understood. If we called for rescue, Kerrigan would insist that Rexortech, not the Secret Service, be the ones to pick us up. And then, on the way to the White House, there'd be another attack by the Brothers of Freedom. We'd never make it to the White House alive.

"Kian, *my mom is there,*" I said. "They said she's in the White House. The Secret Service are probably too scared to let her leave to visit my dad, like after I was shot. That means she's *right there with Kerrigan's guys!*"

He pulled me close, folding me into his arms. "She'll be okay. She doesn't know what Kerrigan's done: she's no threat to him."

My stomach churned. I could see the sense in what he was saying but I hated to think of her there, unaware that she was now right in the middle of the lion's den. "We could call someone we trust," I said in a small, scared voice. "Harlan. Even Miller. Get them to bring us in."

Kian shook his head. "Remember, Rexortech are tied into all the White House communications equipment. They'd intercept the call... and they still have people cruising the streets looking for us. They'd get here before the Secret Service could. Even if we *could* get to the White House, the place is filled with

Rexortech guys. That building is the most dangerous place in the world for you, right now. All he'd have to do is get someone to slip something in your drink or inject you with something while you slept. I can't protect you there."

My last hopes crumbled. The one place I always thought was safe was now a trap. I buried my face in Kian's chest. "What are we going to do?" I whispered.

His hands tightened around my back. "I don't know," he said. "But I swear to you, I'll get you out of this." I was still shaking—from the fear and from the cold. I'd been sitting there in my freezing, soaked dress the whole time. "God, you're freezing," he told me.

He picked me up and carried me, taking most of my weight on his good arm, then put me down in the tiny bathroom. He turned on the shower, waited until the water ran hot, then pulled off my heels and pushed me inside, still in my dress. I gasped as the water sluiced down over my scalp and shoulders, almost too hot to bear... but then the warmth started to soak into my bare arms and it felt good. While I warmed up, he worked at getting my soaked dress off me—not easy, because the fabric was clinging to me, but he gradually managed to work it up over my head and off. My breasts sprang free, the flesh chilled and the nipples hard from the cold. Then the water hit them, too, and I caught my breath as they started to warm up.

Kian hooked his thumbs into the waistband of my panties and stripped them down my legs and off— even they were soaked. The water ran down my stomach, over my thighs, gradually warming me from the top down. My toes were numb from trudging along in the freezing rain but they started to thaw, burning and tingling. I hugged my arms around myself and lifted my face up to the water, letting the heat sink into me. I felt better... but not right. Inside, I was still trembling.

I reached out toward Kian. "Please," I said. "Hold me."

He stripped off his pants and shoes and stepped into the shower, his big body hulking over me. For a second, he blocked the spray and I went cold... but then the water cascaded down from his shoulders and hit me, warming both of us. He pulled me into his arms and cradled me there, my cheek against his chest, and we let the water flow down our backs while our fronts warmed each other. My trembling slowed and finally stopped.

I began to run my hands up and down his arms. I needed to feel him, needed to reassure myself that he was real. He was the one thing I had left to hang onto now that everything else had been ripped away.

And he was the only thing I needed.

My palms smoothed over his shoulders, taking in their wideness and the hard bulk of the muscle there. They swept down, remembering to dodge the bandaged wound, and my fingers skimmed the slippery-wet bulges of his biceps. The size of him, the sheer power of his body made me feel safe... and made me go weak. My hands worked back around him, tracing the contours of his back, my fingers so delicate next to him: I was a vine, clinging to a rock face.

He responded, pushing my wet hair back away from my face and gathering it into a rope so that he could bend over me and kiss my neck. I pushed against him, my breasts pillowing against his chest, as his lips worked their way down behind my ear, his teeth nibbling at my shoulder. He drew back and we nuzzled against each other, noses brushing cheeks, lips brushing chins. I could feel the tension in his body, his hands starting to squeeze as he worked them down my sides and onto my hips. We were at the tipping point, sliding from *comforting* to raw and sexual.

I parted my lips... and that was all it took to tip us over the edge.

Immediately, he was kissing me, his tongue teasing the edges of my lips and then plunging deep to own me. I moaned through it, running my hands down his body. Back in my bedroom at the White House, he'd done most of the touching. Now I was free to explore him, feeling the hardness of his ass and the brute power of his thighs. As I shifted against him, I felt his cock swelling against my thigh, already half-hard. I reached down and curled my fingers around it and he gasped. God, so thick, so hot, stiffening and growing under my fingers in a way that made my chest flutter. I started to stroke it and he growled and pushed me back against the tiled wall.

"Christ," he muttered, and that gleam of Irish silver was thick in his voice. "You've got no feckin' idea how much I want you."

His hand slid down my wet stomach and then on down between my thighs. I caught my breath and parted my legs for him. His fingers brushed through the damp curls of my hair and found my lips. He rubbed me there and then pushed slowly inward, one thick finger sliding up into me. I groaned in response, mashing my ass back against the tiles. His palm was hard against my clit and I rocked against it.

We pressed our bodies together, him fingering me and me stroking him as the water sluiced down on us, trapping us in our own little world of heat and comfort. His finger moved faster and then he added a second finger, stretching me just right. My nipples were hard again, scarlet threads of pleasure lashing through me every time they scraped against his wet chest. I kissed a line between his nipples, burying my lips in the deep center line that ran down his chest. He growled, then pushed back and looked into my eyes.

"Don't move," he told me. He stepped out of the shower, retrieved something from his discarded pants then stepped back against me. He tore open the packet, rolled on the condom and then he was stepping between my legs, knocking them wider with his knees. The tip of him rubbed up against my lips, throbbing and hot, and I grabbed for his shoulders. Then he was easing into me, one glorious, heated millimeter at a time.

This time, I didn't have to worry about making a noise. In fact, with the water pounding down all around us and the fact we were in a tight little room within a room, in theory I could really let loose. *If only I was like that,* I thought. I'd never dared to be vocal with the few boyfriends I'd had: I was too self-conscious. Even now, I—

The head of his cock reached its widest point, stretching me, and then slipped in. "*Ah!*" I gasped, unable to stop myself. Immediately, I flushed. But Kian was staring down at me with nothing but lust in his eyes. He *wanted* to hear me.

He pressed me back hard against the wall, pinning my shoulders there with both hands, and started to move deeper, never moving faster than a few millimeters a second. I began to pant: the sensation of being steadily filled, of being made aware of how damn wet I was, was indescribable. Pleasure blossomed outward, making me claw helplessly at his arms.

His thighs pressed between mine, his groin coming closer and closer to my body as he lunged up into me. My eyes opened wide, staring into his, and it began as a low, guttural cry of pleasure that rose and rose. "*Kiiiiiaaann!*" My eyes squeezed tight shut as I felt him go *deep...* and then fluttered open as I felt his groin kiss my body and realized he was in me completely.

He lowered his head to mine and kissed me like that, deep and hungry, my wet hair cushioning my head against the tiles as we twisted and turned, our kisses open-mouthed and desperate. Every tiny movement we made moved me around his cock, making me gasp and shudder. The last vestiges of who I used to be—or who I *thought* I used to be—slipped away. I was still the President's daughter, but I didn't feel like a good girl, anymore.

He moved his hands to my hips, holding me fast against the tiles and tilting me up to meet him. At his first slow, deep stroke I felt the pleasure tighten, squeezing into a red-hot ball. Then, as those powerful hips began to slam between my thighs, his groin grinding against my clit, I began to twitch and mumble, eyes closed, water sluicing down my face. "God, *yes!* Yes, yes, yes!"

Every time I spoke, it seemed to inflame him more. When I opened my eyes, I saw his body growing harder, every muscle standing out, his lips drawn back over his teeth in a snarl of lust. When one hand came up to maul my slippery breast and I said his name, I heard him moan in response, sounding almost helpless. The idea that I could do that to him, that the sound of my voice could make a man like him lose control, made me heady.

He sped up, his body slamming into mine. All I could think about was the hot, silken slide of him inside me, every thrust pushing me faster and faster towards my peak. My fingertips clawed at the slick tiles: I wanted to tear out great hunks of wall, it felt so good.

He put his mouth to my ear, never slowing his thrusts. That hint of Irish silver in his voice again: he was *incredibly* turned on. "I never want to stop fucking you," he said, every syllable a hot little rush of pleasure in my ear. "I want to wake up and fuck you. I want to fuck you all day and I want to fuck you before you go to sleep at night. You. Are. Mine."

I wanted to tell him how much I wanted him, too. I wanted to tell him how good that sounded. But my orgasm was seconds away and all I could manage was: *"Yes!"*

And then he buried himself inside me and I felt the heat of him as he came. His possessive growl in my ear sent me over the edge and I screamed out my climax, grabbing his shoulders and squeezing him tight as I rocked and spasmed around him.

FORTY-THREE

Kian

I'D WRUNG OUT our clothes and cranked up the room's air conditioning to blow warm air at them, but it would take hours for them to be anything like dry. So we lay naked in the bed, me on my back and Emily cuddled into my side using my chest as a pillow. I could hear a helicopter in the distance but otherwise it was quiet, even the traffic dying down outside.

I felt... *peaceful*. It was more than just the afterglow. The simple pleasure of being alone with her, without having to hide our feelings, was a release unlike anything I'd ever felt. We were on the run with the whole world against us and yet, with Emily's soft, damp hair against my chest and each slow breath she took wafting warmly against me, I felt calm.

And that meant that, for the first time, I could think about opening up. The idea of reliving things made my chest tighten... but I'd promised myself I'd do this, if I got her back. I knew that if I didn't, if I kept myself locked up and closed off, there was no future for us... and no way was I giving her up.

What tipped me over the edge was when she reached out in the darkness and took my hand, tilting her head and looked up at me. A car went past outside, its headlights lighting up her face, and her expression said, *it doesn't matter how bad it is. I'm here for you.* Just like I'd been there for her, at Camp David.

I swallowed. And began.

"It was in Iraq," I said. "But that's not the whole story." I stopped for a second. Iraq was a more recent wound, painful to talk about but near the surface. What happened before that was dug in deep, right down in my soul. I'd never talked to *anyone* about that.

But I wanted her to know all of me.

"I come from a big family," I said. "Lots of brothers. Irish dad, American mom. We moved around a lot when I was a kid, back and forth between Ireland and the US. Some of us were raised mostly over there; I was born here and raised mostly over here. It was sort of crazy: my dad travelled a lot and we were never in the same school for more than six months. But we all took care of each other and my folks loved each other."

Emily looked up at me, listening. She could hear it in my voice: something bad was coming.

"I was still in high school when it happened. My dad was away working so we were living with my mom for a whole summer. She met these people—just friends, she said. And she started spending more and more time with them. Us kids didn't think much of it. We figured she was lonely without my dad and needed the company. So she'd disappear all day and we'd... you know, mess around and get into trouble, like kids do." I swallowed. "Only... it turned out, they weren't friends at all. They were this organization. A cult."

She slid one arm around me. "A *cult?*"

I nodded. "By the time we realized, she'd been sucked pretty deep into it. She'd disappear for days at a time and she'd come back happy... but she'd look terrible, as if she hadn't slept or eaten the entire time she'd been away." My voice tightened. "I'm pretty sure they were giving her drugs."

"Jesus... what did you do?"

"What could we do? We were just a bunch of kids. I tried to talk some sense into her but she wouldn't hear a word against the cult—she actually came close to hitting me, when I criticized it, and she'd *never* done that before. We didn't want to call the cops: none of it was illegal, at least nothing we could prove. And we thought child services might take us into care." I stared up at the ceiling. "It got worse and worse. Guys started coming around to our house, not just to talk to mom but to talk to *us*. Really creepy questions, about what we wanted to do with our lives. And they gave us tests."

"Tests?"

"Like personality tests. And they took photos. That scared the crap out of me. I started to ask around and I started to hear things... nobody dared to say much but there were rumors about what they did to children."

Emily covered her mouth with her hands.

I swallowed and closed my eyes. I was back there, reliving that day. I could feel the summer heat throbbing through the open kitchen door, smell the eggs I'd cooked everyone for breakfast. "My mom's changed," I narrated. "I mean, changed completely. She's talking about taking us to live full-time with the cult at one of their camps. But before that, she tells us that one of our brothers—Bradan—is going to—" I swallowed again, my voice catching. "He's going to *not live with us* for a while. He's going on a special trip, with some of her friends."

"Oh my God," said Emily.

"And we all... *know.* I mean, we're just kids but we know that something really, really bad is going to happen to our brother. But we can't stop her. She's our *mom,* what are we going to do: hit her? We follow her outside and we're grabbing her arms and trying to stand in front of the car and Bradan's in the back seat screaming that he can't get the door open and—"

Goddammit, my eyes were hot. I wasn't going to cry. Fuck that.

"And she drove off and I never saw Bradan again."

I didn't open my eyes but I could feel Emily staring at me in absolute horror. I felt for her hand, found it and squeezed it. I needed that squeeze to be able to carry on but I wanted to be able to reassure her, too. She didn't know there was worse to come.

"My dad arrives home and we tell him what's happened. Now he's been away for months: he hasn't seen my mom since before she joined the cult. So at first, he can't understand what the fuck we're talking about. But then she gets home and he tries to talk to her. She's convinced he's evil: the cult turn you against outsiders. She says she's going to take the rest of us, right now, and starts pushing us into the car. Her and my dad have this almighty row. And... she grabs a kitchen knife."

I opened my eyes and looked down at Emily. "He wrestles with her but she's fighting like crazy, she won't let go of the knife. So he has to—" My voice caught. "He knocks her head against the floor. Hard." I was having trouble getting the words out, now. "And she just goes limp."

We just lay there in silence for a moment as she digested it.

"It tore my brothers and me apart. Losing Bradan, losing my mom... and then they sent my dad to prison and called it murder and some of us sided with him and some with my mom. We tried to hold the family together: that's when we got the shamrock tattoos, to remind us we still had each other. But it didn't work. We all went in different directions: some of us went into foster care, Carrick ran away... and I signed up with the Marines. Had to wait until I was seventeen, but I was waiting outside the recruitment office when it opened on my seventeenth birthday."

I stroked Emily's hair. "I'd lost everything: my mom, my dad, my whole family. The military seemed like it'd give me... *something.*" I paused. "They make you get parental consent, if you're seventeen," I said bitterly. "I had to go to the prison to see my dad—the only time I ever visited him. I didn't say a word to him, just slapped the form down in front of him and waited until he'd signed it, then walked off. Haven't seen him since." I took a deep breath and let it out. "I get it. I've worked it through my head a million fucking times: he had to do it, he had no choice, he was trying to save us. But *he still killed my mom.*"

Emily shook her head slowly. I understood—there were no words.

"So I signed up. Did four years in the marines.

When I started I was pretty messed up but you know what? *It worked.* The military's pretty good at building you back up. After a while, the guys around you start to feel like brothers. I had a family again. By the end of four years in Iraq, we were *tight.*"

She nodded and gave me a tentative smile. "That's good."

I nodded... but then she saw the pain in my eyes and her face fell. "Oh, no...."

"End of the day," I said. "Sun's going down. We're in a pretty safe area of town, one we've been in plenty of times before." I closed my eyes. I could feel the warm breeze on my face. "We're laughing and joking and talking about how much we'd like a cold beer right now. We've been around there so many times, the locals know us: they're friendly." Then this call comes in: they want us to check out a store. Some moron claims that insurgents are storing explosives there. But I know this place: the guys a cobbler, for God's sake. I know him. He fixed my boots for me. He doesn't have anything more dangerous in his store than boot polish. But the guys on the radio won't listen, so we all troop over there."

I actually smiled as I remembered. "We're like, *we're sorry, but we have to check,*" and the store owner's like, *didn't I fix your boots for you? Were the boots not right?*" He's not even pissed off, he's *laughing* about it because we can both see how ridiculous it is. But we make a show of searching his store and, of course, there's nothing there and I apologize and we all troop out again."

I swallowed and opened my eyes. "I come out first, because I want to get on the radio and tell the guy back at base what an asshole he is. But just as I walk out into the street, the store blows up."

Emily was staring at me but I couldn't look at her anymore. I was deep in my memories, feeling the scratch of the sand against my face and smelling the smoke in the air. "See, the intelligence had been wrong... and right. The insurgents *were* storing explosives..in the store next door. They assumed we were working our way down the street and we'd go into their store next so they ran out the back and used a remote detonator to blow the whole place. Took out three stores, killed five locals... and every one of my unit except me."

I finally managed to meet her eyes. It was easier because we had something in common. "That's how I knew what you were going through," I said. "I was damaged, too, just in a different way. Couldn't let myself care about anyone again. Quit the marines. Went into the Secret Service. And I was *angry*. I was mad that I survived. I never stopped being angry. Not until I met you."

She slid on top of me and hugged me tight, wrapping her arms around me and pressing her cheek to my chest.

"That's what I am," I told her. "That's why I am how I am." I looked down at her. "That's what you get. If you want me."

She immediately slid up my body, leaned down and kissed me hard. "I *do* want you."

We stayed like that for a while, enjoying the closeness. I felt better, as if I'd cut out some toxic part of myself that had been slowly poisoning me. I didn't have to throw it away; I could hold onto it, remember the people I'd lost. But it was out of me. And the anger that had controlled me for so long... now it felt a little more like I controlled it.

And that made me feel as if, if we could get out of this thing alive, maybe I could offer Emily the sort of relationship she deserved.

She reached down and rubbed my cheek. "This is the latest I've ever been out with you," she murmured. She rasped her thumb slowly across my stubble. "I think I prefer you like this, not clean-shaven. This is more... *you.*"

I grinned and kissed her. Then I sighed. "We should turn on the TV," I said. "See what they're saying."

When I turned it on, though, I wished I hadn't. A different news anchor had taken over and a photo of a man's face filled half the screen next to her.

"—and *extremely* dangerous," the news anchor was saying. "If seen, do *not* approach him. Dial 911 immediately."

It's deeply disconcerting, seeing your face on national TV, like they've stolen a piece of you that you'll never get back. The creeping horror of knowing that tens of millions of people are suddenly aware of you.

"Once again," said the news anchor, "Kian O'Harra, wanted in the kidnapping of Emily Matthews, the President's daughter—"

I stabbed at the remote and the screen went black.

When I looked at Emily, she'd gone white. "But you didn't—Why would they think—"

I ran a hand through my hair, suddenly feeling every single hour I'd been awake. "I was the last one to be seen with you. I'm the only Secret Service guy not accounted for."

"But you warned my dad! You saved those agents

at the museum when they were cornered!"

"No one knows that. No one else made it out of the museum alive except your dad and we don't know what shape he's in." *Or if he died before he got to the hospital and they just haven't announced it yet,* but I wasn't going to even entertain that thought. "Kerrigan's in control, now. If the new President tells everyone to hunt me down, who's going to argue with him?" I sighed. Now we had the entire country looking for us. And if the police didn't shoot me on sight, as soon as I was in custody, Kerrigan's Rexortech guys would get to me. *What the hell are we going to do?* Lie low, then try to get to the media and get the story out? But we had no hard evidence, and the man we were accusing was now the goddamn President....

I heard the helicopter again, coming closer and closer. Right overhead. It was loud enough to make the windows rattle. *They must be flying low.*

I looked at Emily and my eyes suddenly went wide. "Shit!" I said. "Get dressed!"

"What?" She darted naked from the bed and grabbed for her clothes. "What's going on?"

I was pulling on my pants. They hadn't had enough time to dry and clung damply to my skin. "I'm a moron," I growled. "That's what." I pulled on my shirt, trying to stretch the wet fabric across my back. I had to grit my teeth as my wounded arm flexed.

Emily had managed to pull on her panties and drag the dress over her head. If anything, the dress looked even wetter than my clothes. She sat on the bed to fasten up her shoes. By now, the helicopter was so low we had to shout to hear each other. "What do you mean?"

I grabbed her arm. "The tracking chip in your arm.

Miller said they could locate it if they swept the city with helicopters." I pointed to the sky. "They found us!"

FORTY-FOUR

Emily

OUR FEET hammered down the metal staircase, throwing up freezing water that chilled our legs. The motel's parking lot was being systematically swept by a searchlight beam that looked like the finger of God. Along the street, the stores were being lit up in red and blue as Secret Service SUVs screamed towards us. Exactly the sight I'd wanted to see, since I heard the first shot at the museum. I had to fight the urge to run towards them. Kian was right: they'd take me back to the White House, where Kerrigan's Rexortech thugs would be waiting for me. And if I tried to tell anyone the truth, it was my word against the new President's.

Kian grabbed my hand and pulled me around the edge of the parking lot, skirting the searchlight, then into an alley. The far end was almost blocked by dumpsters and we had to slow down to squeeze through. Behind us, I could hear running footsteps and then the clang of boots on the metal staircase. We were barely out of the alley when I heard the crunch of wood as the motel room door was kicked down. They were seconds behind us.

We ran, splashing through alleys awash with rainwater, cutting left and right to try to throw them off our trail. But the helicopter kept buzzing overhead, homing in on me and alerting the men on foot. We'd run for half a block but, as soon as we hid and stopped to get our breath, the footsteps behind us would return, closer than ever.

Kian was always there to drag me on and catch me when I stumbled. But after a solid twenty minutes of running and hiding I was freezing, exhausted, and almost hysterical. I'd started crying at some point, the tears invisible in the rain. They weren't going to stop. They were never going to stop, not until Kian was in custody and I was back in the White House... and there we'd be easy prey for Kerrigan's Rexortech guys. "I can't go on," I panted, shaking my head.

Kian nodded grimly and pointed to an all-night convenience store. "Come on."

He marched right inside. The clerk working the store had the TV on, tuned to a 24-hour news channel, which wasn't good. "Foil," Kian asked him immediately. "Aluminum foil. Got any?"

The clerk gaped at the man in the torn, bloody shirt and the woman in the evening gown who'd just walked into his life. "...*what?*"

Kian glanced at the door and the noise of the helicopter outside, then pulled his gun. "*Foil,*" he said again. "Like for wrapping a turkey. *Do you have any?*"

The clerk raised his hands and pointed. I ran to the aisle he pointed at and grabbed a roll. Kian dug in his pocket, pulled out a sodden five dollar bill and slapped it on the counter.

Outside, we could see the glare of flashlights approaching. We had to run all over again to regain our lead, our lungs burning and muscles screaming. Then Kian slowed and grabbed the roll of foil from me. "Which arm did they put the chip in?" he asked.

I looked down at my arms. I started to say *left* but, as soon as I thought it, I started to doubt myself. They'd put the chip in me as soon as my dad had taken office: it had been *years*. Had it been left, or right? "I'm not sure," I said, cursing myself.

He nodded quickly and started wrapping my left arm in aluminum foil, all the way from shoulder to wrist. He used half the roll and then did my right arm.

"Will this work?" I asked.

"No idea. It might buy us some time."

We ran on down the alley. After a minute or two, the footsteps chasing us seemed to drop back. The helicopter returned, louder than ever, making passes above us. It was so low it was almost brushing the rooftops. But it didn't seem to be zeroing in on me quite so confidently.

Kian seemed to be searching for something, checking the front of each darkened building. Finally, he found the one he wanted and led me around back, then used a brick to smash a window.

He climbed in first, then me, taking care on the broken glass. I blinked in the gloom, then looked around in confusion. "A bar? How does this help?

He ran behind the bar and collected a few things, then searched the floor until he found a trapdoor leading to the cellar. He heaved it up and ushered me down. When he found the light switch, I saw that we were in a plain breezeblock room filled with broken chairs and crates of beer. Kian closed the trapdoor behind us and looked around. "This might block the signal when we take the foil off," he said.

"I don't get it," I told him. "What are we—"

Then I looked down at his hands and saw what he was holding: a bottle of vodka and the little knife the bartender used to cut lemons. When I looked up again, I could see the pain in his eyes—pain at the idea of hurting me.

"Oh, shit," I said.

"We don't have a choice," he told me, his voice tortured. "I don't know if the foil's working and, even if it is, they'll come back with stronger tracking equipment. They'll zero in on us while we're asleep and not moving. We have to cut the chip out."

I stared at the knife... and nodded. I sat down on a chair, my eyes glued to the blade. I watched as Kian poured vodka over it to sterilize it. It still felt unreal: *he's not really going to... he can't actually....*

Kian looked at me. "There's no anesthetic," he said. "Take a slug of this." He passed me the bottle and that's when it became real. I took a big slug of the liquor, then coughed and choked as it burned my throat. I thought about what was about to happen and took another.

Kian unwound the foil from my arms, looking up towards the ceiling and the faint noise of the helicopter outside. When my arms were bare again, he started to work his way down my left arm from my shoulder, his big, warm fingers probing at my muscles. "I got it," he said, pressing a point halfway down my upper arm. "It's not deep."

"Just do it," I said, my voice tight. I looked away, focusing on a huge cardboard carton of peanuts.

When I felt him come close with the knife, I started to suck in air through my nostrils, my breathing loud in the silent room. Then the tip of the blade touched my skin and I tensed. "Talk to me," I blurted. "Talk to me while you're doing it."

Silence for a second. Then, "You're the most beautiful thing I've ever seen in my life."

A burning pain as the knife cut into me. My toes tried to dig through my shoes and into the floor, but I focused on that deep, growling voice with its hint of Irish silver. "When I saw you at the park," he said, "I knew I had to have you. Didn't matter how ridiculous it was for a guy like me to get someone like you." The knife felt like it had been dipped in red-hot lava but his words vibrated through me, lifting me to another place. "I. *Had to*. Have you. And now I've got you, I'll do whatever it takes to protect you."

Just as the tears welled up, the pain stopped. "I got it," he said, his voice hoarse.

I turned to see him holding a thing the size and shape of a grain of rice. Before I knew it, he'd grabbed the front of my dress and hauled me forward for a kiss. He kissed me with all the heat and burning hunger I'd come to know, but with something else, too. A warmth that was about more than just protecting me.

He moved back, my eyes opened and we stared at each other, both relieved it was over. Then his hand suddenly dived down the front of my dress, palming my naked breast and squeezing, his thumb rubbing. I jerked and my mouth fell open in shock... but my body needed him just as much as always and I felt the heat slam down my body towards my groin, my thighs pressing together—

I cried out and jerked away from him, my arm burning and stinging. I smelled vodka and, when I looked around, he had the bottle upended over my arm: he'd just poured it over the wound. "Sorry," he said. "Figured it'd be better if you were distracted."

I panted through the pain and then whacked him hard in the arm. As he tore another strip off his shirt and used it to bandage my arm, I looked at the tracking chip. "What now?" I asked. "We destroy it?"

He shook his head and looked up. I could still hear the helicopter outside. "If the signal stops, they'll just surround the area and go house-to-house until they find you. I have to lead them away."

It took me a few seconds to realize what he was planning. "No! *NO!*"

"It's the only way. You'll be able to slip away while they're chasing me. I'll give you as long as I can. Get out of the city. Go far away."

"*No!*" I threw my arms around him. "They think you kidnapped me! They'll put you in jail... or worse! Or Kerrigan's men will get to you!"

"It's the only way, Emily. If I don't do this, you won't survive the night."

I was sobbing, now. "You said you'd never leave me again!"

"And I said I'd always protect you. This is what I have to do to do that." He closed his fist around the tracking chip and stood up.

I jumped to my feet and wrapped my arms around him, my hot tears falling to soak his shirt. "Please," I said, "Please don't do this!"

He kissed me once, twice, three times... and then pushed me gently back. "I love you," he said.

And then he ran up the stairs, flung open the trapdoor, and was gone.

FORTY-FIVE

Kian

UPSTAIRS, I kept moving. I didn't want to give myself time to think about it: wrenching myself away from her was already too damn painful. Should I have told her I loved her? It made no sense: I knew I'd never see her again. And the words had come out so suddenly they'd shocked me... but I knew it was the truth.

I found a set of car keys under the bar and spotted a banged-up red pickup out in the parking lot. Some customer had probably gotten too drunk that night and taken a cab home. I could hear the helicopter and it sounded like it was getting closer: I looked down at the chip in my hand. As soon as I'd come out of the cellar, they'd picked up the signal again.

I took a deep breath and ran out into the rain. I didn't even have the pickup's engine started before the searchlight was on me, turning night into day and making me screw my eyes closed against the glare. I looked over my shoulder—luckily, it was a crew cab and the back seats were full of junk. Hopefully, they'd mistake one of the dark shapes there for Emily.

I roared out onto the street, skidding on the surface water. Behind me, I could hear sirens: but that was good, that was exactly what I wanted. I just had to lead them as far away from the bar as I could before they caught me.

A pickup on an almost-deserted street is a lot easier to see from the air than a couple of people in alleys and the helicopter kept me pinned in its searchlight. I'd only gone a block when the first Secret Service SUV slewed out of a side street and picked up the chase, then another and another. How long until they set up a roadblock ahead? Two minutes? Three?

I put my foot down and blasted straight down the street and onto the on-ramp to the highway. Seconds later I was speeding towards the outskirts of DC with a full ten vehicles behind me and the helicopter above. I made it three miles before I saw the hastily-assembled roadblock ahead: a line of cop cars stretching across the highway and police officers with guns lined up behind them. *Shit!* I'd given Emily maybe five minutes. I'd just have to hope it was enough.

I hit the brakes... but I'd underestimated how wet the road was. With a sickening screech of tires, the pickup skidded and careened towards the roadblock, cops dodging back out of the way. I finally came to a stop with the front bumper a hair's breadth from one of the cars.

I raised my hands in the air and waited for whatever came next.

FORTY-SIX

Emily

I STUMBLED UP THE STAIRS to the bar, poked my head out of the trapdoor and listened. I could hear the helicopter and sirens but both sounded like they were retreating into the distance. Kian had done it.

He loves me. I knew I had to move fast but it kept ringing in my head like the clapper of a bell. I hadn't had a chance to say it back to him. And now I never would.

Focus. I had to get out of there or it was all for nothing. But as I moved towards the window and glanced down, I caught sight of my soaked dress and stopped. I was going to stick out like a sore thumb as soon as I went out there... and even more, once dawn broke. I had to change my appearance.

I found a room behind the bar that seemed to be a combination office, break room and storeroom. I was hoping to find a jacket but fate wasn't that kind. I did find a pair of outsize men's pants, paint-splattered and worn but at least dry, and a hooded top stenciled with some rock band's name that stretched down nearly to my knees. I scrambled into them and the simple luxury of feeling dry cloth next to my skin made me want to weep.

I stopped at the window to listen again. This time it was completely silent. I climbed carefully out and jumped down to the ground, then put my hood up to cover my face, picked a direction at random and started walking.

It took me until the end of the alley for it to sink in: I was all alone. For the first time since I'd persuaded Kian to guard me, it was just me. That would have been scary in the White House but out here, in a bad neighborhood in the middle of the night, with Kerrigan's men hunting me, it was terrifying.

It was still raining and my new clothes were soaked in minutes. I could have sheltered in a doorway but I knew that, once they caught Kian and found he was alone, they'd double back and look for me here. I had to be long gone by then... but I had no idea where to go. Out of the city? *Where?* There was nowhere I could go where my face wasn't known. Could I get to an embassy and seek asylum in another country, then try to convince the world of Kerrigan's plans? *How?* He was the President, now, and I was just a—

I was just a woman with a history of mental illness, demonstrated live on TV when I'd freaked out and ran for the limo outside the John F. Kennedy Center. Who the hell would believe me?

This isn't meant to be me! I was completely unsuited to taking on someone like Kerrigan. My dad was the strong one. He was the President—the *real* President. I was just his daughter.

The rain seeped through to my skin but the cold soaked further, right down to my bones. I was losing it fast. I could feel the black fear rising and, just like in my nightmares, Kian wasn't there to help. It was worse than it had ever been. Even in those dark days immediately after the park, I'd had a safe haven in the White House; now, there was nowhere to hide.

I realized that I was walking further and further from the streetlights, deeper into the network of unlit alleys. With the clouds covering the moon it was almost pitch black ahead. But I didn't have any choice: if I strayed close to the street, I might be seen by a surveillance camera.

Tears rolling down my cheeks, I plunged into the darkness.

FORTY-SEVEN

Kian

AFTER THEY dragged me out of the pickup and started cursing because Emily wasn't there, they pulled me into a Secret Service SUV and drove me straight to the White House. As they led me through the hallways, I saw uniformed Rexortech goons everywhere. I'd been right: Kerrigan had wasted no time bringing them in. And all of them would be under orders from him to quietly eliminate Emily, if she was brought here.

As we passed a doorway, the First Lady emerged, flanked by Secret Service agents. Her face was deathly pale, her eyes red from crying. Then she saw me and started towards me. "You son of a bitch!" she yelled. "I saw how you were looking at her! Where is she? *Where is she?*"

It took both Secret Service agents to hold her back as we passed. I kept my eyes on the floor. Even on the off-chance I could get her to believe me, all I'd be doing was painting a target on her back.

I wound up sitting on a plastic office chair in an empty room with my hands cuffed behind my back. No doubt there was one hell of an argument going on over who had jurisdiction: the FBI would be trying to muscle in but the Secret Service wouldn't give up for at least another few hours, not with their agents dead at the scene and the President's daughter missing. So it was no surprise when Miller walked in. I only needed a split-second to see how utterly enraged he was, his whole body shaking with tension.

He got started right away. Before I'd even had time to open my mouth, he punched me so hard I felt a tooth loosen. My head snapped to the side and the room spun a few times.

"You piece of shit," Miller spat at me. "You fucking piece of shit. How much did they pay you?"

I knew it was useless. I knew no one would believe me, but I had to try anyway. "You're being duped. I didn't kidnap Emily. It's Kerrigan. It's all Kerrigan, he set up the Brothers of Freedom. They're all Rexortech guys, private military contractors."

Miller held a black and white photo in front of my face. Ah, shit. It was worse than I thought.

The picture was of me, sitting in a cafe. Sitting next to me, was a big guy in a hooded top and a baseball cap. He was showing me something and I was looking down at it, frowning.

"It's a setup," I said weakly. "It's a fucking crossword puzzle he's showing me."

"That's Gavin Fiss," said Miller. "A known associate of the Brothers of Freedom, one of the few we've managed to get an ID on."

"Who sent you the photo? An anonymous tip? No, wait: I bet it was someone at Rexortech Security."

Miller squatted down so that he was at my eye level. "Let me lay it out for you, O'Harra. You have a history of misconduct and violent outbursts. You show up out of nowhere, just at the right time to save the President's daughter and she's just scared enough to hire you, against our wishes, which conveniently gives you access to her, the President, and all our security procedures. The First Lady told me she's pretty sure you're sleeping with her daughter. That's a common terrorist move, to find some naive young thing and seduce her, to gain access to the inner circle. Then you disappear for a whole afternoon, right before an attack, and no one knows where you are. The shooting starts and the next thing the team at the White House hears is *this*."

He played an audio file on his phone and I heard the radio transmission from the Secret Service agent outside the museum. *"I can see Liberty! She's with O'Harra!"* The agent had been surprised by our sudden appearance... but it was easy to hear it as shock that I was involved with some plot, if you were already thinking that way.

"Then you disappear with Emily and no one can find you until we track down her chip. Then we stop your car and she's not there: you've deliberately led us away. Did you stash her somewhere, or are your friends moving her out of the country right now?"

I shook my head but I wasn't listening to Miller: I was cursing myself for not seeing it sooner. This is why Powell and his men had left me alive outside the museum: I was going to be their patsy. Kerrigan must have thought it up once he saw me and her were getting close. *Goddammit! This is my fault! If I'd just stayed away from her....* I'd played right into their hands.

Miller took my silence for guilt. His voice became conciliatory. "You are going to jail for the rest of your life," he said slowly. "But maybe, *maybe,* if you tell me where Emily is *right now,* I can save you from the death penalty."

There was nothing I could say that was going to get me out of this. I was dead: either by lethal injection with the whole country cheering or a rigged suicide or heart attack at the hands of Kerrigan's people. I didn't care anymore. My whole focus was on someone else.

"I have no idea where she is," I told Miller. "But I hope to God she's safe."

FORTY-EIGHT

Emily

I STUMBLED THROUGH THE DARKNESS for what felt like hours. The alleys seemed to be filling up with trash the further from the street I went. I couldn't see it, but I could feel it underfoot: the wet cardboard mulch from hundreds of fast food containers, the jagged, tinkling shards of broken bottles. As I got colder and colder, it got worse: my feet started to go numb so I couldn't feel what I was walking on and I'd start to slip and slide before I could react. My high heels made it even more treacherous but I didn't dare take them off with so much broken glass around. I was shaking—I couldn't stop shaking, but I couldn't wrap my arms around me to keep warm because I needed them to feel for the alley walls.

If I stayed cold and wet for much longer, I was at risk of exposure. I had to get somewhere warm... could I do what Kian had done and rent a motel room, if I kept my hood up and didn't look at anyone? I knew I couldn't use a credit card because they might be monitoring it, but if I paid cash—

I stopped in my tracks. *What cash?* I suddenly realized I had nothing: my purse was in the museum somewhere. I didn't have a dime on me.

I forced myself to start walking again because I knew that, if I didn't, I was going to just sink to the ground and curl up and go to sleep, and if I let that happen I'd die there.

Eventually, I saw lights ahead of me and the trash started to thin out. I was approaching a road: I had no choice but to cross it. I kept my head bowed, letting the hood cover my face, and willed myself not to look up: I didn't know if there were cameras on the street but, if I looked up to check and saw one, it would be too late.

Waiting to cross was terrifying. Every set of headlights that swept towards me could be Kerrigan's people, about to screech to a stop and pull me in. Every set of footsteps I heard could be one of *them.* And I couldn't even look up to see.

This is what it's going to be like for everyone, when Kerrigan goes through with his plan, I realized. Not *if, when.* Because who was going to stop him now?

I hurried across the street. The rain was so heavy that the water was sloshing over my toes but I was already so cold, I barely noticed. My teeth had stopped chattering and I wasn't shaking so much... I just felt sleepy. Wasn't that supposed to be a bad sign?

And then I smelled something that made no sense: soup. Tomato soup. I glanced furtively around but there were no restaurants, at least none that were open at this hour.

I heard voices, too. I followed them along the street

and then into an alley. And there, in a vacant lot behind some buildings, I found a crowd of twenty or so people standing around sipping paper cups of soup. A ragged tent that might have belonged to the army about fifty years ago sheltered a couple more people and they were ladling soup into cups. I stumbled closer. I had no plan in mind: my legs just instinctively carried me forward.

One of the two people serving glanced up and saw me. I immediately looked at the ground, hiding my face. "Hungry?" she asked. I'd had a quick glimpse of a woman in her sixties, with short dark hair.

I didn't know whether I dared speak. Would she recognize my voice? "I don't, um... have any money," I mumbled.

"It's free, honey." Her voice was gentle. Something in my voice must have told her I was ready to bolt.

I slowly came closer and reached out my hands. She slipped a cup of soup between my palms and I looked down at it in wonder. I could feel the heat throbbing out of it and creeping through my body. My hands stung as they thawed but I welcomed it: pain meant I was alive. And the smell of the soup was even better. I realized I hadn't eaten in about sixteen hours. "Thank you," I croaked. I wanted to look at her, wanted her to see how grateful I was, but I didn't dare.

"That's okay, honey," she said. "There's a dry spot over there if you need somewhere to sit."

I looked around and found the concrete steps she was talking about. The overhang of a building protected them: they were hard and freezing cold but it was such a blessed relief to be out of the rain for a few minutes that I didn't care. I sipped the soup and then gulped it, finishing the whole thing in seconds and then panting as the warm glow spread through me. The sleepy feeling went away for a moment but then came back. What I really needed now was a place to warm up and crash.

A hand touched my shoulder and I jerked around, startled. A guy around my age with sandy-blond hair. I'd looked him in the face before I could stop myself. *Shit!* But he didn't seem to recognize me. "You got somewhere to sleep?" he asked.

I shook my head dumbly.

"C'mon. I know a spot. Nice and warm."

He took my hand, just like Kian used to, and drew me to my feet. Something in my brain started screaming at me but it was so very far away and I was *so* cold.

The guy led me around the back of the building and moved a board out of the way to reveal the dark, gaping maw of an empty window. I climbed through and, inside, it *was* warmer. And around the corner I found blankets and a tiny battery-powered lantern.

"There," he said, grinning. "See?" He put his hand on my cheek, his warmth throbbing into me. "We'll be all cozy, afterwards."

Afterwards? My brain was still screaming at me. He wasn't like the woman serving soup. He wasn't dressed like her *or* like one of the homeless, more like a college kid slumming it.

"Let's get you unwrapped," he said. And lifted the hem of my dripping hooded top. He had it almost to my breasts before I realized what was going on and slapped his hand away.

He sighed as if I was being ungrateful and then his hand cracked across my face so hard I spun to the side and fell to my knees. Too late, I tuned into the warning cries in my brain. I saw him now for what he was. He knew when the soup kitchen came around and he'd had this spot all picked out and ready. He'd waited for a lone woman he could tempt away from the pack....

He grabbed me by the shoulders and hauled me up. The fear spread through my chilled body, making my limbs heavy. This was exactly what I'd always dreaded: alone, with no one to help me and a man about to hurt me.

Kian isn't here.

The man started to lift my top again.

Kian isn't here.

He stepped closer so that he could haul the dripping fabric up my back.

Kian isn't here. The black fear overwhelmed me, spilling down into my lungs and killing my screams. It wasn't just what the man was about to do to me: it was that everything was over. Kian was gone. My country was gone. My dad was gone. Why not just give up?

But....

Time seemed to slow down. My whole body was filled with the black fear, churning and surging like the depths of the ocean. But right at the center of my chest there was a pinprick of light that refused to go out. A deep, rough-hewn voice with a trace of Irish silver. *I'll be right here with you, Emily.*

Kian couldn't be with me. But, somehow, he was still there.

I felt my top catch on my breasts, about to rise higher, and I suddenly knew what I had to do. I stepped forward, my leg between his and pressed up against his thigh. And then twisted my hips and brought my knee up as hard as I could.

He screamed a horrible, choking scream and folded, his hands going to his crotch. By the time he collapsed to the floor, I was already at the window. That tiny point of light was expanding faster and faster, pushing back the blackness. I climbed out into the night. I was still cold, still exhausted but I no longer felt alone. Kian was with me. He'd always be with me.

It was time to stop running and *fight*. No, I wasn't anyone's idea of a hero. No, I wasn't equipped to take on someone like Kerrigan. But if I didn't, who would? Kian had sacrificed himself for me: now it was up to me.

It was the first time I'd been able to think clearly since I'd fled the motel. Kian had said that Kerrigan would want to kill both of us, because we were the only two who knew the truth. But there was a third... my dad. If he was still alive and lying in a hospital somewhere, Kerrigan would try to eliminate him. And his guards wouldn't realize the threat they faced.

I had to save him.

FORTY-NINE

Emily

George Washington University Hospital was a half hour's walk away. Fortunately, it had stopped raining and the sun was starting to lighten the sky, so I could make faster progress. I was still chilled to the bone but moving helped to keep me warm and I had adrenaline on my side, now.

I knew that he might be dead: the news may just not have been released, yet. But I had to try.

I kept my head down and tried to stay off the main streets as much as I could to avoid the cameras. At least I didn't look much like *me,* anymore, in the paint-splattered pants and hooded top.

When I neared the hospital, I slowed down and peeked around the corner to look. They'd closed off an entire floor, according to the news, moving the regular patients elsewhere. Every entrance was guarded by Secret Service agents, which should have made me feel better. But they didn't know what to watch for. They didn't know who the real enemy was.

There was no way I could get in without being seen and, if they saw me, they'd take me straight back to the White House and Kerrigan. I imagined being hauled into a Secret Service SUV while I tried to convince them the conspiracy was real. They might even get a doctor to give me a sedative shot to calm my "hysteria." Then, back at the White House, I'd be easy pickings.

I was starting to despair... but then I saw Harlan come out of the main entrance and talk to another agent. I sidled up to the police do-not-cross tape they'd used to seal everything off and then, at the last minute, ducked under it.

"Hey!" I heard another agent yell behind me.

I ran to Harlan, grabbed his arm and, as he turned, looked up at him so that he could see my face. His jaw dropped.

"Let go of him! Right now!" The other agent, behind me. I was pretty sure he was pointing his gun at me.

"It's okay!" said Harlan quickly. "It's—"

He broke off as I shook my head.

"It's okay," he said again. I pulled on his arm and nodded to the doors. He hesitated for a second and my stomach tightened... but then he sighed and ushered me inside.

The hospital was weirdly empty: there were plenty of Secret Service agents around but not nearly enough to make up for all the missing patients and doctors who'd been shuffled to other floors. The sharp tang of disinfectant made my nose prickle and I felt my stomach knot in fear. I hadn't had time until now for this part of it to hit me: he wasn't just the President, he was my *dad,* and he was somewhere here, dead or dying—

Harlan pulled me into the doctor's lounge and closed the door. "What the hell is going on?" he demanded. "Are you okay?"

"My dad," I asked immediately. "Is he alive?"

"He's out of surgery... but they don't know if he'll wake up."

I slumped. *Jesus.*

"What the hell happened at the museum?" asked Harlan. "How did you get away from O'Harra?"

I shook my head. "Kian's not the enemy. He saved us!"

Harlan leaned close. "Emily, I have to take you in. I'm on orders direct from the Vice—"—he corrected himself—"from the *President.* I don't know what O'Harra told you but he's involved with the Brothers of Freedom. They already have him in custody: he can't hurt you anymore."

"*Hurt* me? He didn't—" I took a deep breath and tried to sound calm and rational. "Harlan, this is *not what you think. Kerrigan* is behind everything."

He blinked at me. "What the hell are you talking about?"

I grabbed his upper arms and looked right into his eyes. "Kerrigan is behind the Brothers of Freedom," I said. "The attack in the park, the one at the museum... it's *all him.* To scare everybody and to steal the Presidency."

Harlan stared at me and then started to shake his head. "Emily, you've been through a lot."

I could feel the tears in my eyes and tried to blink them away because crying wouldn't help my case. "Goddammit, Harlan, *listen to me. Please!*"

"Emily, let me have someone take you back to the

White House. You can calm down, say your piece, we can look into... all of this."

I closed my eyes for a moment in frustration and turned away from him. How the hell could I convince him? I had no evidence and no way to get it.

I opened my eyes and, for a second, I was looking out of the little window of the doctor's lounge, onto the hallway. That's when I saw him: a Rexortech security guy, strolling through the lobby.

I spun to face Harlan. "Rexortech have guys here?"

Harlan nodded. "They handle security for the hospital anyway, but they sent extra guys to help lock the place down." The Rexortech guy was standing in front of the glass security door that led from the lobby into the hospital. As I watched, he swiped a pass card, the door slid open for him and he strolled through.

I grabbed Harlan's arm and dragged him out of the lounge and across the lobby. "Rexortech is Kerrigan's old company," I told him. "The people he has at the White House, the people he sent here, they're in on it!"

Harlan just stared at me. On the other side of the sliding door I could see the Rexortech guy walking away down the hallway.

"*Please,* Harlan!" I begged. "I know how this sounds! But I swear to you, this is real. You've known me for years, have I *ever* seemed crazy, or delusional?"

He looked at me for a long time. "No...."

"Then *please,* don't let that guy go near my dad!"

He hesitated, shook his head... then sighed and nodded. We walked over to the sliding door and Harlan swiped his pass card. Too late, I saw the white Rexortech camera above it. *Shit!* I looked away, but not in time. Somewhere, a computer would be flashing up an alert to Kerrigan's people. How long did I have now—minutes?

I led the way down the hallway. I didn't need to ask which room because I could see the Rexortech guy entering a door. I started to jog, my legs aching with exhaustion, but the hallway seemed to go on forever. The Secret Service agents standing outside my dad's room came alive and put their hands on their guns when they saw me running towards them... but then they saw who it was and just gawped. Harlan waved them aside as we barreled through the door.

The Rexortech guy was standing beside my dad's bed... but however hard I tried, I couldn't focus on him. I just stood there staring at my dad, my heart shrinking down to a tight, hard ball.

He'd always looked so strong but, in that bed with the bandages on his chest and all the machines around him, he looked like a fallen giant. His skin was horribly pale and his breath was a weak rasp.

I finally looked up and saw the Rexortech guy staring at me in horror. He'd recognized me. He snatched his hand away from my dad, holding it down below the level of the bed so we couldn't see it. But I'd seen something in his hand. "What is that?" I demanded. "What are you doing in here?"

"I'm *meant* to be in here," he said. "I have to walk the whole floor, check every room. Just doing my job."

"He has something in his hand," I told Harlan. "I saw it!"

The man frowned at me. "What the *fuck?*" He was so confident, so convincing. He made me sound like a crazy person.

Next to me, I could see Harlan wavering,

uncertain. This guy was going to talk his way out of there, then come back later when my dad was alone and defenseless.... "Harlan, I swear," I said. "I saw it."

The Rexortech guy shook his head angrily and started for the door, one hand down by his side where we couldn't see it.

"Harlan, *please,*" I begged.

Harlan took a long look at me... and suddenly drew his gun and pointed it at the Rexortech guy. "Stop," he said. "Show me your hands."

The guy stopped, glowering at us. He slowly raised one hand... and we saw the syringe he'd been concealing.

Then, while we were distracted, he pulled his gun with his other hand. He did it with military speed. He would have gotten the drop on anyone else.

But not Harlan. He never hesitated, just raised his gun and fired two shots, hitting the guy in the chest with both and sending him slamming back against the wall. He slumped to the floor, dead.

The door opened and the room was suddenly full of Secret Service agents, guns drawn. "What the *fuck?*" asked one of them, seeing the body.

I pulled Harlan to one side. "You believe me *now?*" I asked.

He nodded. His whole demeanor had changed. I might have always thought of Harlan as an old, faithful Labrador but now he'd gone into full-on attack mode... and he was *furious* that he hadn't seen this danger until now.

"I need you to trust no one," I told him. "Not a goddamn soul. You don't let *anyone* near my dad. Can you do that?"

He straightened up. "Yes ma'am."

Another agent stepped forward. "Miss Matthews, we need to take you back to the White House."

I backed away from them and out through the door.

"Miss Matthews, it's for your own safety!"

I caught Harlan's eye over the agent's shoulder. The full horror of it was hitting him, now: the White House under Kerrigan's control and full of Rexortech's people. He understood, now: it wasn't safe for me there, anymore.

Run, he mouthed.

I ran. Down the hallway, back towards the sliding door. I could hear footsteps behind me but they'd hesitated for a vital few seconds and I'd gotten a head start. I slapped the door release button for the sliding door and sprinted through the lobby, then out of the main doors and around the side of the building.

Too late, I saw the black SUV speeding towards me. I swerved but it pulled up right in front of me, cutting me off. The rear door swung open and I saw Powell, a grin of satisfaction on his face. As I desperately tried to backpedal, he lunged forward and grabbed me, dragging me inside. A cloth bag was rammed over my head and everything went black.

FIFTY

Kian

"Sir?" An agent passed Miller a phone. "Harlan for you, from the hospital. *She was there!*"

I'd been sitting slumped in my plastic chair, hands still cuffed behind my back, but now I sat bolt upright, straining my ears. I could only hear Miller's end of the conversation but it told me all I needed to know: Emily had been to the hospital and there'd been another attempt on the President's life. I shook my head, mad at myself: I should have realized Kerrigan would try to finish the President off. But what the hell had she been thinking, putting herself at risk like that?

Then I saw Miller's face go white. Twisting, sickening fear hit me right in the guts. With every second that he stood there silently listening, it climbed higher. I'd never felt so utterly powerless.

When he hung up, he just stared at me, his expression unreadable. *"What?"* I yelled.

"Emily's been taken," he said. "Right outside the

hospital. The Brothers of Freedom have her."

The fear deepened and darkened. I had to get out of there and after her... *now*. I felt the familiar anger start to take over, comforting as a favorite blanket. Emily needed me and this asshole was in the way. "Let me help," I said desperately.

He didn't answer. He pulled a chair across the room, its legs shrieking on the linoleum, and straddled it backwards. Then he just looked at me. For the first time in hours, I felt the tiniest shred of hope.

He was starting to doubt the official story. I could see it in his eyes. For years, this guy had obeyed every single order he'd been given. But you don't get hired by the Secret Service unless you're smart and he was starting to see the holes in what Kerrigan was saying.

"I swear to God," I told him, "everything I told you is true. I'm on your side. Get me out of these cuffs and *let me help!*"

"Harlan shot a guy at the hospital, a guy in a Rexortech uniform. Rexortech are saying they have no record of him working for them: they say he must have stolen a uniform and a pass card."

"Kerrigan's not stupid. That guy probably *doesn't* work for Rexortech, to give them deniability if he gets caught. But they'll have given him the uniform and the pass card, just like they supplied the weapons to the Brothers of Freedom."

"She ran from the Secret Service," Miller said, almost to himself. "That's what I can't figure out. Why would she do that?"

"Because she knew they'd take her right back here!" Over Miller's shoulder, I saw one of the Rexortech guys in the hallway. I jerked my head. "Surrounded by *them*."

Miller turned and looked at the guy but his expression was still unreadable. I was getting more and more frustrated—I didn't have time for this!

"She said some stuff to Harlan," said Miller, lowering his voice. "Told the same story about the Vice President."

"Yes!" I yelled, the anger rising. *"Because it's true!"*

Miller crossed his arms. He was wavering between believing me and not believing me and now I'd pushed him back the other way. "Or because you've brainwashed her into believing it. Is that what this is? You work your way into her bed and then fill her head with conspiracy theories?"

I saw a little flicker of anger in his eyes when he said *bed.* That's the first time I realized he was a little bit in love with her, probably had been for years. What man wouldn't be—it was *Emily,* for God's sake. Of course, he'd never done anything about it, which must have made it all the worse when he'd realized I was sleeping with her. And now he thought I'd *used* her. Oh, great. Yet another reason for him to hate me.

I was about to lose it. *She's going to die while I sit here trying to convince him!* I didn't care how it would look, how much it would damn me. I was going to haul myself to my feet, and headbutt the fucker. Every muscle in my body went hard, the adrenaline pounding through me.

I leaned forward. Miller leaned forward, too, and that's when it hit me. I realized he *wanted* me to get mad. He wanted me to be behind all this. If I raged and yelled and stayed his enemy, his world could stay safe and neat and understandable. I had to stay calm, had to reason with him but there was no way in hell I could—

And then I felt her hand, cool and delicate, right between my shoulder blades, a safety valve that let all the rage hiss safely out of me. I smelled her clean, warm skin as she leaned into me and told me I could do it.

My hands bunched into fists... and then relaxed again.

"You know Emily," I said quietly.

Miller was silent.

"You know how smart she is," I said. "Do you really think an asshole like me could brainwash her?"

He stared at me. "No."

"This all *came from Emily*. She was the one who figured out what Kerrigan was doing, not me. Go to her room—there are notes there in her handwriting from when she was investigating him." I forced my voice to be level. "Miller...."—I forced myself to say it—"*Sir*. This is real. You've looked at my history more than anyone. I'm an asshole... but I'm not a traitor."

He just sat there watching me. I couldn't tell what was going on in his head.

"Sir, *please*." I think it was the quietest I'd ever spoken. "We have to find her. *Right now*. Or she's going to die."

He stared at me for a second longer and then stood up. "Stand up."

I got to my feet. "You going to hit me again, sir?"

He put a hand on my shoulder and pushed, spinning me around. Then I felt my cuffs loosen and fall away.

"If you're lying to me," said Miller, "I will personally relish putting a bullet right between your eyes. You hear me?"

I turned to face him, rubbing my wrists. "Yes, sir."

"And stop calling me *sir*. It doesn't suit you."

I nodded.

"You got any idea where those bastards are holding her?" He lifted his chin a little, assessing me. He still didn't trust me—maybe never would. But he was willing to risk everything to find her and so was I.

"They were using an old Rexortech warehouse to plan their ops, but they won't take her there: they know I know about that place. But they've got to be running things from somewhere. Emily had all sorts of notes on Kerrigan. We should start there."

We turned towards the residence and started to run.

Helena Newbury

FIFTY-ONE

Emily

Slow breath in. Slow breath out.

I kept repeating it in my head like a mantra. If I breathed fast, the black cloth bag sucked against my lips and smothered me and, with my hands bound behind my back with what felt like a zip-tie, I couldn't push it away again. It made me panic and that made me breathe faster, a cruel vicious cycle. Already, I'd nearly passed out twice and each time I'd heard the men either side of me laugh. There was an air of victory in the car.

The SUV was still moving. I had no way to guess the time but I was sure we'd been driving for at least fifteen minutes: we could be anywhere. I'd long ago lost track of all the turns we'd taken and, even if I'd known, the phone Kian had given me was gone, lost somewhere in the mad dash from the motel.

At last, we started to slow. With my eyes covered, my ears strained for any clue as to where we might be. I could still hear traffic in the distance, so we were still inside the city. But when I was bundled out of the car I could feel a cold wind whip across my bare arms, as if I was standing on a wide open plain. That made no sense.

I was pushed from behind and staggered forward. Walking with the bag over my head was terrifying, every step a potential plunge into nothingness. That cruel laughter returned, as they saw how scared I was. Then we were inside and I was shoved into a hard wooden chair.

The bag was pulled from over my head, leaving me spluttering and blinking. As my eyes adjusted, I gaped at my surroundings.

It looked like a ballroom, the kind you get in very old, very fancy hotels. It seemed insane but that's what it appeared to be. And the place was falling apart: the long red velvet drapes around the edges of the room were worn paper-thin and full of moth holes. The wood paneling was coated in graffiti and a huge chandelier overhead didn't have a single functioning bulb. When I breathed in, I nearly choked on the combination of dust and sharp, dank mold.

Powell walked around in front of me. "Hello, Emily," he said. "Time to talk."

My heart started thudding against my ribs. I kept my mouth shut.

"Our boss wants to know everything you do," he told me. "And who you've told it to. Any recordings you've made or pictures you've taken." He squatted so that we were eye-to-eye. "You're going to tell me *all* about it."

FIFTY-TWO

Kian

WE WERE in Emily's bedroom, sifting through her notes. Well, Miller was sifting: lifting up one fucking piece of paper at a time, looking at it and carefully placing it back on a pile as if we had all the time in the world. I was tearing through the pile, scattering papers across the room. But neither of us was making any progress.

"We need to narrow it down," said Miller. "We need some clue, any clue, as to the sort of place we're looking for. Anything you saw when you went to the first warehouse. Anything you heard."

I shook my head angrily. "One of them mentioned a woman, but that could be anyone."

"What woman?"

"*Isabella.*" Despite my frustration, I felt my hopes rise for a second. "Why? Does that mean anything to you? Maybe someone connected with Kerrigan, one of his staff who's in on this?"

Miller shook his head. "There's no one called

Isabella on the VP's staff... and there must be thousands of Isabellas in DC. What else can you tell me?"

"Nothing!" I hurled a fistful of papers across the room and they fluttered down like snow. The rage was back, full force. This was a waste of time! Emily was out there somewhere and we were sitting here looking at papers!

Miller came over and stood in front of me. For a moment I thought he was going to yell at me, but his voice was gentle. "O'Harra," he said, "*think*. Any little clue."

Think. That's what Emily would do, instead of raging and yelling. *What if I never see her again?*

I tried to be like her. I sucked in a long breath and let it out, going back in my mind to each time I'd seen Kerrigan's guys: the park, the warehouse, the museum....

And *after* the museum, when they'd kidnapped Emily and I'd intercepted them. They'd been following a road north, probably heading for the same place they'd taken her to now. We had a direction. "North," I said. "I think it's on the north side of the city."

"Good. What else?"

I closed my eyes and tried to pick through the details. Anything on their clothes, their guns? But they'd all been standard military issue, probably straight from Rexortech—

"That doesn't make sense," I said, frowning.

"What doesn't?"

"All their clothes were new but... when I got close to Powell, his clothes smelled musty."

Miller dug through the papers until he found what he was looking for: lists of property Rexortech owned.

"Most of these places are pretty new," he said, running his finger down the page. "And they're in use. We need somewhere *disused*."

I had a sudden thought. "What about derelict places? They'd be musty. Have they bought any land to build on, and the old buildings are still standing?"

He rooted around again and then stopped and grabbed a printout from a website. A news story about Rexortech buying up a huge plot of land in northern DC on which to build a new office complex. A photo showed the construction site: it looked like the surface of the moon, just gray rubble stretching on forever.

Aside from one building, standing all on its own near the center. One that had been subject to a preservation order that Rexortech had only just managed to overturn. The sign over the door said *Hotel Isabella*.

FIFTY-THREE

Emily

THE BALLROOM had huge windows but they'd been boarded up long ago. Tiny holes in the boards let in pinpricks of sunlight from outside, stabbing like lasers through the air and showing just how much dust was floating around. Then there was one place, high up, where a board had fallen away entirely and a lozenge of bright light spilled from it onto the floor. That's where Powell had dragged my chair, right into the light. Presumably so that he could see my reactions as he interrogated me.

Interrogated me. I wanted to be sick. I'd read about things done to prisoners overseas. There'd even been allegations that Rexortech contractors had been involved.

"What I want to know," said Powell, "is who you've told. Who believes you."

I thought of Harlan. And Kian. And my dad.

"No one," I said.

He pursed his lips and shook his head. "See, that's

the wrong answer," he said. "We know you at least told your boyfriend. You're *lying* to me. That means you get punished."

The other men had been sitting on one of the big, circular tables that still lined the edges of the room, mostly hidden in shadow as they watched. Now they stepped forward. Two of them could almost have been brothers, shorter than the leader but powerfully muscled, with light brown hair. Both of them grinned down at me, their eyes crawling over my body. *Oh God. Not that.* I was helpless, my wrists bound. I wouldn't be able to fight back.

I didn't think it was possible to be more scared. Then I saw the third one.

He was taller than the others, taller even than the leader, pale and wiry with a long, pointed black beard. He didn't look at me with lust, like the other two. His eyes were utterly impassive, just mildly... *interested.* As if I was a lab experiment.

My chair suddenly tipped back and I screamed. I'd forgotten about Powell. He started dragging my chair backwards on two legs across the room, the wooden legs screeching across the floor.

"See, back in the park," said Powell mildly, "I told you it was just business. And it was, back then."

I twisted and strained but I couldn't see where we were going. *Oh Jesus. Oh fuck. Kian, where are you?*

"But now, after making us run around after you all night? After your boyfriend killed so many of my men? *Now?* Now, I'm going to enjoy this."

A door banged open and I glimpsed ancient black and white tiles and porcelain urinals. The men's bathroom. Why would—

The chair was dropped back onto all four legs, hard

enough that my teeth clacked together. While I was still reeling, Powell lifted me, cut the ziptie binding my wrists and then dropped me on my back onto a piece of board that was lying on the floor. I looked up at him and the other men, terrified. *Oh Jesus, they're going to—*

But they didn't. They grabbed my wrists and ankles and tied them with zipties to drilled holes in the board so that I formed a "T," my arms outstretched but my legs together. And they didn't make any move to take off my clothes. Instead, they lifted the foot of the board so that my feet were higher than my head.

I heard a rubbery sound. Looking up, I got an upside-down view of the bearded one twisting a rubber hose onto a faucet. He adjusted it until he had a steady flow of water coming out of the tube.

That's when I got it.

They were going to waterboard me.

FIFTY-FOUR

Kian

WE RAN. But before we were even out of Emily's bedroom, Miller was keying his radio. "All units," he began. Then I slammed him into the wall to shut him up. He gaped at me but I was already tearing the radio from him and jerking the earpiece from his ear. "What the *fuck?*" he spluttered.

I leaned into him. "Kerrigan's men have been ahead of you since the start. Rexortech replaced all your communications gear, remember? They're tapped into your radios. They'll be gone before we get there and then we'll *never* find her. If we're going to do this, we're going to have to do it my way: off the grid."

For a second he stared at me like he wanted to kill me. Then I saw the uncertainty take over. The guy had never disobeyed an order in his life. Freeing a prisoner and taking him on an unauthorized mission, telling no one where we were going... this was way beyond his comfort zone.

"Fine," he said at last, and stuffed the radio in his pocket. "Come on."

We ran on, heading for the garage, but I slowed as we passed the armory. "I need a gun," I said. "They took mine when they arrested me."

I expected him to grab me one of the Secret Service pistols. But instead, he unlocked a gun safe, reached in and threw me the holster and gun that were inside.

My holster and gun. The Desert Eagle he'd taken off me the day I'd arrived. I grabbed it the way a kid grabs their favorite blanket. Then we were running again, not stopping until we were in a Secret Service SUV. Miller slammed it into gear and we tore out of the garage so fast the barrier barely had time to lift.

I just prayed we were in time.

FIFTY-FIVE

Emily

"No," I said.

They ignored me. The one with the beard picked up a piece of cloth and shook it out, then walked towards me.

"No," I said again. This time it wasn't a plea so much as a denial. I didn't want to believe this could happen.

The bearded man settled the cloth over my face, the weave rough against my lips.

I started to pull—really pull—against the zipties but they held fast. "*No!*" I yelled through the cloth.

And the water started.

Ever since the park, I'd always felt my fear like black water rising around me, threatening to reach my mouth and nose and spill down inside me, drowning me. This was the real thing. The cold water hissed out of the tube, soaked through the cloth and spread across my forehead. My eyebrows. My nose. My—

I was drowning. I spat and coughed and gagged but

there was always more water in my mouth and nose. I was inhaling it, feeling it burn its way down my airway and into my lungs and *Jesus oh Jesus I'm going to die.* The most basic fear of them all. This was worse than anything I'd ever known and there was nothing I could do to stop it—I couldn't even speak until they chose to turn the water off.

I stopped being rational. I stopped thinking at all. I was a screaming, choking animal that only wanted it to stop. My hands tore at the air and my feet twisted and kicked so hard that I pulled something and pain shot up my leg.

Then the water went away and the cloth was lifted off my face, folded up onto my forehead and left there as a reminder. I took in a huge gulp of air and immediately choked, the air searing my lungs. I coughed and coughed. I hadn't realized I was crying but tears were streaming down my face.

Powell leaned over me, a cruel smile on his face. "Now. Who did you tell? And did they believe you?"

I opened my mouth to tell him but stopped. I wasn't being brave. I wasn't trying to protect Harlan or Kian or my dad. I was way past that, way too scared. But I knew that, as soon as I told him, they'd kill me. Right now, that was frightening enough to make me hesitate but I knew that, given another session, the balance would swing the other way: death would become a welcome escape. I'd give him the names, Kerrigan would win... and I'd have helped usher in a new world where torturing innocents like this was normal.

"Okay, then," he said.

I'm never going to see Kian again.

The cloth came down over my face.

And the black fear finally won.

FIFTY-SIX

Kian

IT WAS just as the photo had shown it: a huge empty lot, filled with rubble, and the hotel standing on its own at the center. I started to see why they'd chosen this place. The windows were boarded up, so they didn't have to worry about prying eyes, and there was enough space for a small army. The best part was, once this op was over, they'd demolish the building and any evidence would be buried underneath a new office building.

We crept closer. Around back, covered with a tarpaulin, was the same black SUV I'd seen at the museum. We were definitely in the right place.

The main door was locked but we pried off the board that covered the empty doorframe at the rear and sneaked in. A hallway led to an echoey, musty ballroom but I couldn't see Emily or any of the bastards who'd taken her. Then Miller nodded towards a doorway, silently indicating that he'd heard something. We both crept up to it... and from inside, I heard Emily sobbing. Not *a woman*: *Emily*. I knew the sounds she made when she was scared. They'd been burned into my mind that day at the park.

I knew we should wait while we checked out the rest of the building. We had no idea how many of them were behind that door or how many others were upstairs. We should stop, assess and call for backup.

But someone was hurting *my woman*.

I charged the door and kicked it almost off its hinges, yelling a wordless cry of rage. Everyone froze for an instant, startled, and I took in the scene: the board, the cloth over Emily's face... *Jesus Christ!*

Powell was bent low over her, his face inches from hers. When he looked up at me, his mouth was still twisted into a faint grin: he'd been enjoying watching her struggle. *Oh, you son of a bitch.*

He focused on my face and saw the pure rage there... and his grin faltered and died.

Time seemed to slow down as I ran at him. He was too close to Emily to risk a shot, but that was fine: shooting was too good for him. As I ran, I squeezed off two shots at the two guys holding the foot of the board. My first shot hit one of them square in the chest and he went flying back against the wall. My second just clipped the other guy but, now that I had my old gun back, the force was enough to spin him around and send him to the ground clutching his shoulder.

And then I was slamming into Powell, my momentum carrying both of us to the floor. Next to me, I was dimly aware of Miller doing the same to the bearded guy.

My first punch caught him right across the jaw. I

followed up with another and another, the anger pouring out of me like lava and bringing words with it. *"You don't touch her!"* I bellowed. *"Nobody touches her!"*

I was fighting wild, without any thought to tactics or defending myself. When I'd been a kid, my brother Aedan had been into boxing and he'd won every play-fight we had because I was too angry, too undisciplined. It had never been a problem before, when I had to tussle with some drunk idiot who was threatening a senator, or some guy in a crowd who got too close to Emily. But Powell was ex-military, like me. He'd been trained.

His fist caught me in the kidneys and I felt one whole side of my body go weak as pain flashed up and down my spine. Then we were rolling over and over until we whacked into the white-tiled wall with him on top. Now *I* was taking the blows, the room spinning as his fists pounded me. *Shit.* I managed to get a few more hits in but brute strength wasn't cutting it, now. I glanced at Emily, still helpless on the board. The cloth still covered her eyes: she couldn't even see what was going on. She must be *terrified*. The thought of it pumped more anger into my veins but anger wasn't helping either.

Aedan's words came back to me across the years, memories I'd pushed to the back of my mind until Emily got me to open up. *"Keep your guard up, you feckin' idiot. Wait for an opening."*

I lifted my arms and started absorbing the blows, going against my instincts and reigning in my need to hit back. I made myself wait, letting Powell grin and get cocky, thinking he'd won. I waited until he drew his arm back to put me down for good.

And then I got in my one good hit, catching him right in the face.

He flew off me as if he'd been hit by a truck and lay groaning. I got up and, next to me, Miller was getting to his feet as well, the bearded guy unconscious under him. We looked at each other, panting, and then nodded.

I could hear boots thumping in the hallways above us. There must be more men here, upstairs, and they'd heard the shots. I raced to free Emily, wrenching the zip ties free from the board and then pulled her into my arms. She was bruised where she'd strained against her bonds and she couldn't speak yet, still coughing up water, but she was alive and we were together again. The pain from the beating I'd taken seemed to fade away. As long as she was safe, everything was okay. "It's alright," I whispered in her ear.

But she didn't respond. My chest tightened.

"We need to move," said Miller. The pounding footsteps were getting closer. It sounded like a small army was approaching.

"Emily?" I said gently. My throat was closing up. She didn't seem to know I was there.

"*Now!*" said Miller. He pointed to Emily's leg and I saw that she was holding one foot off the floor, unable to put any weight on it. "I don't think she'll be able to walk."

I stared down at Emily, taking in what those bastards had done to her. My anger swelled into huge, crimson clouds that filled my mind. I scooped my arms under her legs and back and then stood, carrying her cradled against my chest. "She doesn't have to," I said.

We ran back into the ballroom. I was hoping we could make it to the door and then back to our car before the reinforcements got downstairs but, when we were less than halfway across the huge room, a door swung open and the first man burst through, leveling his gun right at us. There was nothing I could do, not with Emily in my arms. I winced and twisted away, waiting to feel the impact on my back, praying that my body would protect hers—

I felt something brush past my back. An instant later, I heard the boom as the gun fired... but I didn't feel any pain. Then Miller was falling against me, nearly knocking me over. I hoisted Emily into one arm and fired back at the gunman, putting him down. Then I stood there blinking, confused. Looking down at myself, I didn't see any blood. Terrified, I checked Emily... but she was fine, too. Had the gunman missed?

Then I looked down at Miller, who was lying on his back at my feet. He was clutching at his chest, wet red blossoming across his white shirt. He'd taken the bullet for us.

I could hear more men approaching. We weren't going to make it to the door before they arrived. I bent and grabbed Miller's jacket and dragged him along with us as I backed towards the corner. "*Asshole!*" I spat at Miller. "Thought you hated me."

"Didn't do it for you," Miller managed. "Did it for her."

I pulled him and Emily behind one of the big, circular tables, then tipped it up on its side to act as a shield. Seconds later, bullets started tearing at the wood. We were safe for a second but now we were trapped, pinned down in the corner of the ballroom with no place to run.

"*Now* can I call for backup?" Miller grunted. He was rapidly going pale.

"Be my guest." We'd managed to take them by surprise by staying off the radio, but now I'd happily take all the Secret Service help we could get. Miller started gasping orders into his radio, stopping every few words to wince in pain. I peeked around the edge of the upended table. *Shit!* Another four guys were already in the ballroom and firing at us and two more were just emerging from the door. I fired a couple of times to hold them back, then had to pull back behind the table as bullets slammed into the wood.

I knew the Secret Service would take at least a few minutes to get there. Miller's breathing was slowing. He might survive but he certainly couldn't fight. And with just me to hold off the bad guys, we weren't going to last that long.

I pulled Emily higher in my arms so I could look at her. If this was the end, I wanted to see her face one last time. I gently pushed her wet hair back but, when I saw those big green eyes staring up at me, my heart tore in two. They were distant and unfocused and that light that I loved had gone, maybe for good. "Emily?" I asked in a broken voice.

She didn't reply. She was breathing, but she wasn't with us. She'd experienced too much and she'd slipped into catatonia. I buried my face in the crook of her neck, raw emotion flooding through me: guilt that I hadn't been able to protect her, anger that Kerrigan was going to win.

It shouldn't end like this.

And then I realized that maybe it didn't have to.

Maybe only one of us had to die.

FIFTY-SEVEN

Emily

WHEN THEY'D STARTED the second round of waterboarding, the black fear had finally risen up over me, joining the water as it poured down into my throat. It had filled my body with impenetrable cold, forcing my mind into a smaller and smaller space to escape until something finally snapped. And suddenly it was as if my mind and my body weren't connected at all. I was aware of the table shaking as bullets slammed into the far side of the wood and the feel of Kian's fingers on my face as he brushed my hair aside, but it felt as if it was happening to someone else.

"I'm sorry," I heard him say against my neck. "I'm sorry, Emily."

I wanted to tell him that it was okay, that it wasn't his fault. But my mind refused to go near my body—it shied away like a dog from an abusive master. My body was a source of fear and pain.

"I'm not going to let them get you," he said. The Irish was thick in his voice, now, gleaming and razor-sharp. He pushed me back from him a little, propping me up against the table, and I sat there like a lifeless doll. I saw him check his gun and then he took Miller's pistol, too, so that he had one in each hand.

No. Oh no. I suddenly realized what he was planning. He was going to burst out from behind the table and run at them, use all that anger and brute strength to charge right at them. They'd cut him to pieces... but he'd draw their fire long enough for me to escape.

He leaned out to fire a few final shots before his suicide run, then returned to me and cupped my cheeks in his hands. "When I go," he said firmly, "*you* have to go. Okay?" He must have known it was probably useless. He could see I was gone, cowering in the shadows of my mind, but he wanted to believe he could give me a chance. "*Run!*" he ordered. But I couldn't respond. Every time I tried to force myself back into awareness, my mind slid away again. I didn't want to be me.

"I love you," he said. "I'll always love you."

I love you, too. But the words wouldn't come out. My body felt as if it was at the end of a mile-long hallway.

He shifted the guns in his hands, readying himself. He was about to sacrifice himself for me and it wasn't even going to work, he was going to die for nothing: he'd run towards them and I'd sit there like a puppet with its strings cut, hearing the bullets hit his body and him slump to the floor. All because I was hiding, hiding from the pain and fear just like a child.

Kian shifted his weight, about to spring out into

view. He was going to die. *He's going to die, Emily, he's going to die, right fucking now unless you do something do something DO SOMETHING—*

I looked into those blue eyes and imagined never seeing them again. Deep inside my mind, I gritted my teeth... and *wrenched.*

I'd been floating free: numb, but light as air and in no pain. Now, suddenly, I was at the bottom of a black ocean, the fear pressing down on me, crushing me. I couldn't breathe, couldn't think. But I knew I needed to swim against the weight and I did, soaring up through it with everything I had.

I broke the surface... and I was back. All the pain slammed into me at once: my injured ankle, the bruises on my wrists but most of all my aching, burning lungs. Taking a breath was sheer agony and there was no way I could speak yet. But I didn't have to speak.

As Kian rose to his feet, I reached out and grabbed his wrist and hung on in a death grip. He snapped his head round and stared at me.

It took me several panting breaths before I dared to try speaking and, when I did, each syllable burned like fire in my lungs and then clawed at my throat. "*Don't,*" I croaked.

He squatted back down next to me. I could see the conflict in his eyes: joy that I was back but aching sadness that he had to leave me. "I have to," he said. I saw him glance at Miller. "It's the only way."

I could hear the shuffle of boots on the other side of the table. They were starting to advance towards us. In another few seconds they'd be on us, and Kian could only guard one side of the table at once.

I reached out and pulled Miller's gun from Kian's

hand. I couldn't speak anymore, so I put my head close to his and whispered, my voice rasping. "You forget where I grew up," I said, and worked the gun's slide.

He stared at me and I stared right back at him, resolute. It was about more than just knowing how to shoot a gun. It was about him understanding that we'd moved beyond him protecting me. I loved him. And that meant I protected him, too.

He nodded and the look of pride in his eyes took my breath away. Then his lips were on mine. We only had a second but it didn't matter: we poured every ounce of ourselves into that kiss. Everything we'd been through, every danger he'd shielded me from, every bit of pain I'd helped him release. We kissed for then and now and for the future because, if we lived through this, we were never letting go of each other again.

Then we were moving apart and he was leaning around the left side of the table while I leaned around the right. It had been a long time since I fired a gun. I closed my eyes for a second, remembering Texas and sunshine and shooting cans with my dad. *Identify your target. Aim and squeeze.*

Muscle memory took over. The gun kicked in my hand and the first guy cried out and fell to the floor, clutching his leg. I aimed again. The second guy's eyes went wide, amazed that a girl was pointing a gun at him... and then he staggered back as I hit him in the shoulder. Kian's huge gun boomed on the other side of the table and another guy fell. There were many more of them than of us, but they were caught by surprise out in the open—they didn't expect to suddenly take fire from both sides. They actually began to retreat.

I had to flinch back behind the table as they started firing back, but with two of us one could hold them at bay while the other repositioned. I crawled behind Kian, careful to stay off my injured ankle, leaned around the bottom of the table and shot from there. I didn't hit anyone, this time, but the shot was close enough to make the guy duck back behind cover. *This might actually work....*

Then my gun clicked empty. Two shots later, so did Kian's. We both dropped back behind the table, staring at each other in horror. Immediately I heard boots pound across the ballroom's wood floor towards us. *We were so close!* I grabbed for Kian's hand and felt those big, warm fingers wrap around mine. I looked up into his eyes. I wanted them to be the last thing I saw.

The first of the gunmen rounded the table, his gun pointed right at us.

And every one of the ballroom's huge windows exploded inwards.

FIFTY-EIGHT

Emily

I SCREWED MY EYES CLOSED, gripped Kian's hand and braced myself against the chaos. The air was full of smoke, shards of glass and charred bits of the board that had once been nailed over the windows. I could hear men converging on us from every direction, swarming in through the windows and doors. There was a hail of gunfire, then frantic shouting. And then everything went still.

When I opened my eyes, I counted at least twenty men: a mixture of Secret Service agents and soldiers. I later learned they'd called in a Marine unit as backup. A medic ran over and started tending to Miller.

As Kian helped me to my feet and I peeked over the top of the table, I saw that most of Powell's men were dead. The two that were still alive were on their knees with their hands clasped behind their heads while the military zip-tied them. Meanwhile, the medics worked to stabilize Miller. When they eventually nodded that he'd live and loaded him onto a stretcher, I threw my arms around Kian's neck and hugged him close. *It's over!*

Moments later, the soldiers brought out three men from the bathroom. Powell and the man with the beard had both regained consciousness and the one Kian had injured was being carried out on a stretcher. They carried the injured one outside, presumably to an ambulance, but the other two were pushed to their knees and restrained along with the others.

Powell looked up at me and smirked, unafraid. A chill went through me. Hadn't we won?

That was when the Secret Service agent approached us. "Ma'am?" he said. "You're to come with us." He gave me his arm to lean on, because I still couldn't put any weight on my injured ankle. But when Kian stepped forward to follow, the agent shook his head. "Not you," he said.

Kian and I looked at each other in confusion.

The Secret Service agent sighed and shook his head. "I'm on orders to take O'Harra into custody," he said. Then he looked down at the semi-conscious Miller. "You, too, sir," he said sadly. "You've been declared enemy combatants."

I gaped as it hit me. I'd been so focused on surviving the firefight, I'd forgotten that Kerrigan was still in charge. "No," I said. "No, Kerrigan is behind all this!" I pointed at Powell. "The evidence is right here: search that man, he'll have a cell phone with a text message from Kerrigan. You need to get hold of his phone, too, you can match them up and—"

The agent was shaking his head. He looked apologetically at Miller again and I realized he must have served under him at the White House. That bastard Kerrigan was making him arrest his own boss.

"Everything will be taken as evidence," he said. "The President's already promised there'll be a full enquiry."

"You asshole," slurred Miller from the stretcher. They must have given him something for the pain. "This is wrong and you know it."

"I'm under orders, sir!" spat the Secret Service agent. "Ma'am, come with me!"

Shit. *Shit, shit, shit!* Kian and I looked at each other. Now I knew why Powell had been smirking: he'd go to jail but so would Kian and Miller. There'd be some long, drawn out enquiry spanning years and no doubt vital evidence would be conveniently lost along the way. Kian would be painted as an accomplice—maybe we could persuade a court of his innocence, maybe not. But whatever happened, Kerrigan wouldn't be linked to any of it. He'd be free to rule the country. "No!" I said desperately. "You *can't do this!*"

The agent gripped my arm and pulled me away from Kian. "It's for your own protection, ma'am."

They'd take me right back to the White House... and with Kerrigan still in control and his thugs everywhere, I wouldn't last more than a day. How easy would it be to arrange an accident, or another sniper attack they could pin on a lone gunman. "No!"

Kian growled and seized my other arm, tugging me back to him. Immediately, both the Secret Service agents and the soldiers swung their guns up to point at him. "Let her go!" snapped the Secret Service agent.

"Not happening," said Kian.

I heard guns being cocked. I knew how this would end. Kian wouldn't let me go, not again. "Please!" I begged.

"I'm sorry," said the agent. And he looked as if he genuinely was. But he was still going to carry out his orders. "I'm on direct orders from the President."

The main doors crashed open. Harlan, pushing a wheelchair, closely followed by a team of doctors.

"*I'm* the goddamn President!" bellowed my dad.

Everyone in the room gaped at him. His entire chest was wrapped in bandages. He had an oxygen tube in his nose and his skin was gray. But he was still a hundred times the leader Kerrigan would ever be.

"All of you men stand down!" he snapped.

The Secret Service agents and soldiers hesitated, unsure whose orders they should be following. So my dad made the decision for them. "*Stand the hell down!*" he yelled, his face turning purple.

Every gun swung away from Kian. The Secret Service agent dropped my arm like it had burned him.

I ran towards my dad. Two steps in, I remembered my injured ankle as pain shot up my leg, but that wasn't going to stop me. I reached the wheelchair and threw my arms around him. "Are you—How are you *here?* Are you going to be okay?" I babbled. Kian ran over and slipped his arm under my shoulders to support me.

My dad tried to speak, but grimaced instead, tensing in his chair. A monitor attached to the wheelchair started bleeping and the doctors raced to surround him. One of them adjusted an IV line. "That should help with the pain, sir," the doctor said. "But we need to get you back to the hospital!"

My dad panted through the pain for a second, his eyes closed. Clearly, those few seconds of shouting had taken everything he had. Then he relaxed a little as the medication hit and shook his head. "After we get all this straightened out," he grunted. He opened his eyes and looked at Kian and, after a moment, he managed to speak again. "I never got a chance to thank you, Mr. O'Harra."

Kian nodded. "Not necessary, Mr. President."

My dad narrowed his eyes. I realized he was looking at the way Kian was standing, pressed right up against me. And I realized he must have heard from Harlan about Kian running off with me and my mom's suspicions. A little more strength returned to his voice. "There something you want to tell me, Mr. O'Harra?"

It was the only time I've ever seen Kian embarrassed. He shuffled his feet, then straightened up. "Uh... I have intentions towards your daughter. Sir."

My dad took a long look at him. "You going to treat her right? Protect her?"

Kian looked at me. "*Yes sir!*"

My dad made him sweat for fully five seconds. Then: "Well, then I guess that's okay."

My heart swelled and I had to grab Kian's hand to stop from tearing up. "What about Kerrigan?" I asked. "Where is he?"

"Aboard Air Force One," said my dad. "They got him airborne as soon as these bastards shot me." Then, through the pain, he managed a smile. "But I called the pilot on my way here. They're landing at Andrews now. He's about to get a real nasty surprise."

I turned to Kian, grabbed his shirt and pulled myself to his chest, resting my cheek on those warm slabs of muscle. Over his shoulder, I saw the Secret Service agent we'd had the stand-off with go over to Powell... who wasn't smirking anymore. The Secret

Service agent patted down his pockets... and pulled out a cell phone. He held it up to show me and nodded respectfully.

We had him. We had Kerrigan.

And suddenly, I felt myself just *wilt*. Kian felt the change in me and caught me before I could fall, scooping me up in his arms. *"Whoah,"* he said. "It's okay. I got you."

I looked up into his eyes. There was so much I wanted to say but I hadn't slept in twenty-four hours and had barely eaten in thirty-six. I'd been drenched, frozen, tortured and I'd walked God knows how many miles. I was utterly, utterly exhausted. So I hauled my head up to his and put my mouth to his ear for just long enough to say, *"I love you,"* because I couldn't wait even another minute to finally say it back to him. And then, as he grinned, I just flopped in his arms and my eyes closed.

"I got you," he said again, stroking my cheek.

He got me.

EPILOGUE

Two Weeks Later

Emily

"Your tie is crooked," I said out of the side of my mouth.

Kian looked down at the blue silk tie as if he wanted to rip it off and shred it. In fact, he looked as if he'd happily just tear off the whole Armani suit and do the photo op in his pants. I doubted he'd ever look fully comfortable in a suit.

But he still looked amazing in one. All those sharp lines only emphasized the power of his arms and back, the soft white shirt stretched tight over the firm slabs of his chest and the tie set off his eyes.

Come to think of it, *I* wanted to rip the suit off him.

But photos first. I straightened his tie. This was going to be our first group photo together and I wanted it to go well.

The first twenty-four hours after the hotel had been insane, the two weeks that followed only slightly less so. Kian and I had been taken to the hospital so the doctors could check us out. My throat and chest were swollen but the doctors said I'd recover within a few days. My ankle injury turned out to be a torn ligament, from twisting and straining against my bonds so hard. They gave me crutches but I preferred to lean on Kian's powerful shoulder, as I was right now. Both of us had about a million little cuts from the glass in the museum, plus the wound where my tracking chip had been removed and the bullet wound in Kian's arm. But nothing that wouldn't heal.

And the psychological wounds? Everyone expected those to be devastating, given what I'd been through. But something had changed in me. Maybe it was that moment behind the table in the hotel when I'd forced myself past my fears. Maybe it was knowing Kian was with me now, forever. But that night after the hotel, I slept like a baby. I still had the occasional nightmare, but nothing like as bad as after the park. The fear would always be there—I'd have to be crazy *never* to be scared. But it didn't own me, anymore.

My mom swept in from the hallway. We were in the Oval Office, waiting to step out into the Rose Garden for the photo op. "You look great, honey," she told me. Then she turned to Kian. "Kian, you brush up well."

"Ma'am," he said in that deep, Irish-tinged growl.

My mom had come around to Kian pretty fast when she discovered what really happened, including giving him a tearful, spontaneous hug when she met us at the hospital. She didn't necessarily *approve* of him in the same way she'd approve of a billionaire

CEO. But that was okay: if Kian had thought she approved of him, he'd probably have been quite offended.

The door from the hallway opened again and my dad strode in. He was still under orders from the doctors to take it easy and he was still ignoring them. "We ready?" he asked. Then he looked at Kian. "*You* ready?"

Kian nodded. "Yes, Mr. President." But I could tell he was nervous. Very little scared Kian, but he didn't want to screw this up and embarrass me, or my folks. I grabbed his hand.

We stepped out into the Rose Garden and turned towards a solid wall of photographers. Camera shutters started clicking at the rate of a hundred a second, almost a continuous buzz.

The media had been going nuts ever since the attack on the museum but, when Jessica gave a press conference the next morning and announced that Edward Kerrigan had been detained in connection with the assassination attempt on the President, they went *insane*. And the entire world wanted to read the story: several news websites actually dropped off the internet for about an hour, unable to cope with the massive increase in traffic.

By mid-morning, every news channel was filled with footage of Kerrigan's arrest. My dad and Jessica had made damn sure that the reporters were there to watch Air Force One touchdown and Kerrigan walk down its steps... straight into the arms of a squad of US Marines. When a couple of Military Police step forward with cuffs, you can see Kerrigan turn around and start spitting orders to his Secret Service detail, only to find them shaking their heads in disgust. My dad had already spoken to them and they were taking orders from their real Commander-in-Chief again. It's a very satisfying moment: I've replayed the clip many times.

No one was sure who had jurisdiction over a White House conspiracy, especially when it involved terrorism. Nothing remotely like it had ever happened before. Eventually, a special team formed from Homeland Security and the FBI took control. The investigation and trial would take months but, whatever happened, Kerrigan was going to jail and the death penalty was a real possibility.

As the initial shock of the conspiracy died away, the media started looking at Kerrigan's plan and Rexortech. Of course, there was a cover up. The Rexortech CEO went on TV to say there'd *categorically* been no involvement whatsoever from anyone at the company. Unfortunately, he made the mistake of giving the speech in front of the Rexortech HQ and if you watch the footage there's a wonderful moment where an FBI agent interrupts him at the podium and hands him a warrant, and then the cameras all swing around to the main doors of the building and you can see about a hundred FBI agents begin to raid the place. Within twenty-four hours, they'd arrested the CEO, three other executives and twenty staff for aiding in the conspiracy. Within forty-eight hours, the company had been delisted from the stock market. Across DC, Rexortech surveillance cameras started coming down.

The Guardian Act was dead. A mass-backpedaling began, with all of the newspapers and TV channels who'd supported Kerrigan suddenly hating the idea of an invasive surveillance state and talking about how we needed checks and balances. It was sickening to watch them do a slick 180, but the public wasn't fooled. We'd come too close to disaster. People would remember, the next time someone like Kerrigan came along.

"Mr. O'Harra!" yelled a reporter. "How does it feel to be dating the President's daughter?"

Kian looked at me. "Great," he said. And the way he said it made me melt inside. It was better than any lengthy speech he could have given.

"Any idea what you'll do now, Mr. O'Harra?" yelled someone else.

I'd rehearsed an answer to that question with him: *I'm going to take some time to think about that.* But now that it came to it, Kian just did a big, unashamed shrug. There was friendly laughter from the reporters. I had a feeling they were going to like Kian: like my dad, he was a straight talker. We'd talked about what he might do next and tossed around a few ideas but we hadn't made any decisions, yet. He'd quit the Secret Service: he couldn't be responsible for guarding me *and* be with me. That meant a new agent took over my bodyguard duties: a blond-haired guy from Nebraska called Jack. Kian gave him a hard time at first, drilling him on everything, but we both liked him. And whoever was officially guarding me, what mattered most was that I had Kian's protection, always.

And me? I'd veered away from the fundraising my mom had been gently steering me towards and was looking into a career with an investigative agency, focusing on political and corporate corruption. It wasn't typical for a President's daughter but I wanted to make a difference: there were too many people out there like Kerrigan and too many corporations willing to help them. I'd roped in my mom to help me with one bit of fundraising, though: we'd raised money for the soup kitchen that had fed me during my night on the streets, and opened a new homeless shelter. I also reported the guy who'd lured me into the abandoned building and the DC police picked him up just days later at a different soup kitchen. He was eventually charged with attacks on four homeless women.

The cameras clicked and clicked but the noise was dying down, the photographers getting their last few shots as the photo op came to an end. "How about a kiss?" yelled one reporter.

Kian and I looked at each other and my face flushed. Kissing him wasn't a problem but kissing him *on camera?* I awkwardly turned to him and tilted my face up. He leaned down towards me and hesitated, as if trying to figure out how to do a chaste little kiss that would look good on the front pages.

Kian didn't do *chaste.*

"The hell with it," he growled under his breath. And suddenly he was tipping me and kissing me full-on, his tongue parting my lips, his chest crushed against my breasts. The camera clicks became a continuous buzz again, the reporters yelling their approval. What they couldn't see was Kian's hand behind me as he squeezed my ass. A rush of heat went through me, twisting and arcing, clouding my brain and then soaking down to my groin. I grabbed his biceps and clung on, losing myself in the kiss. For long seconds, I didn't care who was watching.

Eventually, we came up for air and reality set in again. I was panting and flushed: embarrassed and thrilled and melting inside, all at the same time. My mom was giving Kian a reproachful look but my dad was trying not to laugh. I mock-glared at Kian. "You're not supposed to do that to the President's daughter," I muttered.

He leaned closer and growled in my ear, each word scalding hot and silver-edged. "Then we got a problem," he said. "Because tonight...."

I tried to keep a sweet, respectable smile on my face for the cameras as he whispered *exactly* what he was going to do to me. He balanced me perfectly: I worried too much about what the press and everyone else thought and he didn't worry about it at all.

"...that alright with you?" he finished.

I swallowed and pressed my thighs together. "Kiss me again," I muttered. "I'm not sure they got the first one."

One Month Later

Emily

I opened the door to my bedroom and walked in on Kian wearing only his jockey shorts, his hard ass outlined through the thin cotton. Unlike the time when he'd walked in on *me,* he wasn't embarrassed at all: he just stood there, all rugged tan body and gleaming blue eyes, and I felt his gaze sweep down my body. I flushed and quickly came in and closed the door behind me. "You're getting changed *now?*" I asked. "We don't have to go until eight."

We were attending a ceremony that night recognizing soldiers injured in the line of duty. I'd already seen him in his tux and he looked fantastic, my very own James Bond. But that was hours away.

He shook his head and went over to the closet. I'd cleared him some space there, since he was practically living in my room, but we were really looking forward to moving into our own place. "I gotta go out," he said. "I'll be back before tonight." I could hear the tension in his voice.

He started grabbing clothes, but not suits or the respectable casualwear my stylist had picked out for him: the jeans and leather jacket he'd been wearing when I first met him. "What's going on?" I asked, a stab of panic going through me.

He nodded at the bed.

There was a letter there, handwritten, the envelope addressed to him. I snatched it up and read as he dressed. My eyes widened as I scanned down the page.

Kian pulled on his jacket. "You don't need to come," he said. "I can do this on my own."

I got up off the bed and walked over to him, then looked up into those big blue eyes. He was trying to hide it, but I could see the pain there, the memories that had been slowly poisoning him until I'd got him to open up. The letter had brought them to the surface again, jagged and sharp. "You don't have to," I told him, and pulled him close.

***

The meeting was set for Anacostia Park: we'd come full circle, since that day I met Kian. By now, it was November and the temperature was dropping fast as the sun went down. But it was a beautiful evening, the sunset turning everything shades of red and gold as it sank below the horizon. I walked hand in hand with Kian as we made our way towards the bench and sat down. Jack and the other Secret Service agents arranged themselves to form a perimeter around us, just far enough away that they wouldn't be able to hear our conversation. I looked around and took a couple of deep breaths. I'd expected to be nervous, coming back to the park, but I seemed to be okay: it was a nice milestone to have reached.

A few minutes later, Kian stood up and nodded at a man walking along the path towards us. He was coming out of the sun and I had to screw my eyes up to see.

"Is that...." I asked, standing and looking at the man.

Kian nodded silently. I saw him swallow, nervous as hell, his hands clenching into fists. I ran a hand lightly up his arm and over his shoulder, rubbing him there until I felt him relax a little. "I'm right here," I murmured.

The man stopped in front of us. I recognized the build and the jet-black hair. I recognized the jawline and the shockingly blue eyes.

"Emily," said Kian after a moment, his voice tight, "this is my brother, Sean."

Neither of them moved. They stared into each other's eyes in silence for long seconds, the tension rising and rising until I was sure they were going to swing at each other. Then they broke at the same moment and pulled each other into a fierce hug.

"Christ," muttered Kian when he let his brother go. "It's been *years*."

Sean nodded. "You sure we're okay here?" His accent was a lot stronger than Kian's, halfway between American and Irish.

I nodded. "The Secret Service won't let any reporters come close. And no one knows it's you we're meeting."

Sean nodded. "Good. I don't want to cause you problems."

"You in trouble with the law?" asked Kian.

Sean ran a hand through his hair, the same gesture I knew so well from Kian. "No more than usual," he said. "But... probably best if no one noses around me for a while." He looked between Kian and me. "I met someone, too. And she was in trouble. I had to help her do something bad... so we could do something good."

Kian shook his head angrily. "For fuck's sake, Sean," he snapped. "If you were in trouble, why didn't you come find me?"

Sean squared up to him. "Same reason you didn't find me."

They stared at each other, neither of them backing down. But slowly, I saw them both soften.

"It's time," said Sean. "Louise—the woman I met—she made me see that. You know what we need to do. That's why I'm here. We've all been out there on our own too long."

Kian lowered his eyes, staring at the ground. I could feel him tensing up again, all the memories flooding back. I found his hand and squeezed it, letting him know that whatever he had to do, I'd be there with him.

Kian looked at his brother. "You're right," he said at last. He took a long, slow breath, and it was almost as if it was the first real breath he'd taken in years.

"We're going to find them," said Sean. "Aedan and Carrick. Wherever they are."

"And Bradan," said Kian, his voice thick with emotion. "Whether he's alive or dead. I want to know what happened to him."

Sean gripped Kian's shoulder and nodded. "Bradan too."

Kian took another deep breath. "Alright, then," he said. "Let's start putting this family back together."

Thank you for reading!

If you enjoyed *Saving Liberty,* please consider leaving a review.

Kian's brothers have their own books. If you'd like to hear about Sean and the "something bad" he had to do to help the woman he fell in love with, pick up *Growing and Kissing.* The story of Aedan, the bad boy Irish boxer, is told in *Punching and Kissing.* I've included the first three chapters in this book, so just turn the page to try it.

Yes, more O'Harra brothers will appear in future books :)

The story of how Arianna, a CIA spy on her first assignment, falls for Luka, the Russian mobster she's meant to betray, is told in *Lying and Kissing.*

The story of how Lily, a forger on the run, meets a cowboy who just won't quit pursuing her, is told in *Texas Kissing.*

Or discover what happens when a Russian hitman looks into the eyes of his female target...and finds he can't pull the trigger. That's *Kissing My Killer.*

Would you like a free steamy ebook novella about a ballerina who falls for a badass biker with a penchant for BDSM? It's called *Losing My Balance* and I wrote it especially (and exclusively) for my newsletter readers - sign up to get your free copy.

Helena Newbury

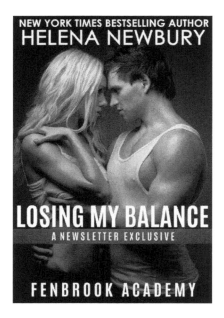

http://list.helenanewbury.com

Preview of Punching and Kissing (Out Now)

ONE

Sylvie

I didn't belong there.

The crowd was a baying, howling mass of wild eyes and open mouths, leaning far over the concrete balcony to gawp. The heat of a hundred frenzied bodies pressed in on me from all sides until I could barely catch my breath.

I had to get out of there but I needed to stay. I owed it to Alec.

I stumbled through the crowd, making my way around the edge of the huge, circular room. I kept my gaze fixed on the graffiti, on the rusted pipes...anything to avoid looking at what was going on below us.

There was a cry of pain and I glanced down before I could stop myself. One man had the other on the floor, fists pummeling his face. There was only one rule: it went on until someone couldn't get up.

Welcome to The Pit.

I looked away, disgusted, and tried to move faster.

Elbowing or pushing isn't in my nature and I was the lone woman in a roomful of hyped-up, drunk men. So I muttered apologies and sneaked through gaps. Luckily, they barely noticed me—not the rich guys who'd come there for an edgy walk on the wild side, not the local guys who were one bad bet away from disaster. Everyone was going nuts, jumping and yelling and punching the air.

No, wait. Not everyone.

I stopped in my tracks as I saw him. He stood like a rock in an ocean, a full head taller than the people around him and moving not even an inch as they ebbed and swelled against him. His broad back was like a cliff and his shoulders seemed twice as wide as mine. He was in a sleeveless top, arms folded across his chest, and the heavy swells of his shoulders and biceps led down to thickly corded forearms. *Big,* and ripped, as well. But it wasn't his size or his muscles that made me stop, nor even the way he stood so still.

His hood was raised, throwing his face into shadow. Who wore a hood, in this heat?

I moved forward and lost sight of him for a moment. When I saw him again, I was closer. I was looking up into that shadowed face, now. I could just catch glimpses: a jaw dusted with dark stubble, a full lower lip pressed into a tight line. He was watching, but he hadn't lost himself like the others. Maybe he was sickened by what was happening downstairs. Maybe, like me, he didn't belong in this place.

I passed behind him, willing myself not to look. I made it three feet beyond him before the urge got too much and I glanced back over my shoulder. At first, I could see only shadows under the hood but then—

As one of the cheap fluorescent tubes flickered, I

caught a glimpse of eyes: savagely blue and brutally hard. Starkly beautiful, they saw every weakness and gave no mercy.

I tore my eyes away, panting like I'd just missed a speeding truck. I'd been wrong. He wasn't immune to this place at all—he was already lost. And if I didn't belong here; he could have been born here.

I tried to move faster through the crowd. A drink. I needed a drink. I headed for the guy I'd seen on the far side of the room, the one who sold sodas out of a cooler at six dollars a time. He knew his market—six dollars was nothing to the guys who came here, the ones who bet thousands of dollars and then drove home in their Lexuses, speed-dialing their wives to apologize for working late. To me, six dollars was a day's food. But I was going to pass out if I didn't drink something.

I bought a Dr. Pepper and ran the cool metal can over my forehead, closing my eyes, letting the chill soak into me and calm me, pushing away the remembered fear from when I'd glimpsed that guy's expression.

Fear and...something else.

The eyes had been gorgeous—coldly beautiful beyond anything I'd ever seen. And that jaw, those lips, that body—the expression had sent ice down my spine but, when it reached my groin, it had turned into something else entirely. Cold had become hot. Fear had become—

I closed my eyes for a second and took a deep breath. *Stupid*. Sure, from the glimpses I'd seen, the guy might just be hot as hell under that hood. But that expression...he was like the distilled essence of this place.

Stay. The fuck. Away.

I popped the top and drank. The cold soda foamed down my throat like liquid sex. A calming chill soaked through me and I felt my heart gradually slowing down.

I drained the whole can before I looked up and saw him. The hooded man. Closer, this time, no more than ten feet away.

And staring right at me.

The momentary cool from the soda boiled away in an instant. A wave of heat shot through me, rippling upward from my groin. I wasn't ready for how deeply sexual his gaze was, how it connected with me right where I lived.

I told myself, *of course he's not looking at you.* I'm not much to look at. My brother's the eye-catching one, all blond hair and muscle, like my dad. I take after my mom—small and slender, with boobs like half-oranges.

I wrenched my eyes from him and stared fixedly into the distance, waiting for him to look away.

But I could still feel his gaze on the side of my face, never wavering for a second.

TWO

Aedan

THERE WERE about a million reasons I shouldn't be there: it was too damn hot; I had to be up early for work the next morning; I didn't want to give *him* the satisfaction of seeing me at one of his fights.

But there was something that mattered more than any of that. That itch, that deep-down itch that can't be scratched any other way but feeling your fists connect. The rush you get as you duck and weave, hands up, taking the punishment and then returning it tenfold.

I don't do that anymore. But the itch is still there. Watching it is the next best thing.

By rights, indulging myself like that should have brought something bad down on me. A lightning bolt from above, maybe. But someone saw fit to send me a whole different kind of divine intervention.

She was the only woman in the place, but she

would have stood out if she'd been in some uptown club filled with supermodels. Long, black hair, maybe even darker than mine, so dark it was almost blue-black. A slender, lithe body that made me want to take the flat of my hand and run it all the way down from her neck to the curve of her calf, like stroking a cat. She was wearing a bubblegum-pink *Curious Weasels* t-shirt and it molded to the soft swells of her breasts in a way that made my breath catch.

No. Not her. I wasn't going to torture myself with a girl like that. Too beautiful. Too pure. I didn't deserve someone like that. Oh, sure, I could grab her wrist and pin her with my Irish eyes and tell her she was coming home with me, *now*. Maybe she'd see what was underneath the hood and freak out, but maybe she'd be okay with it. Then we could go back to my apartment. My body between those sweet thighs, driving up into her, those cute little tits filling my hands—

Jesus, would that really be so bad?

Yeah, it would. In the morning, she'd realize I wasn't some fantasy bad boy; I was just *bad*. Not an exciting walk on the wild side but a full-on savage, only good for two things. She'd look down at my big, calloused hands as they roved over her naked breasts and start to think about what else they'd done—how much pain and damage I'd dealt. She'd panic and make excuses and run back to her safe little life, wherever the hell that was, and it'd be over. Or, worse, she'd hang around just long enough for me to fuck up her life. I wasn't going to risk that. No matter how perfect her tits were.

I watched her moving through the crowd. Damn, she was just a scared little thing. Why didn't people make way for her? I pegged her for about twenty, five years younger than me. It was only when she glanced my way again that I saw the pain in her eyes. She *was* about twenty, but she'd seen more bad shit than someone her age should.

She bought a soda and ran the can over her forehead—right there, in front of me, like it was nothing at all. I drank in every detail: the slow roll of the can as it kissed her skin, the soft, long lashes as she closed her eyes in pleasure, the drop of ice water that fell from the bottom of the can and fell—

Jesus onto her upper boob and then trickling down into the scoop neck of her t-shirt, painting a trail of moisture over the soft flesh.

I could feel my cock swell against my thigh. *Damn,* she was hot.

She opened her eyes and I finally got a look at them. Big and liquid and the color of some lush, enchanted forest grove. And her lips! Soft, perfect pillows, flawless and pink. She popped the top of the can and drank. I couldn't take my eyes off that elegant throat, flexing and swallowing. God, she was beautiful. What the hell was she doing here? Some rich kid, slumming it? Her clothes didn't look expensive, but she must be some rich guy's girlfriend. What else would a woman be doing here? This was a guy's world—women had more sense.

And then she looked up and, for maybe half a second, she was looking right at me. A jolt went through my body, as if I'd touched a live wire. I felt every muscle go tense, my hands making fists so tight my knuckles ached. It was like I'd dropped right into a fantasy world for an instant, a heaven where I knew her, where we could be together. I felt like I was coming alive, the last few years beginning to slough off and fall away from me.

An angel. Fate had sent me an angel.

Then she came to her senses and looked away and I felt like an idiot for staring at her. I was pretty sure she couldn't see much, under the hood, but maybe she'd seen. Or maybe she'd sensed what I was like and that had scared her even more.

I couldn't tear my eyes from her, though. I drank her in because it might be the last time I ever saw her. I watched until she finally finished her soda and headed out of the main room, down the long, dark hallway that led to the bathroom. I caught my breath. The sight of her ass in those jeans, pert and tight and just the right size of my hands...I had a new favorite part of her.

She disappeared into the shadows and the spell was broken. Reality returned like a punch to the side of my head. *Yeah, and you'll never even touch her, you feckin' idiot.*

I liked her and that was why I had to stay away from her. Because if I got tempted and actually got close, all I was going to do was hurt her.

And then I frowned, because I saw another guy watching her retreating back. Not one of the rich guys in a suit, one of the locals. He nodded to his two buddies and all three of them disappeared into the shadows.

Oh God, no.

THREE

Sylvie

THE PIT was some kind of industrial building, once. Most of it is just bare concrete and graffiti, but some of the fluorescent lights still work and there's running water. The crowd has to be able to see; the organizers have to hose the blood off the floor.

Hidden away down a long hallway, in what I guess used to be the office area, there's a bathroom. Not many people know about it. I normally avoid it because I don't like being off on my own in The Pit. But after draining a whole Dr. Pepper, I suddenly needed to go.

The roar of the crowd died away as I turned one corner, then another, hurrying past disused rooms with broken windows. It wasn't much cooler than the rest of The Pit, but at least there was space to think.

Had that guy really been staring at me? It didn't seem likely—no one ever looked at me. I couldn't help thinking someone could have rolled the genetic dice better. I could have been some tall, leggy blonde with bags of confidence and my brother could have been short, dark and shy.

Because then maybe he wouldn't be downstairs, waiting to take his turn in the ring.

I locked myself in the bathroom. There was only one in the whole place, so it's a good thing people don't know it's there or it'd get pretty nasty in there on fight night. I pushed my jeans and panties down around my knees. A few seconds later...*relief*.

I understood why Alec was doing it. Without the cash from fighting, we'd be on the street already. But watching him risk his life each month was almost unbearable. I hated The Pit. But sitting waiting for him at home...that would be even worse.

I was just about to stand up when the door rattled. Not hard, just like someone was leaning against it, but it made me jump. I cleared my throat. "*Occupied!*" I called out, wishing my voice didn't sound so high and nervy.

A low laugh, the sort that's shared between friends. And then I saw the bolt on the door slide back.

I grabbed for it, but it was too late. The door was swinging wide and the guy was already inside. Not much taller than me but wider, with heavy muscle under a layer of fat. He was still holding the coin he'd used to open the lock from the outside.

I started to get up. I wasn't all that scared, yet. My mind was still occupied with humiliation, one hand reaching for my jeans while the other tried to cover my groin. In my head, it was more on the level of some high school prank where the guys invade the girls' bathroom and laugh at them.

Then his hand slapped across my mouth, his

sweaty palm tight against my lips. With his other hand, he lifted me off the toilet and pressed me against the wall. Two more men were crowding in, almost filling the small room. And the true horror of it began to sink in.

One guy closed and locked the door. I could barely hear the roar of the distant crowd, now—even if I could scream, no one would hear me. *And no one knows I'm in here.*

The guy holding me had wiry brown hair that lay in tangled curls. His foot, when he stamped it down on my jeans and panties to ram them down my legs, was in a work boot, white with dust. I felt my legs bared, then his knee between them, stopping them from closing.

I tried to scream, but my lungs couldn't get any air. In his excitement, the guy had pushed the edge of his hand right up against my nostrils. I tried to kick, but my ankles were still tangled in my jeans and the bundle of cloth was pinned to the floor by his foot. I heaved myself away from the wall, but his chest was pressed hard against me.

I still couldn't breathe. Every panicked attempt just sucked his hand tighter against my nose and mouth.

His other hand pushed between my legs. Fingers on me. God...*in* me. I wanted to throw up. I clawed with my hands and managed to scratch his neck, but then one of the other men grabbed my wrists and pressed my hands hard against the wall. All three of them were laughing, the sound ringing in my ears. I heard a belt buckle being unfastened.

I was still straining against their grip, but my vision was going dark. I wondered if I was going to pass out before it happened.

The door gave a single, solitary creak, as if someone was leaning against it. I looked towards it—anything was better than looking at the men's faces.

With a sound like the end of the world, the door was ripped off its hinges and lifted away, trailing shattered wood. Then it was tossed aside and I saw—

Him. The man who'd been staring at me.

The lead guy's two buddies ran at my savior, yelling at him. Now my arms were free, but I barely had the strength to lift them away from the wall. My body had gone limp, my lungs burning for air.

The hooded guy grabbed the first man by the t-shirt and hurled him across the hallway as easily as if he was tossing a garbage bag into a dumpster. The man hit the wall with a sickening crack and went down.

The other man tried to land a punch. Mystery guy blocked it easily, then slammed his fist into the man's side, right over his kidney. The man crumpled, just in time to get a knee to his chin.

My vision had narrowed to a tunnel. My face was wet with sweat, my life measured in seconds, now. The guy holding me glanced between me and my rescuer like a predator unwilling to let go of its meal. He finally released me and turned to run.

The hooded guy took a single step forward and slammed a fist up into the man's chin. The uppercut lifted him off his feet and his head smacked into the top of the door frame. He crashed unconscious to the floor.

I slid to the floor. I was wavering at the edge of consciousness, barely capable of taking a breath, but my tortured lungs managed one weak little gasp. The fetid air of The Pit poured down my throat and it tasted like it came from the Swiss Alps. I took another breath and another, each one a little stronger, until I was gulping it down. It took long seconds for my vision to clear and, when it did, nausea followed it. I wrapped my arms around myself and just sat there, staring at the floor.

My rescuer's boots stepped into my vision. Then his knees appeared as he crouched down. I didn't look up at him—I couldn't. I felt as if I was going to throw up. My jeans and panties were still around my ankles but I couldn't pull them up while I was sitting and it didn't feel like my legs would hold me if I tried to stand. I settled for pressing my knees together and hugging my calves tight to my thighs. I hoped most of me was hidden in shadow.

I could feel him watching me. Waiting. Giving me time.

I was shaking. I couldn't stop shaking.

He didn't say anything and he didn't attempt to touch me. I think I would have screamed, if he had. He just crouched there next to me, guarding me. I don't know how long I sat there—minutes, at least. Once, I heard someone approach down the corridor and saw his head snap up. *"Fuck off,"* he snapped, and the person scurried away.

Except it didn't sound like *Fuck off*. It sounded more like *Feck off*. He had an unfamiliar accent that reminded me of cold, unyielding rock.

At last, I felt strong enough to try to stand. I pushed myself unsteadily to my feet, trying to pull my jeans up at the same time, knowing that whatever I did, he was going to catch a glimpse of my pussy.

But instead, as he stood up with me, I saw him twist and look off down the hallway. He kept his eyes averted while I got my jeans pulled up and only looked back when all the rustling of clothes had ceased.

Now that I was standing, I could see more of him—all the way up to his chest. But I still didn't dare look up at his face. I was burning up inside with humiliation and raw, sick fear. I knew, on some level, that it was over and that I was safe, now. But I'd been shaken on a deeper level. I'd thought I'd known how shitty the world was, how terrifyingly, casually evil men could be, but I'd been wrong.

I was safe, but I'd never feel safe again.

And then he did something—he put his hand out towards me. A big, calloused hand, each finger easily twice the thickness of mine. He didn't touch me with it. He just rested it in the air, an inch away from cupping my shoulder. He left it there, saying nothing.

And I felt a warmth flow through me, expanding outward from that almost-touch. Reassurance that he wasn't like them. That he'd never, ever hurt me.

It shouldn't have been possible from someone who'd just dealt such violence. But I knew it was true.

I finally looked up at him. His hood was still up, his face hidden in shadow. His comforting hand was still almost touching my shoulder, but it wasn't enough. I needed to see *him,* not a mystery savior.

I stared up into the shadows, my eyes pleading.

Slowly, reluctantly, he pulled back his hood just enough to show his face.

Soft black hair cut short and messed up. His strong brow was creasing into a frown at having to reveal himself. But he didn't look angry—not with me, at least. His gorgeous, electric blue eyes seemed to burn with concern. It was when he glanced down at the three men on the floor that I saw the look change to hatred.

The dark stubble on his cheeks made his skin look even paler. Black hair, white skin, blue eyes and that strong brow...I knew that look, but I was way too messed up, right then, to place it.

I saw the fight again in my head. It had been so *quick!* I'd seen plenty of fights in The Pit, but nothing like that. He'd hit with unstoppable power. It had been like watching the men get hit by a truck.

I was still shaking, but it seemed to be dying down. I wrapped my arms around myself and that felt better. But his presence felt better still. It made no sense. I'd seen him destroy those three guys—I should have been terrified of him. But I felt...protected.

"Are you okay?" he asked. That granite-hard accent again, brutal yet beautiful.

He kept glancing down at the guy on the floor—the leader, the one who'd had me pinned against the wall. He was giving the guy such a look of pure, undiluted *hate* that I thought the floor was going to start bubbling and melting. The guy was still breathing—for now. But I realized with a lurch that whether he lived or died depended on my answer.

It scared the hell out of me...but it was strangely reassuring, too. I nodded.

"You're crying," he said tightly. The accent went with his looks, somehow, but my overloaded brain refused to process it. This time his gaze swept around all three of the fallen men, as if he was considering snapping each of them over his knee in turn. *Ending* them, so they could never hurt anyone again.

"I'm okay," I said. I pawed at my cheeks. I *was* crying. Big, fat tears of despair or relief—I didn't know when they'd started, but they seemed to be stopping.

He stared down at me, his eyes full of sadness. And he moved his hand back from my shoulder and offered it to me.

I slowly took it, my small hand almost disappearing as he clasped it in his much bigger one. He drew me away from the bathroom, leading me down the corridor with a gentleness completely at odds with his strength. With every step we took, I breathed a little more easily. I knew that what had happened was going to live on in my nightmares for a long time—maybe forever—but I felt the strength returning to my body.

As we moved through the dimly-lit corridor, I started to glance up at him. The sheer size of him, up close, was imposing. It wasn't just that he was big; it was the hardness of him, as if he was carved from rock under his jeans and hooded top. He didn't seem to have an ounce of fat on him but he probably weighed close to twice what I did. And I swore he wasn't even breathing hard, as if beating those guys up had been nothing at all.

"Thank you," I said, because I realized I hadn't said it yet.

He shrugged awkwardly, glancing back at the three men on the floor.

I was slowly taking in how gorgeous he was. The strong jaw and heavy brow, softened just enough by high cheekbones...and those eyes, pale blue and alive with a fierce, protective fire. I flushed at the memory of how I'd lusted after him when I'd seen him in the crowd. It was fate's cruel trick—the man who'd seen me at my worst was the one I would have liked to see me at my best. As I blinked back the last of the tears, I pleaded silently, *don't remember me like this.*

He stared at me...and then he nodded. As if he could read my mind, as if we'd known each other for years. His grip was warm and comforting and, looking at where we joined, it felt...*right,* somehow. I didn't feel as if I was in danger, despite everything I'd seen him do.

"What's your name?" I asked. "I'm Sylvie."

"Aedan," he said reluctantly. And the name finally helped my brain make the connection between his looks and that flint-like accent. *Irish.* "You going back in there?" he asked, jerking his head down the hall towards the fight. "It's not safe."

"I have to. My brother's in the next fight," I blurted.

He stared at me, probably confused by the lack of family resemblance. "The blond fella? *Koning?*"

I nodded, surprised that he actually knew our surname. Real names weren't used much. The fight organizers gave people stage names to hype them up. Alec was *The Dutchman.* For Aedan to know his surname, he must be pretty close to the scene, more than just another spectator—

Of course. He was a fighter, or maybe an ex-fighter. I didn't recognize him, but then I'd only been going to the fights since Alec got involved.

Aedan shook his head, looking even more troubled, now. The shake dislodged the hood and it fell the rest of the way, exposing his neck. He'd been....*ruined* there. It wasn't just a simple, raised scar. I could see where something had cut deep and then twisted, tearing as it went. Then the wounds had been inexpertly stitched up and thick scars had formed, stretching down under his collar.

I felt my heart tear in two. It wasn't that it was ugly. It was that someone had done something so vicious and cruel to him. I wanted to tell him that it was okay, that it didn't make him any less beautiful. But like an idiot, I just stood there, staring.

He caught me looking and jerked his hood back up, throwing his face into shadow. I cursed myself, trying to think of a way to apologize, but the damage was done.

"I gotta go," he said, and dropped my hand.

I felt something wrench, soul-deep. This was wrong. I knew, somehow, that he was important—maybe the most important person who'd ever walked into my life. But he was already walking, his powerful shoulders squared as if to fend off any attempt to stop him. With his hood up and his back turned, he was suddenly closed off and distant.

And alone.

"Wait!" My hand was tingling where he'd held it. I grabbed it in my other hand, not wanting to lose that warm glow. "How do I find you again?"

He kept walking. I could hear the sudden bitterness in his voice. "You don't."

Punching and Kissing is out now

CONTACT ME

If you have a question or just want to chat, you can find me at:

Blog: http://helenanewbury.com

Twitter: http://twitter.com/HelenaAuthor

Facebook: http://www.facebook.com/HelenaNewburyAuthor

Goodreads: http://www.goodreads.com/helenanewburyauthor

Pinterest: http://pinterest.com/helenanewbury/

Amazon Author Page http://www.amazon.com/author/helenanewbury

Don't be shy! :)

18797858R00227

Printed in Great Britain
by Amazon